Three Short Novels

by C O L E T T E

COLETTE

*Translated from the French
by Roger Senhouse and Patrick Leigh Fermor
Introduction by Judith Thurman*

FARRAR, STRAUS AND GIROUX • NEW YORK

Gigi

Julie de Carneilhan

Chance Acquaintances

Farrar, Straus and Giroux
18 West 18th Street, New York 10011

Translated from the French, *Gigi, Julie de Carneilhan,* and
    Chambre d'hôtel
Printed in the United States of America
Second Farrar, Straus and Giroux paperback edition, 2001

Library of Congress Cataloging-in-Publication Data
Colette, 1873–1954.
    [Selections. English. 2001]
    Gigi ; Julie de Carneilhan ; Chance acquaintances / Colette ;
[translated from the French by Roger Senhouse and Patrick
Leigh Fermor].
        p.   cm.
    ISBN 0-374-52785-7 (pbk. : alk. paper)

    ISBN 978-0-374-52785-3

    1. Colette, 1873–1954—Translations into English.   I. Title: Gigi ;
Julie de Carneilhan ; Chance acquaintances.   II. Senhouse, Roger.
III. Fermor, Patrick Leigh.   IV. Colette, 1873–1954. Julie de
Carneilhan. English.   V. Colette, 1873–1954. Chambre d'hôtel.
English.   VI. Title: Julie de Carneilhan.   VII. Title: Chance
acquaintances.   VIII. Title.

PQ2605.028 A27 2001
843'.912—dc21

                                                    2001033697

www.fsgbooks.com

P1

CONTENTS

Sidonie-Gabrielle Colette was born in the Burgundian village of Saint-Sauveur-en-Puisaye on January 28, 1873, and died in Paris, on her fur-covered divan in the Palais-Royal, on August 3, 1954. She was given a state funeral—the first for a *citoyenne* of the Republic—and mourned as a national treasure.

Death's protocols, however, had always repelled her and aroused her instincts for impiety. Colette was a pagan whose life and appetites were Olympian in their vitality, as was her oeuvre. She published nearly eighty volumes of fiction, memoir, drama, essays, criticism, and reportage, among them perhaps a dozen masterpieces. *Gigi*—written in the bleakest months of World War II—is the best known to English-speaking readers, somewhat unfortunately, if only because its promise of happiness so misrepresents Colette's view of love.

Like Proserpina, she has two guises: one as a daughter, one as a queen. The daughter of Ceres is our guide to the earthly paradise: the quintessential countrywoman, poet of nature, epicure, coquette, traveler, animal lover, gardener, athlete, collector of butterflies, and connoisseur of sensual pleasures. The realm of the queen is an erotic underworld where love is perdition, where those who give pleasure can't receive it, or those who take it can't give it, and "restless ghosts" crash "headlong and sidelong against that barrier reef, mysterious and incomprehensible, the human body" (*The Pure and the Impure*).

Literary masters as diverse in temperament as Marcel Proust and François Mauriac knew Colette well and considered her great. Her influence is ubiquitous in Simone de Beauvoir's *The Second Sex*. Henry de Montherlant condescended to call Colette France's greatest "natural" writer, though the modifier is something of a slight, not to say a misapprehension—for she was a consummate, even lapidary, stylist who slaved over her sentences and revised prodigiously.

But for the last quarter of a century, Colette has been out of fashion and, in translation, often out of print—or, to borrow an image from *La Naissance du jour* (*Break of Day*), which is probably her most innovative and profound novel—"hiding, like Poe's [purloined] letter, in plain sight." What accounts for her eclipse, particularly during a period when scholars and readers have been so avid to rescue even minor women writers from oblivion?

Colette has always been admirable for reasons that have nothing to do with political correctness. "Me, a feminist?" she scoffed in a 1910 interview. "I'll tell you what the suffragettes deserve: the whip and the harem." She saw no contradiction between supporting conservative positions and living her life as an "erotic militant" in revolt against them. Better worlds and just rewards were of no more consequence to her than the prospect of an afterlife. Preferring "passion to goodness," she seduced her teenage stepson and neglected her only child.

The paradoxes of great literature are those of human nature, and Colette is nothing if not human. "She eagerly picked the fruits of the earth without discriminating those which were forbidden," wrote her stepson as an old man. Accessible and elusive; greedy and austere; courageous and timid; subversive and complacent; scorchingly honest and sublimely mendacious; an inspired consoler and an existential pessimist—these are the qualities of the artist and the woman. It is time to rediscover them.

The provincial backwater where Colette spent her childhood was known as "the poor Burgundy," to distinguish it from the rich Burgundy of the great vineyards. Both her parents were outsiders, even pariahs, in the village where they had settled. Her father, Captain Jules Colette, was an officer of the Zouaves from Toulon who, after his service in the wars of the Second Empire, had retired to Saint-Sauveur with a wooden leg and a sinecure as the local tax collector. He proceeded to dabble in science, poetry, education, finance, and politics, but failed at everything he attempted, including paternity—his children considered him a sibling rival. After his death, they discovered he had spent his retirement tinkering with a "phantom opus": the luxuriously hand-bound volumes in his study were, beyond their title pages, entirely blank.

Mme Colette—the splendid earth mother known to Colette's readers as Sido—was born into a family of mixed African and Creole descent. Colette would describe her maternal antecedents as "cocoa-harvesters from the colonies" (Martinique) and her grandfather as a "ginger-colored gorilla." But Sido had been educated by her elder brothers, distinguished liberal journalists who had emigrated from France to Belgium. Her wit, atheism, extravagance, and modernity had outraged the villagers nearly as much as the love affair she had conducted with Captain Colette while she was still married to her alcoholic first husband. This gentleman died opportunely, leaving her a fortune that the captain squandered on his improvident dreams.

The "Madame Bovary" of Saint-Sauveur had boundless ambitions for her youngest daughter and "second self," Gabrielle, and these never included domestic—or sentimental—drudgery. Sido called marriage, only half-ironically, a "heinous crime," and would rejoice in Colette's liaison from 1905 to 1911 with a cultivated and melancholy lesbian transvestite, the Marquise de Morny, largely because "Missy's" generosity and solicitude were so wholesome for Colette's fiction. Nor was Sido's "precious jewel," childless until forty, ever encouraged by her mother to procreate.

"Balzac has invented everything," Colette wrote in *L'Etoile vesper* (*The Evening Star*), and the writer whom she called "my cradle" and "my forest" could easily have invented the Colettes. The family's dramas in Saint-Sauveur—adulteries, lawsuits, bankruptcies, and suicide attempts—would enthrall its inbred and petty-minded society. However much, in later life, Colette would rhapsodize about her sense of place, and define herself in *Les Vrilles de la vigne* (*Tendrils of the Vine*) as a woman who belonged "to a natal village I have left behind," her voice and character were shaped by her conviction of being "a special case" and her feeling of superiority of the village and its inhabitants.

The young Gabrielle Colette was a rugged, radiant tomboy with sea-green eyes and an auburn plait longer than she was tall. In 1893, at twenty, after a long engagement stalked by scandal, she married Henry Gauthier-Villars, a well-born Parisian rake and journalist of thirty-six who signed his salacious novels and amusingly savage music criticism "Willy." It was a not very well kept secret that all of these extravagantly publicized works had been "improved" by other hands, if not entirely ghostwritten by struggling young writers or provincial academics. It was less well known that Willy had also put his "child bride" to work—and, indeed, Colette would become the most productive draft horse in his stable.

As a nubile literary debutante toiling anonymously for her pudgy *érotomane* of a husband, who not only signed her bestselling Claudine novels[1] and pocketed the royalties but kept her enthralled in more primal ways, Colette invented the century's first teenage girl: rebellious, secre-

---

1. These are *Claudine at School*, *Claudine in Paris*, *Claudine Married*, *Claudine and Annie*, and *Retreat from Love* (*La Retraite sentimentale*), published between 1900 and 1907, which, as a series, are one of the greatest French bestsellers of all time, if not the greatest.

tive, erotically reckless and disturbed, determined to be an individual in her own right, but confused about how, or if, one can actually become both a person and a woman. That is a challenge she would take on in her fiction for the next fifty years.

The last fin de siècle was an anarchic and fertile period that generated the anxieties about meaning, authority, and the integrity of the self that we still live with. It was also, not coincidentally, an era of nearly bulimic sexual consumption and pervasive misogyny. Male writers from the most reactionary to the most avant-garde were haunted by the specter of a "virilized," "vampiric" New Woman who, by asserting her rights not only to autonomy but to pleasure, was responsible for the degeneracy of the culture. Women, in turn, were haunted by the consequences of this male fear. Colette, for one, would always struggle valiantly to impersonate a "real" woman (as defined by the old men of her youth), while feeling, as she puts it, like a "mental hermaphrodite."

Writing was the way that a supremely vital and gifted but fragile young woman with a weakness for bondage discovered her true value and disengaged from an exploitive master. It was not, however, the only bridge to liberation. Colette had perceived, precociously, that the beauty of a woman's muscles is identical with their purpose, which is self-support. By 1902, she had installed a private gymnasium with a trapeze and parallel bars in the studio upstairs from the luxurious conjugal apartment on the rue de Courcelles that Willy had financed with her earnings. And here she began training for the profession she would take up after their divorce.

"Colette Willy," as she signed the first book Willy gave her leave to avow—*Dialogues de bêtes* (1904)—also entertained her own small circle of intimates in this "bachelor pad." Most of them were young, stylish, and "acid-tongued" gay men—the "valiant of voluptuousness," as Cavafy would call them. Colette admired their erotic ruthlessness and shared their sense of marginality. They confirmed her sense—articulated with such eloquence in the Claudines— that gender is impure; that children of either sex have drives to dominate and yearnings to be possessed; that a society which demands too much conformity in the realm of desire irrevocably warps its young.

In 1905, the year her marriage foundered and she went off, very publicly, with Missy, Colette also abandoned the salons of polite society (which closed their doors to her) and embarked on a stage career. She became a tough, self-promoting music-hall star—a mime, dancer, and actress— who was never averse to a skimpy costume or a kitschy production. It was an interlude for which the mandarins would never quite forgive her, and every time in later life her name was proposed for some official honor, a chorus of elders—recalling how she had bared her flesh to the leering throng in the two-franc seats and haggled expertly over her contracts—protested.

Colette's experience of a trouper's life inspired *La Vagabonde* (*The Vagabond*; 1910), a novel that anticipates, by ninety years, the contemporary fashion for wry, first-person narratives by single, thirty-something career women. Its heroine examines her addictions to men with amused detachment, and flirts, alternately, with abstinence and temptation. Is there love without complete submission and loss of identity? Is freedom really worth the loneliness that pays for it? These are Colette's abiding questions.

Her own life as a vagabond and divorcée had exposed her to poverty as she had never known it, and Colette was one of the first middle-class women of her generation to know what it takes—how much passionate steeliness—to earn a living. The frugality of Virginia Woolf's five hundred a year and a room of one's own had as much allure for her as the ideals of Woolf's feminism, which is to say, none at all. Colette's models were never the gentlewomen of letters living on their allowances but the courtesans and artistes she had frequented in her youth, whose notion of a bottom line was fifty thousand a year and a villa of one's own—with a big garden, a great chef, and a pretty boy. They also came closest to fulfilling the ideal of the Amazons: to live unfettered yet sexually fulfilled.

Yet Colette, who entitled her sequel to *The Vagabond*, *L'Entrave* (*The Shackle*), always found it difficult to live unfettered. She had lovers of all ages and both sexes, but as her friend Natalie Barney was to put it in "The Colette I Have Known," "Torn between the desires of her two contrary natures, to have a master and not to have one, she always opted for the first solution." The day she turned forty, Colette was four months pregnant and still performing. By now she had abandoned the selfless Missy to marry her baby's father, Baron Henry de Jouvenel, one of the most influential and sexually charismatic political journalists in Paris.

The child, born in July of 1913, was a daughter to whom Colette gave her own name and her own nickname but not much else, abandoning her to the care of a dour English nanny. She wrote fondly, at times ecstatically, about Colette II, as she sometimes called her, but they only ever shared a roof for the odd month in summer, and the little girl was sent to boarding school at eight, then farmed out to various women friends who acted as Colette's surrogates. "The danger which threatens the writer, elevated to a happy and tender parent, [is that] of becoming a mediocre author," she asserted in *The Evening Star*. There was only one way that Bel-Gazou could make herself exist for her mother, and that was to become her greatest disappointment.

Jouvenel was then the editor of a major Paris daily, *Le Matin*, and in 1911 Colette joined the paper as a columnist, eventually becoming its drama critic and literary editor. Had she never written a word of fiction, she would still be remembered as one of the most original French journalists of the century. Her focus was intimate, but her range was wide. She would be one of the first women to report from the front lines of World War I—having traveled incognito to Verdun in the autumn of 1914 to join her husband, who was fighting with the French army. One of her specialties would be crime, particularly domestic violence and criminal psychology. She wrote about fashion with a knowledgeable irreverence that still sounds provocative today. She penned advice columns on love, food, exercise, decorating, and other traditional woman's-page subjects, but she was lucid and often scathing about the plight of women in brutal marriages and degrading jobs.

In 1916, while on assignment for *Le Matin* in Rome—the center of the nascent European film industry—Colette also became one of the first twentieth-century novelists to adapt her work for the new medium. During the same period, she composed her incandescent libretto for Ravel's opera *L'enfant et les sortilèges*. But love and war distracted her from serious fiction. It was not until 1919 that she began to contemplate the story of a beautiful bad boy living with a courtesan old enough to be his mother. "For the first time in my life," Colette told a friend when she had just begun to serialize *Chéri*, "I felt morally certain of having written a novel for which I need neither blush nor doubt."

Not all the critics would agree, some calling her incomparable portrait of the Belle Epoque demimonde "soulless," "vulgar," and "perverse." The prevailing opinion, however, was summed up concisely by André Gide in a now famous fan letter: "What a wonderful subject you have taken up," he told Colette. "And with what intelligence, mastery, and understanding of the least-admitted secrets of the flesh."

After his distinguished wartime service both as a soldier and a diplomat, Henry de Jouvenel decided to enter politics and ran—successfully—for the Senate. Colette's erotic legend now became an embarrassment, though not quite so great an embarrassment as the affair that she had been conducting with Henry's son by his first marriage. Bertrand de Jouvenel was a bookish virgin of sixteen when his stepmother "made him a man" at her beach house among the dunes of Brittany. She was still smoldering and Venusian at forty-seven, even if she did weigh nearly one hundred and eighty pounds. Her husband, himself a rapacious womanizer, had tormented Colette with his infidelities while complaining (not unjustly) of her "monstrous innocence." When he finally discovered her five-year-long liaison with his son and asked for a divorce, Colette was depressed and outraged, but sought solace, as she generally did, by eating "methodically"—her lust for food, she told a friend, "directed primarily at shellfish."

The affair with her stepson and his concurrent romance with a schoolmate his own age inspired *Le Blé en herbe* (*The Ripening Seed*), one of Colette's most sensuously written novels. In comparing the first sexual experiences of a teenage boy and girl, Colette rejects the received wisdom about what the "loss" of their virginity means to men and women. It is the boy who feels most deeply violated and transformed by his initiation. Here, as throughout her oeuvre, the male of the species is the weaker but nobler creature, while the female monopolizes the "will to survive."

Bertrand, who, like his father, had never much liked the "*louche milieu*" of Colette's fiction, wanted her to write something more uplifting. (How exquisitely French: a pimply schoolboy who was honing his sexual technique on the body of his father's wife objected to the absence of any moral feeling in her writing!) In part to appease him, Colette wrote a chaste and celebratory memoir of Sido and her own provincial childhood—*La Maison de Claudine* (*My Mother's House*)—which has become one of the best-loved works in her canon.

Jouvenel and his first wife eventually contrived to separate their son from Colette. She continued to live tumultuously and to write tirelessly, as well as to lecture, travel, edit, and perform. In 1925, during the rehearsals of *Chéri*—she had dramatized the novel and was playing the heroine, Léa—mutual friends introduced her to a worldly Jewish bachelor of Dutch descent named Maurice Goudeket. He wrote poetry and sold pearls, and he had worshipped Colette's writing since his adolescence. She, in turn, breathed oxygen into his depressive character and stifled existence. They embarked upon a torrid adventure that would in time become the serene and enduring mutual devotion she had yearned for but never known.

The great writer was fifty-two when she fell in love with the thirty-five-year-old Maurice. After their first idyll in a rented villa on the Côte d'Azur, Colette bought a house in Saint-Tropez and settled into the happiest and most fecund period of her life. This "vintage time" produced *Break of Day*, *Sido* (a sequel to *My Mother's House*), *La Fin de Chéri* (*The Last of Chéri*—a bleak and ambitious portrait of the lost generation), and a first draft of *Le Pur et l'impur* (*The Pure and the Impure*—originally called *Ces Plaisirs . . .*), the work Colette herself judged most worthy of enduring. It is not only, as she puts it, "my personal contribution to the sum total of our knowledge of the senses," but her definitive treatise on the bonds of love—and on the voracity that bondage seeks to contain.

When the Depression started, Goudeket's jewelry venture failed, and the lovers—who would marry in 1935 and honeymoon in New York—decided to embark on a joint "second career." Rich friends staked them to an *institut de beauté* on the rue Miromesnil, where Colette did celebrity makeovers in a white lab coat. They also launched a line of beauty products: "Colette" potions and cosmetics. The elegant little boxes bore her signature and her likeness. "I find the women beautiful as they emerge from beneath my writer's fingers," she wrote, "and I enjoy touching the living flesh . . . inspired by a kind of benevolent, maternal feeling." But Colette's genius was not maternal, and less benevolent than one might suppose. Perhaps that's why the beauty shop was a failure: the aging actresses who entrusted her with their faces emerged from their makeovers looking twice as old as when they had gone in.

After this strenuous, costly, and disappointing experiment, Colette resumed her primary vocation with renewed vigor. In 1935, she was elected to L'Académie Royale de Langue et de Littérature Françaises de Belge, and the same year her peers voted her the greatest living master of French prose. That virtuosity is nowhere more evident than in *Mes apprentissages* (*My Apprenticeships*; 1936), the most confessional of her memoirs, sober in its power, cold in its passion, in which she takes exquisite revenge on Willy for having destituted her of the Claudines. What sweeter recompense for the frauds perpetrated by a hack than to make him the villain of a masterpiece?

Given her lifelong indifference to politics, it is not sur-
prising that Colette's work of the 1930s ignores the rise
of fascism, the general strikes, the unemployment crisis.
Her trio of Depression novels—*La Chatte* (*The Cat*), *Duo*,
and *Le Toutounier*—are variations on one of her constant
themes: the tragic incompatibility of men and women. Yet
the superb short stories collected in *Bella-Vista* (1937)
manifest a social conscience that is rare if not unique out-
side her journalism, and their achievement has been com-
pared with the "social portraiture" of Gorky.

The novella, as Goudeket would put it in his memoir,
Près de Colette (*Close to Colette*), "was henceforth her
preferred genre. It represented neither an impoverish-
ment nor a loss of patience, but a willed divestment." And
he is right: readers searching for Colette at her purest will
find her in the late novellas. It is as if she were adjusting
her style, like a diet, to a more sedentary and less flam-
boyant life.

By the outbreak of the Second World War, Colette was
suffering from the excruciating arthritis of the hip—an ail-
ment common among so many dancers—that would even-
tually cripple her entirely. In 1940, she and Goudeket
briefly sought refuge from the German invasion with her
daughter, who owned a ruined castle in the Corrèze and
was active in the Resistance. Without any means of sup-
port, however, they returned to the capital, where they
had recently moved to an apartment at 9, rue de Beaujo-
lais, on the *étage noble* of the Palais-Royal—Colette's last
and most famous Parisian address. For a while, they both
naïvely believed her eminence would protect Maurice

from persecution by the Nazis, and for the next four years Colette would practice what she liked to call *"le sage repliement sur soi"*—the wise retreat into one's private bastion—which also translates, less poetically, as lying low.

Colette's work, and even her letters from the Occupation, contain no outrage, and indeed very little apparent cognizance of the war's obscenity. The Paris she observed from her windows overlooking Richelieu's gardens was peopled by a race of beasts and humans with her own virtues of old-fashioned stoicism and female resourcefulness. And like so many of her peers, she contributed her fiction and her journalism to the organs of the pro-Vichy and pro-Nazi press.

Never are Colette's "powers of denial," as she put it, greater than in her short fiction of the 1940s: *Gigi, Le Képi, Le Tendron (The Tender Shoot), L'Enfant malade (The Sick Child)*—and never is she more endearing or accessible. Perhaps that is why the old sinner who narrates these tales, and who, like Gigi's Aunt Alicia, is so rich in erotic wisdom, has been the writer most widely revered and remembered. Colette escapes from war, old age, and debility into an innocent and lighthearted past. She reveals the smiling face she begrudged the camera throughout her life, and the maternal tenderness that she feared so terribly to show her child. They signal a sickbed conversion of sorts. It's not quite to a solid faith in love, in lasting happiness, or in redemption—Colette was too inveterate an unbeliever and too vigilant an artist to let herself go so far. But she allows that in an affair of the heart there may be no victims, and that lust may coexist with devotion.

Introduction

Maurice Goudeket survived a six-week internment in the concentration camp at Compiègne, and Colette's reputation survived her ambiguous collaboration with the Occupation press. (Indeed, one feels she would have collaborated with the Devil himself to ensure the survival of the being most essential to her—the man she called "my best friend.") In 1945, she was elected to the Académie Goncourt—the second woman member in its history—and in 1949 her *confrères* chose her as their president.

After the liberation of Paris, Colette had ten years left. She spent most of them on the daybed she called her "raft," where she worked and slept. Her reading lamp had an improvised shade made of her blue writing paper. At night it marked her window to anyone passing through the Palais-Royal gardens. She would call her last memoir *Le Fanal bleu* (*The Blue Lantern*).

Age, corpulence, and unremitting pain forced Colette to give up vagabondage, and she says that she renounced "egotism." But she could never renounce coquetry, and she could never "learn how not to write." "Perhaps the most praiseworthy thing about me," she concluded in an interview with Glenway Wescott two years before she died, "is that I have known how to write like a woman, without anything moralistic or theoretical, without promulgating." And by the end of the woman's story that Colette spins as she lives, she is unbeholden to the gods of men.

G I G I

Gigi is probably the best known and loved of Colette's late novellas, at least in America, partly because it is—atypically—a delectably comic romance with a happy (and moral) ending, but also because it was adapted as a successful and long-running play by Colette and Anita Loos starring Audrey Hepburn in the title role and, later, as a cinematic musical with Leslie Caron and Louis Jourdan playing the two lovers. *Gigi*, however, was written in the darkest months of the Occupation—the summer of 1942. The mass deportations of French Jews had begun that July, and Colette's third husband, Maurice Goudeket, who had been released from the concentration camp at Compiègne the previous February, had gone into hiding in the South of France.

Tormented by anxiety about the fate of her *meilleur ami*, and by the agonies of her crippling and intractable arthritis, Colette revisits, in *Gigi*, that hothouse milieu of retired fin de siècle cocottes which she had explored with considerably more acidity in *Chéri*. The charm of the tale—and its narrative tension—reside in the incongruity between the thorough and proper "finishing" that the virginal *jeune fille* receives from her exigent Aunt Alicia, and its aim: to make her into the most desirable and expensive of kept women. Yet Gigi proves to be more subtle—and more ambitious—than her tutors: she holds out for true love, and for the prestige of marriage to the most eligible of Parisian bachelors. (It is, however, somewhat disenchanting to learn that the originals of Colette's ingenue and playboy were eighteen and sixty, respectively).

Toward the beginning of the story, Alicia gives her niece a lesson in gemology, dismissing all semiprecious or "artistic" baubles as unworthy. "There are precious stones and pearls," she concludes, "white, yellow, blue, blue-white, or pink diamonds. Then there are rubies—when you can be sure of them; sapphires when they come from Kashmir; emeralds, provided they have no fatal flaw." It's a sublimely ironic little lecture about professional pride that applies equally well to the gem of a story Colette is telling, and to the jewel box of her prose, which contains, at this late stage, nothing flawed, nothing showily "artistic," nothing unworthy.

Like all work published under the Occupation, *Gigi* had to pass muster with the Nazi censors. In the autumn of 1943, Colette sold first serial rights to *Présent*, a pro-Vichy journal, noting that she was happy enough never to have seen a copy. As the title piece of a collection that included "Noces," "Flore et Pomone," and "La Dame du photographe," the novella was published in Lausanne by the Guilde du Livre in 1944, and republished by Ferenczi in liberated Paris a year later.

Gigi

Translated by ROGER SENHOUSE

Gigi

Don't forget you are going to Aunt Alicia's. Do you hear me, Gilberte? Come here and let me do your curls. Gilberte, do you hear me?"

"Couldn't I go there without having my hair curled, Grandmamma?"

"I should think not," said Madame Alvarez, quietly. She took an old pair of curling-irons, with prongs ending in little round metal knobs, and put them to heat over the blue flame of a spirit-lamp while she prepared the tissue-papers.

"Grandmamma, couldn't you crimp my hair in waves down the side of my head for a change?"

"Out of the question. Ringlets at the very ends—that's as far as a girl of your age can possibly go. Now sit down on the footstool."

To do so, Gilberte folded up under her the heron-like legs of a girl of fifteen. Below her tartan skirt, she revealed ribbed cotton stockings to just above the knees, unconscious of the perfect oval shape of her knee-caps. Slender calf and high arched instep—Madame Alvarez never let her eyes run over these fine points without regretting that her granddaughter had not studied dancing professionally. At the moment, she was thinking only of the girl's hair. She had corkscrewed the ends and fixed them in tissue-paper, and was now compressing the ash-blonde ringlets between the heated knobs. With patient soft-fingered skill, she gathered up the full magnificent weight of finely kept hair into sleek ripples which fell to just below Gilberte's shoulders. The girl sat quite still. The smell of the heated tongs, and the whiff of vanilla in the curling-papers, made her feel drowsy. Besides, Gilberte knew that resistance would be useless. She hardly ever tried to elude the authority exercised by her family.

"Is Mamma singing Frasquita today?"

"Yes. And this evening in *Si j'étais Roi*. I have told you before, when you're sitting on a low seat you must keep your knees close to each other, and lean both of them together, either to the right or to the left, for the sake of decorum."

"But, Grandmamma, I've got on my drawers and my petticoat."

"Drawers are one thing, decorum is another," said Madame Alvarez. "Everything depends on the attitude."

"Yes, I know. Aunt Alicia has told me often enough," Gilberte murmured from under her tent of hair.

"I do not require the help of my sister," said Madame Alvarez testily, "to instruct you in the elements of propriety. On that subject, thank goodness, I know rather more than she does."

"Supposing you let me stay here with you today, Grandmamma, couldn't I go and see Aunt Alicia next Sunday?"

"What next!" said Madame Alvarez haughtily. "Have you any other *purposal* to make to me?"

"Yes, I have," said Gilberte. "Have my skirts made a little longer, so I don't have to fold myself up in a Z every time I sit down. You see, Grandmamma, with my skirts too short, I have to keep thinking of my you-know-what."

"Silence! Aren't you ashamed to call it your you-know-what?"

"I don't mind calling it by any other name, only . . ."

Madame Alvarez blew out the spirit-lamp, looked at the reflection of her heavy Spanish face in the looking-glass above the mantelpiece, and then laid down the law.

"There is no other name."

A skeptical look passed across the girl's eyes. Beneath the cockle-shells of fair hair they showed a lovely dark blue, the color of glistening slate. Gilberte unfolded with a bound.

"But, Grandmamma, all the same, do look! If only my skirts were just that much longer! Or if a small frill could be added!"

"That *would* be nice for your mother, to be seen with a great gawk looking at least eighteen! In her profession! Where are your brains!"

"In my head," said Gilberte. "Since I hardly ever go out with Mamma, what would it matter?"

She pulled down her skirt, which had rucked up towards her slim waist, and asked, "Can I go in my everyday coat? It's quite good enough."

"That wouldn't show that it's Sunday! Put on your serge

coat and blue sailor-hat. When will you learn what's what?"

When on her feet, Gilberte was as tall as her grandmother. Madame Alvarez had taken the name of a Spanish lover now dead, and accordingly had acquired a creamy complexion, an ample bust, and hair lustrous with brilliantine. She used too white a powder, her heavy cheeks had begun to draw down her lower eye-lids a little, and so eventually she took to calling herself Inez. Her family pursued their fixed orbit around her. Her unmarried daughter Andrée, forsaken by Gilberte's father, now preferred the sober life of a second-lead singer in a State-controlled theatre to the fitful opulence of a life of gallantry. Aunt Alicia—none of her admirers, it seemed, had ever mentioned marriage—lived alone, on an income she pretended was modest. The family had a high opinion of Alicia's judgment, and of her jewels.

Madame Alvarez looked her granddaughter up and down, from the felt sailor-hat trimmed with a quill to the ready-made cavalier shoes.

"Can't you ever manage to keep your legs together? When you stand like that, the Seine could flow between them. You haven't the shadow of a stomach, and yet you somehow contrive to stick it out. And don't forget your gloves, I beg of you."

Gilberte's every posture was still governed by the unconcern of childish innocence. At times she looked like Robin Hood, at others like a carved angel, or again like a boy in skirts; but she seldom resembled a nearly grown-up girl. "How can you expect to be put into long skirts, when you haven't the sense of a child of eight?" Madame

Alvarez asked. And Andrée sighed, "I find Gilberte so discouraging." To which Gilberte answered quietly, "If you didn't find *me* discouraging, then you'd find something else." For she was sweet and gentle, resigned to a stay-at-home life and seeing few people outside the family. As for her features, no one could yet predict their final mould. A large mouth, which showed beautiful strong white teeth when she laughed, no chin to speak of, and, between high cheekbones, a nose—"Heavens, where did she get that button?" whispered her mother under her breath. "If you can't answer that question, my girl, who can?" retorted Madame Alvarez. Whereupon Andrée, who had become prudish too late in life and disgruntled too soon, relapsed into silence, automatically stroking her sensitive larynx. "Gigi is just a bundle of raw material," Aunt Alicia affirmed, "it may turn out very well—and, just as easily, all wrong."

"Grandmamma, there's the bell! I'll open the door on my way out. Grandmamma," Gigi shouted from the passage, "It's Uncle Gaston!"

She came back into the room with a tall, youngish looking man, her arm linked through his, chattering to him with the childish pomposity of a school-girl out of class.

"What a pity it is, Tonton, that I've got to desert you so soon! Grandmamma wishes me to pay a call on Aunt Alicia. Which motor-car are you using today? Did you come in the new four-seater de Dion-Bouton with the collapsible hood? I hear it can be driven simply with one hand! Goodness, Tonton, those are smart gloves, and no mistake! So you've had a row with Liane, Tonton?"

"Gilberte," scolded Madame Alvarez, "what business of yours can that be?"

"But, Grandmamma, everybody knows about it. The whole story was in the *Gil Blas*. It began: *A secret bitterness is seeping into the sweet product of the sugarbeet.* . . . At school all the girls were asking me about it, for of course they know I know you. And I can tell you, Tonton, there's not a soul at school who takes Liane's side! They all agree that she's behaved disgracefully!"

"Gilberte!" repeated Madame Alvarez, "Say goodbye to Monsieur Lachaille, and run along!"

"Leave her alone, poor child," Gaston Lachaille sighed. "She, at any rate, intends no harm. And it's perfectly true that all's over between Liane and me. You're off to Aunt Alicia's, Gigi? Take my motor-car and send it back for me."

Gilberte gave a little cry, a jump of joy, and hugged Lachaille.

"Thank you, Tonton! Just think of Aunt Alicia's face! The concierge's eyes will be popping from her head!"

Off she went, with the chatter of a young filly not yet shod.

"You spoil her, Gaston," said Madame Alvarez.

But in this she was not altogether speaking the truth. Gaston Lachaille did not know how to "spoil" anyone—even himself. His luxuries were cut and dried: motor-cars, a dreary mansion on the Parc Monceau, Liane's monthly allowance and birthday jewels, champagne and baccarat at Deauville in the summer, at Monte Carlo in the winter. From time to time he would drop a fat check into some charity fund, or finance a new daily paper, or buy a yacht only to resell it almost at once to some Central European monarch: yet from none of this did he get any fun. He would say, as he looked at himself in the glass, "That's the face of a man who is branded." Because of his rather long nose and large dark eyes he was regarded on all sides as easy game. His commercial instinct and rich man's caution stood him in good stead, however; no one had succeeded in robbing him of his pearl studs, of his massive gold or silver cigarette-cases encrusted with precious stones, of his dark sable-lined topcoat.

From the window he watched his motor-car start up. That year, fashionable automobiles were being built with a slightly higher body and a rather wider top, to accommodate the exaggerated hats affected by Caroline Otero, Liane de Pougy, and other conspicuous figures of 1899: and, in consequence, they would sway gently at every turn of the wheel.

"Mamita," said Gaston Lachaille, "you wouldn't make me a cup of camomile?"

"Two rather than one," answered Madame Alvarez. "Sit down, my poor Gaston."

From the depths of a dilapidated armchair she removed some crumpled illustrated papers, a stocking waiting to be darned, and a box of liquorice candies known as *agents de change*. The jilted man settled down into the chair luxuriously, while his hostess put out the tray and two cups.

"Why does the camomile they brew at home always smell of faded chrysanthemums?" sighed Gaston.

"It's simply a matter of taking pains. You may not believe it, Gaston, but I often pick my best camomile flowers in

Paris, growing on waste ground, insignificant little flowers you would hardly notice. But they have a taste that is *unesteemable*. My goodness, what beautiful cloth your suit is made of! That deep-woven stripe is as smart as can be. Just the sort of material your father liked! But, I must confess, he would never have carried it so elegantly."

Never more than once during the course of a conversation did Madame Alvarez evoke the memory of an elder Lachaille, whom she claimed to have known intimately. From her former relationship, real or invented, she drew no advantage other than the close relationship of Gaston Lachaille, and the pleasure to be derived from watching a rich man enjoying the comforts of the poor when he made himself at home in her old armchair. Under their gas-blackened ceiling, these three feminine creatures never asked him for pearls, chinchillas, or solitaire diamonds, and they knew how to converse with tact and due solemnity on scandalous topics traditional and recondite. From the age of twelve, Gigi had known that Madame Otero's string of large black pearls were "dipped," that is to say, artificially tinted, while the three strings of her matchlessly graded pearl necklace were worth "a king's ransom"; that Madame de Pougy's seven rows lacked "life"; that Eugénie Fougère's famous diamond bolero was quite worthless; and that no self-respecting woman gadded about, like Madame Antokolski, in a coupé upholstered in mauve satin. She had obediently broken her friendship with a school friend, Lydia Poret, after the girl had shown her a solitaire, set as a ring, presented by the Baron Ephraim.

"A solitaire!" Madame Alvarez had exclaimed. "For a girl of fifteen! Her mother must be mad!"

"But, Grandmamma," pleaded Gigi, "it's not Lydia's fault if the Baron gave it to her!"

"Silence! I'm not blaming the Baron. The Baron knows what is expected of him. But plain common sense should have told the mother to put the ring in a safe at the bank, while waiting."

"While waiting for what, Grandmamma?"

"To see how things turn out."

"Why not in her jewel-case?"

"Because one never knows. Especially as the Baron is the sort of man who might change his mind. If, on the other hand, he has declared himself openly, Madame Poret has only to withdraw her daughter from her studies. Until the matter has been properly cleared up, you will oblige me by not walking home with that little Poret. Who ever heard of such a thing!"

"But supposing she marries, Grandmamma?"

"Marries? Marries whom, pray?"

"Why, the Baron!"

Madame Alvarez and her daughter exchanged glances of stupefaction. "I find the child so discouraging," Andrée had murmured. "She comes from another planet."

"My poor Gaston," said Madame Alvarez, "is it really true, then, that you have broken with her? In some way, it may be the best thing for you; but in others, I'm sure you must find it most upsetting. Whom can one trust, I ask you!"

Poor Gaston listened while he drank the scalding camomile. The taste of it gave him as much comfort as the sight of the plaster-rose on the ceiling, still black from the hanging lamp now "converted to electricity," still faithfully retaining its shade—a vast frilly bell of palest green. Half the contents of a work-basket lay strewn over the dining-room table, from which Gilberte had forgotten to remove her copy-book. Above the upright piano hung an enlarged photograph of Gilberte at eight months, as a pendant to a portrait in oils of Andrée, dressed for her part in *Si j'étais Roi*. The perfectly inoffensive untidiness, the ray of spring sunshine coming through the point-lace curtains, the warmth given out by a little stove kept at a low heat,—all these homely things were like so many soothing potions to the nerves of a jilted and lonely millionaire.

"Are you positively in torment, my poor Gaston?"

"To be exact, I'm not in torment. I'm just very upset, as you say."

"I have no wish to appear inquisitive," said Madame Alvarez, "but how did it all happen? I've read the papers, of course; but can one believe what they say?"

Lachaille tugged at his small waxed moustache, and ran his fingers over his thick, cropped hair.

"Oh, much the same as on previous occasions. She waited for the birthday present, then off she trotted. And, into the bargain, she must needs go and bury herself in such a wretched little hole in Normandy—so stupid of her! Any fool could have discovered that there were only two rooms at the inn, one occupied by Liane, the other by Sandomir, a skating-instructor from the *Palais de Glace*."

"He's Polaire's tea-time waltzing partner, isn't he? Oh,

women don't know where to draw the line nowadays! And just after her birthday, too! Oh! it's so tactless! What could be more unladylike!"

Madame Alvarez stirred the teaspoon round and round in her cup, her little finger in the air. When she lowered her gaze, her lids did not quite cover her protuberant eyeballs, and her resemblance to George Sand became marked.

"I'd given her a rope," said Gaston Lachaille. "What you might call a rope—thirty-seven pearls. The middle one as big as the ball of my thumb."

He held out his white, beautifully manicured thumb, to which Madame Alvarez accorded the admiration due to a middle pearl.

"You certainly know how to do things in style," she said. "You came out of it extremely well, Gaston."

"I came out of it with a pair of horns, certainly."

Madame Alvarez did not seem to have heard him.

"If I were you, Gaston, I should try to get your own back on her. I should take up with some society lady."

"That's a nice pill to offer me," said Lachaille, who was absent-mindedly helping himself to the *agents de change*.

"Yes, indeed, I might even say that sometimes the cure may prove worse than the disease," Madame Alvarez continued, tactfully agreeing with him. "Out of the frying-pan into the fire." After which she respected Gaston Lachaille's silence.

The muffled sounds of a piano penetrated through the ceiling. Without a word, the visitor held out his empty cup, and Madame Alvarez refilled it.

"Is the family all right? What news of Aunt Alicia?"

"Oh, my sister, you know, is always the same. She's smart enough to keep herself to herself. She says she would rather live in a splendid past than an ugly present. Her King of Spain, her Milan of Serbia, her Khedive, her rajahs by the half-dozen—or so she would have you believe! She is very considerate to Gigi. She finds her a trifle backward for her age, as indeed she is, and puts her through her paces. Last week, for instance, she taught her how to eat *homard a l'Américaine* in faultless style."

"Whatever for?"

"Alicia says it will be extremely useful. The three great difficulties in a girl's education, she maintains, are *homard a l'Américaine,* a boiled egg, and asparagus. Bad table manners, she says, have broken up many a happy home."

"That can happen," said Lachaille dreamily.

"Oh, Alicia is no fool! And it's just what Gigi requires—she is so greedy! If only her brain worked as well as her jaws! But she might well be a child of ten! And what breathtaking scheme have you got for the Battle of Flowers? Are you going to dazzle us again this year?"

"O Lord no!" groaned Gaston. "I shall take advantage of my misfortune, and save on the red roses."

Madame Alvarez wrung her hands.

"Oh, Gaston, you mustn't do that! If you're not there, the procession will look like a funeral!"

"I don't care what it looks like," said Gaston gloomily.

"You're never going to leave the prize banner to people like Valérie Cheniaguine? Oh, Gaston, we can't allow that!"

"You will have to. Valérie can very well afford it."

"Especially since she does it on the cheap. Gaston, do you

know where she went for the ten thousand bunches thrown last year? She had three women tying them up for two days and two nights, and the flowers were bought in the flower market! In the market! Only the four wheels, and the coachman's whip, and the harness trappings bore the label of Lachaume."

"That's a dodge to remember!" said Lachaille, cheering up. "Good Lord! I've finished the liquorice!"

The tap-tap of Gilberte's marching footsteps could be heard crossing the outer room.

"Back already!" said Madame Alvarez. "What's the meaning of this?"

"The meaning," said the girl, "is that Aunt Alicia wasn't in good form. But I've been out in Tonton's 'tuf-tuf.' "

Her lips parted in a bright smile.

"You know, Tonton, all the time I was in your automobile, I put on a martyred expression—like this—as if I was bored to death with every luxury under the sun. I had the time of my life."

She sent her hat flying across the room, and her hair fell tumbling over her forehead and cheeks. She perched herself on a rather high stool, and tucked her knees up under her chin.

"Well, Tonton? You look as if you were dying of boredom. What about a game of piquet? It's Sunday, and Mamma doesn't come back between the two performances. Who's been eating all my liquorice? Oh, Tonton, you can't get away with that! The least you can do is to send me some more to make up for it."

"Gilberte, your manners!" scolded Madame Alvarez.

"Your knees! Gaston hasn't the time to bother about your liquorice. Pull down your skirts. Gaston, would you like me to send her to her room?"

Young Lachaille, with one eye on the dirty pack of cards in Gilberte's hand, was longing simultaneously to give way to tears, to confide his sorrows, to go to sleep in the old armchair, and to play piquet.

"Let the child stay! In this room I can relax. It's restful. Gigi, I'll play you for twenty pounds of sugar."

"Your sugar's not very tempting. I much prefer sweets."

"It's the same thing. And sugar is better for you than sweets."

"You only say that because you make it."

"Gilberte, you forget yourself!"

A smile enlivened the mournful eyes of Gaston Lachaille.

"Let her say what she likes, Mamita. And if I lose, Gigi, what would you like? A pair of silk stockings?"

The corners of Gilberte's big childish mouth fell.

"Silk stockings make my legs itch. I would rather. . . ."

She raised the snub-nosed face of an angel towards the ceiling, put her head on one side, and tossed her curls from one cheek to the other.

"I would rather have an *eau-de-nil* Persephone corset, with rococo roses embroidered on the garters. No, I'd rather have a music-case."

"Are you studying music now?"

"No, but my older friends at school carry their copy-books in music-cases, because it makes them look like students at the Conservatoire."

"Gilberte, you are making too free!" said Madame Alvarez.

"You shall have your case, and your liquorice. Cut, Gigi."

The next moment, the heir of Lachaille-Sugar was deep in the game. His prominent nose, large enough to appear false, and his slightly negroid eyes did not in the least intimidate his opponent. With her elbows on the table, her shoulders on a level with her ears, and her blue eyes and red cheeks at their most vivid, she looked like a tipsy page. They both played passionately, almost in silence, exchanging occasional insults under their breath. *"You spindly spider! you sorrel run to seed!"* Lachaille muttered. *"You old crow's beak!"* the girl countered. The March twilight deepened over the narrow street.

"Please don't think I want you to go, Gaston," said Madame Alvarez, "but it's half-past seven. Will you excuse me while I just see about our dinner?"

"Half-past seven!" cried Lachaille, "and I'm supposed to be dining at Larue with de Dion, Feydeau, and one of the Barthous! This must be the last hand, Gigi."

"Why one of the Barthous?" asked Gilberte. "Are there several of them?"

"Two. One handsome and the other less so. The best known is the least handsome."

"That's not fair," said Gilberte. "And Feydeau, who's he?"

Lachaille plopped down his cards in amazement.

"Well, I declare! She doesn't know who Feydeau is! Don't you ever go to a play?"

"Hardly ever, Tonton."

"Don't you like the theatre?"

"I'm not mad about it. And Grandmamma and Aunt Alicia both say that going to plays prevents one from thinking about the serious side of life. Don't tell Grandmamma I told you."

She lifted the weight of her hair away from her ears, and let it fall forward again. "Phew!" she sighed. "This mane does make me hot!"

"And what do they mean by the serious side of life?"

"Oh, I don't know it all off by heart, Uncle Gaston. And, what's more, they don't always agree about it. Grandmamma says: 'Don't read novels, they only depress you. Don't put on powder, it ruins the complexion. Don't wear stays, they spoil the figure. Don't dawdle and gaze at shop windows when you're by yourself. Don't get to know the families of your school friends, especially not the fathers who wait at the gates to fetch their daughters home from school.' "

She spoke very rapidly, panting between words like a child who has been running.

"And on top of that, Aunt Alicia goes off on another tack! I've reached the age when I can wear stays, and I should take lessons in dancing and deportment, and I should be aware of what's going on, and know the meaning of 'caret,' and not be taken in by the clothes that actresses wear. 'It's quite simple,' she tells me, 'of all the dresses you see on the stage, nineteen out of twenty would look ridiculous in the paddock.' In fact, my head is fit to split with it all! What will you be eating at Larue this evening, Tonton?"

"How should I know! *Filets de sole aux moules*, for a change. And of course, saddle of lamb with truffles. Do get on with the game, Gigi! I've got a point of five."

"That won't get you anywhere. I've got all the cards in the pack. Here, at home, we're having the warmed up remains of the *cassoulet*. I'm very fond of *cassoulet*."

"A plain dish of *cassoulet* with bacon rind," said Inez Alvarez modestly, as she came in. "Goose was exorbitant this week."

"I'll have one sent to you from Bon-Abri," said Gaston.

"Thank you very much, Gaston. Gigi, help Monsieur Lachaille on with his overcoat. Fetch him his hat and stick!"

When Lachaille had gone, rather sulky after a regretful sniff at the warmed up *cassoulet*, Madame Alvarez turned to her granddaughter.

"Will you please inform me, Gilberte, why it was you returned so early from Aunt Alicia's? I didn't ask you in front of Gaston. Family matters must never be discussed in front of a third person, remember that!"

"There's no mystery about it, Grandmamma. Aunt Alicia was wearing her little lace cap to show me she had a headache. She said to me, 'I'm not very well.' I said to her, 'Oh! Then I mustn't tire you out, I'll go home again.' She said to me, 'Sit down and rest for five minutes.' 'Oh!' I said to her, 'I'm not tired. I drove here.' 'You drove here!' she said to me, raising her hands like this. As you may imagine, I had kept the motor-car waiting a few minutes, to show Aunt Alicia. 'Yes,' I said to her, The four-seater de-Dion-Bouton-with-the-collapsible-hood, which Tonton lent me while he was paying a call on us. He has had a rumpus with Liane.' 'Who do you think you're talking to?' she says to me, 'I've not yet got one foot in the grave! I'm still kept informed about public events when they're important. I know that he has had a rumpus with that great lamp-post of a woman. Well, you'd better run along home, and not bother about a poor ill old creature like me.' She waved to me from the window as I got into the motor-car."

Madame Alvarez pursed her lips.

"A poor ill old creature! She has never suffered so much as a cold in her life! I like that! What . . ."

"Grandmamma, do you think he'll remember my liquorice and the music-case?"

Madame Alvarez slowly lifted her heavy eyes towards the ceiling.

"Perhaps, my child, perhaps."

"But, as he lost, he owes them to me, doesn't he?"

"Yes, yes, he owes them to you. Perhaps you'll get them after all. Slip on your pinafore, and set the table. Put away your cards."

"Yes, Grandmamma. Grandmamma, what did he tell you about Madame Liane? Is it true she ran out on him with Sandomir and the rope of pearls?"

"In the first place, one doesn't say 'ran out on' anyone. In the second, come here and let me tighten your ribbon, so that your curls won't get soaked in the soup. And finally, the sayings and doings of a person who has broken the rules of etiquette are not for your ears. These happen to be Gaston's private affairs."

"But, Grandmamma, they are no longer private, since

everyone's talking about them, and the whole thing came out in *Gil Blas.*"

"Silence! All you need to know is that the conduct of Madame Liane d'Exelmans has been the reverse of sensible. The ham for your mother is between two plates: you will put it in the larder."

Gilberte was asleep when her mother—Andrée Alvar, in small type on the Opéra-Comique play-bills—returned home. Madame Alvarez, the elder, seated at a game of patience, inquired from force of habit whether she was not too tired. Following polite family custom, Andrée reproached her mother for having waited up, and Madame Alvarez made her ritual reply.

"I shouldn't sleep in peace unless I knew you were in. There is some ham, and a little bowl of warm *cassoulet.* And some stewed prunes. The beer is on the window-sill."

"The child is in bed?"

"Of course."

Andrée Alvar made a solid meal—pessimists have good appetites. She still looked pretty in theatrical make-up. Without it, the rims of her eyes were pink and her lips colorless. For this reason, Aunt Alicia declared, Andrée never met with the admiration in real life that she gained on the stage.

"Did you sing well, my child?"

"Yes, I sang well. But where does it get me? All the applause goes to Tiphaine, as you may well imagine. Oh dear, oh dear, I really don't think I can bear to go on with this sort of life."

"It was your own choice. But you would bear it much better," said Madame Alvarez sententiously, "if you had someone! It's your loneliness that gets on your nerves, and you take such black views. You're behaving contrary to nature."

"Oh, Mother, don't start that all over again, I'm tired enough as it is. What news is there?"

"None. Everyone's talking of Gaston's break with Liane."

"Yes, they certainly are! Even in the green room at the Opéra-Comique, which can hardly be called up-to-date."

"It's an event of world-wide interest," said Madame Alvarez.

"Is there talk of who's in the running?"

"I should think not! It's far too recent. He is in full mourning, so to speak. Can you believe it, at a quarter to eight he was sitting exactly where you are now, playing a game of piquet with Gigi? He says he has no wish to attend the Battle of Flowers."

"Not really!"

"Yes. If he doesn't go, it will cause a great deal of talk. I advised him to think twice before taking such a decision."

"They were saying at the *Théâtre* that a certain music-hall artiste might stand a chance," said Andrée. "The one billed as the Cobra at the Olympia. It seems she does an acrobatic turn, and is brought on in a basket hardly big enough for a fox-terrier, and from this she uncurls like a snake."

Madame Alvarez protruded her heavy lower lip in contempt.

"What an idea! Gaston Lachaille has not sunk to that level! A music-hall performer! Do him the justice to admit that, as befits a bachelor of his standing, he has always confined himself to the great ladies of the profession."

"A fine pack of bitches!" murmured Andrée.

"Be more careful how you express yourself, my child. Calling people and things by their names has never done anyone any good. Gaston's mistresses have all had an air about them. A liaison with a great professional lady is the only suitable way for him to wait for a great marriage, always supposing that some day he does marry. Whatever may happen, we're in the front row when anything fresh turns up. Gaston has such confidence in me! I wish you had seen him asking me for camomile! A boy, a regular boy! Indeed, he is only thirty-three. And all that wealth weighs so heavily on his shoulders."

Andrée's pink eyelids blinked ironically.

"Pity him, Mother, if you like. I'm not complaining, but all the time we've known Gaston, he has never given you anything except his confidence."

"He owes us nothing. And thanks to him we've always had sugar for our jams, and, from time to time, for my *curaçao;* and birds from his farm, and odds and ends for the child."

"If you're satisfied with that!"

Madame Alvarez held high her majestic head.

"Perfectly satisfied. And even if I was not, what difference would it make?"

"In fact, as far as we're concerned, Gaston Lachaille, rich as he is, behaves as if he wasn't rich at all. Supposing we were in real straits! Would he come to our rescue, do you suppose?"

Madame Alvarez placed her hand on her heart.

"I'm convinced that he would," she said. And after a pause, she added, "But I would rather not have to ask him."

Andrée picked up the *Journal* again, in which there was a photograph of Liane the ex-mistress. "When you take a good look at her, she's not so extraordinary."

"You're wrong," retorted Madame Alvarez, "she is extraordinary. Otherwise she would not be so famous. Successes and celebrity are not a matter of luck. You talk like those scatterbrains who say, 'Seven rows of pearls would look every bit as well on me as on Madame de Pougy. She certainly cuts a dash—but so could I.' Such nonsense makes me laugh. Take what's left of the camomile to bathe your eyes."

"Thank you, Mother. Did the child go to Aunt Alicia's?"

"She did indeed, and in Gaston's motor-car, what's more! He lent it to her. It can go forty miles an hour, I believe! She was in seventh heaven."

"Poor lamb, I wonder what she'll make of her life. She's quite capable of ending up as a mannequin or a saleswoman. She's so backward. At her age, I—"

There was no indulgence in the glance Madame Alvarez gave her daughter.

"Don't boast too much about what you were doing when

you were her age. If I remember rightly, at her age you were snapping your fingers at Monsieur Mennesson and all his flour-mills, though he was perfectly ready to make you your fortune. Instead, you must needs bolt with a wretched music master."

Andrée Alvar kissed her mother's lustrous plaits.

"My darling mother, don't curse me at this hour, I'm so sleepy. Goodnight, Mother. I've a rehearsal tomorrow at a quarter to one. I'll eat at the dairy during the entr'acte; don't bother about me."

She yawned and walked in the dark through the little room where her daughter was asleep. All she could see of Gilberte in the obscurity was a bush of hair and the Russian braid of her nightdress. She locked herself into the exiguous bathroom and, late though it was, lit the gas under a kettle. Madame Alvarez had instilled into her progeny, among other virtues, a respect for certain rites. One of her maxims was, "You can, at a pinch, leave the face till the morning, when travelling or pressed for time. For a woman, attention to the lower parts is the first law of self-respect."

The last to go to bed, Madame Alvarez was the first to rise, and allowed the daily cleaning woman no hand in preparing the breakfast coffee. She slept in the dining-sitting room, on a divan-bed, and, at the stroke of half-past seven, she opened the door to the papers, the quart of milk, and the daily maid—who was carrying the others. By eight o'clock she had taken out her curling-pins, and her beautiful coils of hair were dressed and smooth. At ten minutes to nine, Gilberte left for school, clean and tidy, her hair well-brushed. At ten o'clock Madame Alvarez was "thinking about" the midday meal, that is, she got into her mackintosh, slipped her arm through the handle of her shopping net, and set off to market.

Today, as on all other days, she made sure that her granddaughter would not be late; she placed the coffee-pot and the jug of milk piping hot on the table, and unfolded the newspaper while waiting for her. Gilberte came in fresh as a flower, smelling of lavender-water, with some vestiges of sleep still clinging to her. A cry from Madame Alvarez made her fully wide awake.

"Call your mother, Gigi! Liane d'Exelmans has committed suicide."

The child replied with a long drawn-out "Oooh!" and asked, "Is she dead?"

"Of course not. She knows what she's about."

"How did she do it, Grandmamma? A revolver?"

Madame Alvarez looked pityingly at her granddaughter.

"The idea! Laudanam, as usual. '*Doctors Morèze and Pelledoux, who have never left the heart-broken beauty's bedside, cannot yet answer for her life, but their diagnosis is reassuring . . .*' My own diagnosis is that if Madame d'Exelmans goes on playing that game, she'll end by ruining her stomach."

"The last time she killed herself, Grandmamma, was for the sake of Prince Georgevitch, wasn't it?"

"Where are your brains, my darling? It was for Count Berthou de Sauveterre."

"Oh, so it was. And what will Tonton do now, do you think?"

A dreamy look passed across the huge eyes of Madame Alvarez.

"It's a toss-up, my child. We shall know everything in good time, even if he starts by refusing to give an interview to anybody. You must always start by refusing to give an interview to anybody. Then later you can fill the front page. Tell the concierge, by the way, to get us the evening papers. Have you had enough to eat? Did you have your second cup of milk, and your two pieces of bread and butter? Put on your gloves before you go out. Don't dawdle on the way. I'm going to call your mother. What a story! Andrée, are you asleep? Oh, so you're out of bed! Andrée, Liane has committed suicide!"

"That's a nice change," muttered Andrée. "She has only the one idea in her head, that woman, but she sticks to it."

"You've not taken out your curlers yet, Andrée?"

"And have my hair go limp in the middle of rehearsal? No thank you!"

Madame Alvarez ran her eyes over her daughter, from the spiky tips of her curlers to the felt slippers. "It's plain that there's no man here for you to bother about, my child! A man in the house soon cures a woman of traipsing about in dressing-gown and slippers. What an excitement, this suicide! Unsuccessful, of course."

Andrée's pallid lips parted in a contemptuous smile: "It's getting too boring—the way she takes laudanum as if it was castor oil!"

"Anyhow, who cares about her? It's the Lachaille heir

who matters. This is the first time such a thing has happened to him. He's already had—let me see. He's had Gentiane, who stole his private papers; then that foreigner, who tried to force him into marriage, but Liane is his first suicide. In such circumstances, a man so much in the public eye has to be extremely careful about what line he takes."

"Hm! He'll be bursting with pride, you may be sure."

"And with good reason, too," said Madame Alvarez. "We shall be seeing great things before very long. I wonder what Alicia will have to say about the situation."

"She'll do her best to make a mountain of a molehill."

"Alicia is no angel. But I must confess that she is long-sighted. And that without ever leaving her room!"

"She's no need to, since she has the telephone. Mother, won't you have one put in here?"

"It's expensive," said Madame Alvarez, thoughtfully. "We only just manage to make both ends meet, as it is. The telephone is of real use only to important businessmen, or to women who have something to hide. Now, if you were to change your mode of life—and I'm only putting it forward as a supposition—and if Gigi were to start on a life of her own, I should be the first to say, 'We'll have the telephone put in.' But we haven't reached that point yet, unfortunately."

She allowed herself a single sigh, pulled on her rubber gloves, and coolly set about her household chores. Thanks to her care, the modest flat was growing old without too many signs of deterioration. She retained, from her past life, the honorable habits of women who have lost their honor, and these she taught to her daughter and her daughter's daughter. Sheets never stayed on the beds longer than ten days, and the combination char- and washerwoman told everyone that the chemises and drawers of the ladies of Madame Alvarez' household were changed more often than she could count, and so were the table napkins. At any moment, at the cry of "Gigi, take off your shoes!" Gilberte had to remove shoes and stockings, exhibit white feet to the closest inspection, and announce the least suspicion of a corn.

During the week following Madame d'Exelmans' suicide, Lachaille's reactions were somewhat incoherent. He engaged the stars of the National Musical Academy to dance at a midnight fête held at his own house, and, wishing to give a supper party, at the Pré-Catalan, he arranged for that restaurant to open a fortnight earlier than was their custom. The clowns, Footit *et* Chocolat, did a turn: Rita del Erido caracoled on horseback between the supper tables, wearing a divided skirt of white lace flounces, a white hat on her black hair with white ostrich feathers frothing round the relentless beauty of her face. Indeed, Paris mistakenly proclaimed, such was her beauty, that Gaston Lachaille was hoisting her astride a throne of sugar. Twenty-four hours later, Paris was undeceived. For in the false prophecies it had published, *Gil Blas* nearly lost the subsidy it received from Gaston Lachaille. A specialized weekly, *Paris en amour*, provided another red herring, under the headline: "Young Yankee millionairess makes no secret of weakness for French sugar."

Madame Alvarez' ample bust shook with incredulous laughter when she read the daily papers: she had received her information from none other than Gaston Lachaille in person. Twice in ten days, he had found time to drop in for a cup of camomile, to sink into the depths of the now sagging conch-shaped armchair, and there forget his business worries and his dislike of being unattached. He even brought Gigi an absurd Russian leather music-case with a silver-gilt clasp, and twenty boxes of liquorice. Madame Alvarez was given a *pâté de foie gras* and six bottles of champagne, and of these bounties Tonton Lachaille partook by inviting himself to dinner. Throughout the meal, Gilberte regaled them rather tipsily with tittle-tattle about her school, and later won Gaston's gold pencil at piquet. He lost with good grace, recovered his spirits, laughed, and, pointing to the child, said to Madame Alvarez, "There's my best pal!" Madame Alvarez' Spanish eyes moved with slow watchfulness from Gigi's reddened cheeks and white teeth to Lachaille, who was pulling her hair by the fistful. "You little devil, you had the fourth king up your sleeve all the time!"

It was at this moment that Andrée, coming back from the Opéra-Comique, looked at Gigi's disheveled head rolling against Lachaille's sleeve, and saw the tears of excited laughter in her lovely slate-blue eyes. She said nothing, and accepted a glass of champagne, then another, and yet another. After her third glass, Gaston Lachaille was threatened with the Bell Song from *Lakmé*, at which point Andrée's mother led her away to bed.

The following day, no one spoke of this family party except Gilberte, who exclaimed, "Never, never in all my life, have I laughed so much! And the pencil is real gold!" Her unreserved chatter met with a strange silence, or rather with "Now then, Gigi, try to be a little more serious!" thrown out almost absent-mindedly.

After that, Gaston Lachaille let a fortnight go by without giving a sign of life, and the Alvarez family gathered its information from the papers only.

"Did you see, Andrée? In the Gossip Column it says that Monsieur Gaston Lachaille has left for Monte Carlo. *The reason for this seems to be of a sentimental nature—a secret that we respect.* What next!"

"Would you believe it, Grandmamma, Lydia Poret was saying at the dancing class that Liane travelled on the same train as Tonton, but in another compartment! Grandmamma, do you think it can be true?"

Madame Alvarez shrugged her shoulders.

"If it was true, how on earth would those Porets know? Have they become friends with Monsieur Lachaille all of a sudden?"

"No, but Lydia Poret heard the story in her aunt's dressing room at the Comédie Française."

Madame Alvarez exchanged looks with her daughter.

"In her dressing room! That explains everything!" she exclaimed, for she held the theatrical profession in contempt, although Andrée worked so hard. When Madame Emilienne d'Alencon had decided to present performing rabbits, and Madame de Pougy—shyer on the stage than any young girl—had amused herself by miming the part of Columbine in spangled black tulle, Madame Alvarez had stigmatised them both in a single phrase, "What! have they sunk to that?"

"Grandmamma, tell me, Grandmamma, do you know him, this Prince Radziwill?" Gilberte went on again.

"What's come over the child today? Has she been bitten by a flea? Which Prince Radziwill, to begin with? There's more than one."

"I don't know," said Gigi. "The one who's getting married. Among the list of presents, it says here, *'are three writing-sets in malachite.'* What is malachite?"

"Oh, you're being tiresome, child. If he's getting married, he's no longer interesting."

"But if Tonton got married, wouldn't he be interesting either?"

"It all depends. It would be interesting if he were to marry his mistress. When Prince Cheniaguine married Valérie d'Aigreville, it was obvious that the life she had led him for the past fifteen years was all he wanted; scenes, plates flung across the room, and reconciliations in the middle of the restaurant Durand, Place de la Madeleine. Clearly, she was a woman who knew how to make herself valued. But all that is too complicated for you, my poor Gigi."

"And do you think it's to marry Liane that they've gone away together?"

Madame Alvarez pressed her forehead against the window pane, and seemed to be consulting the spring sunshine, which bestowed upon the street a sunny side and one with shade.

"No," she said, "not if I know anything about anything. I must have a word with Alicia. Gigi, come with me as far as her house; you can leave me there and find your way back along the quais. It will give you some fresh air, since, it would seem, one must have fresh air nowadays. I have never been in the habit of taking the air more than twice a year, myself, at Cabourg and at Monte Carlo. And I am none the worse for that."

That evening Madame Alvarez came in so late that the family dined off tepid soup, cold meat, and some cakes sent round by Aunt Alicia. To Gilberte's "Well, what did she have to say?" she presented an icy front, and answered in clarion tones.

"She says that she is going to teach you how to eat ortolans."

"Lovely!" cried Gilberte. "And what did she say about the summer frock she promised me?"

"She said she would see. And that there's no reason why you should be displeased with the result."

"Oh!" said Gilberte, gloomily.

"She also wants you to go to luncheon with her on Thursday, sharp at twelve."

"With you, too, Grandmamma?"

Madame Alvarez looked at the willowy slip of a girl facing her across the table, at her high, rosy cheekbones beneath eyes as blue as an evening sky, at her strong even teeth biting a fresh-colored but slightly chapped lip, and at the primitive splendor of her ash-gold hair.

"No," she said at last. "Without me."

Gilberte got up and wound an arm about her grandmother's neck.

"The way you said that, Grandmamma, surely doesn't mean that you're going to send me to live with Aunt Alicia? I don't want to leave here, Grandmamma!"

Madame Alvarez cleared her throat, gave a little cough, and smiled.

"Goodness gracious! what a foolish creature you are! Leave here! Why, my poor Gigi, I'm not scolding you, but you've not reached the first stage towards leaving."

For a bell-pull, Aunt Alicia had hung from her front door a length of bead-embroidered braid on a background of twining green vine-leaves and purple grapes. The door itself, varnished and revarnished till it glistened, shone with the glow of a dark brown caramel. From the very threshold, where she was admitted by a "man-servant," Gilberte enjoyed in her undiscriminating way an atmosphere of discreet luxury. The carpet, spread with Persian rugs, seemed to lend her wings. After hearing Madame Alvarez pronounce her sister's Louis XV little drawing room to be "boredom itself," Gilberte echoed her words by saying: "Aunt Alicia's drawing room is very pretty, but it's boredom itself!" reserving her admiration for the dining room, furnished in pale almost golden lemon wood dating from the Directoire, quite plain but for the grain of a wood as transparent as wax. "I shall buy myself a set like that one day," Gigi had once said in all innocence.

"In the Faubourg Antoine, I dare say," Aunt Alicia had answered teasingly, with a smile of her cupid's bow mouth and a flash of small teeth.

She was seventy years old. Her fastidious taste was everywhere apparent: in her silver-grey bedroom with its red Chinese vases, in her narrow white bathroom as warm as a hot-house, and in her robust health, concealed by a pretence of delicacy. The men of her generation, when trying to describe Alicia de Saint-Efflam, fumbled for words and could only exclaim, "Ah, my deah fellow!" or "Nothing could give you the faintest idea . . ." Those who had known her intimately produced photographs which younger men found ordinary enough. "Was she really so lovely? You wouldn't think so from her photographs!" Looking at portraits of her, old admirers would pause for an instant, recollecting the turn of a wrist like a swan's neck, the tiny ear, the profile revealing a delicious kinship between the heart-shaped mouth and the wide-cut eyelids with their long lashes.

Gilberte kissed the pretty old lady, who was wearing a peak of black Chantilly lace on her white hair, and, on her slightly dumpy figure, a tea-gown of shot taffeta.

"You have one of your headaches, Aunt Alicia?"

"I'm not sure yet," replied Aunt Alicia, "it depends on the luncheon. Come quickly, the eggs are ready! Take off your coat! What on earth is that dress?"

"One of Mamma's, altered to fit me. Are they difficult eggs today?"

"Not at all. *Oeufs brouillés aux croutons.* The ortolans

are not difficult, either. And you shall have chocolate cream. So shall I."

With her young voice, a touch of pink on her amiable wrinkles, and lace on her white hair, Aunt Alicia was the perfect stage marquise. Gilberte had the greatest reverence for her aunt. In sitting down to table in her presence, she would pull her skirt up behind, join her knees, hold her elbows close to her sides, straighten her shoulder blades, and to all appearances become the perfect young lady. She would remember what she had been taught, break her bread quickly, eat with her mouth shut, and take care, when cutting her meat, not to let her fore-finger reach the blade of her knife.

Today her hair, severely tied back in a heavy knot at the nape of her neck, disclosed the fresh line of her forehead and ears, and a very powerful throat, rising from the rather ill-cut opening of her altered dress. This was a dingy blue, the bodice pleated about a let-in piece, and to cheer up this patchwork, three rows of mohair braid had been sewn round the hem of the skirt, and three times three rows of mohair braid round the sleeves, between the wrist and the elbow.

Aunt Alicia, sitting opposite her niece and examining her through fine dark eyes, could find no fault.

"How old are you?" she asked suddenly.

"The same as I was the other day, Aunt. Fifteen and a half. Aunt, what do you really think of this business of Tonton Gaston?"

"Why? Does it interest you?"

"Of course, Aunt. It worries me. If Tonton takes up

with another lady, he won't come and play piquet with us any more or drink camomile tea—at least not for some time. That would be a shame."

"That's one way of looking at it, certainly."

Aunt Alicia examined her niece critically, through narrowed eyelids.

"Do you work hard, in class? Who are your friends? Ortolans should be cut in two, with one quick stroke of the knife, and no grating of the blade on the plate. Bite up each half. The bones don't matter. Go on eating while you answer my question, but don't talk with your mouth full. You must manage it. If I can, you can. What friends have you made?"

"None, Aunt. Grandmamma won't even let me have tea with the families of my school friends."

"She is quite right. Apart from that, there is no one who follows you, no little clerk hanging round your skirts? No schoolboy? No older man? I warn you, I shall know at once if you lie to me."

Gilberte gazed at the bright face of the imperious old lady who was questioning her so sharply.

"Why, no, Aunt, no one. Has somebody been telling you tales about me? I am always on my own. And why does Grandmamma stop me from accepting invitations?"

"She is right, for once. You would only be invited by ordinary people, that is to say, useless people."

"And what about us? Aren't we ordinary people ourselves?"

"No."

"What makes these ordinary people inferior to us?"

"They have weak heads and dissolute bodies. Besides, they are married. But I don't think you understand."

"Yes, Aunt, I understand that we don't marry."

"Marriage is not forbidden to us. Instead of marrying 'at once,' it sometimes happens that we marry 'at last.' "

"But does that prevent me from seeing girls of my own age?"

"Yes. Are you bored at home? Well, be a little bored. It's not a bad thing. Boredom helps one to make decisions. What is the matter? Tears? The tears of a silly child who is backward for her age. Have another ortolan."

Aunt Alicia, with three glittering fingers, grasped the stem of her glass and raised it in a toast.

"To you and me, Gigi! You shall have an Egyptian cigarette with your coffee. On condition that you do not wet the end of your cigarette, and that you don't spit out specks of tobacco—going *ptu, ptu*. I shall also give you a note to the *première vendeuse* at Béchoff-David, an old friend of mine who was not a success. Your wardrobe is going to be changed. Nothing venture, nothing gain."

The dark blue eyes gleamed. Gilberte stammered with joy.

"Aunt! Aunt! I'm going to . . . to Bé—"

"—choff-David. But I thought you weren't interested in clothes?"

Gilberte blushed.

"Aunt, I'm not interested in home-made clothes."

"I sympathize with you. Can it be that you have taste? When you think of looking your best, how do you see yourself dressed?"

"Oh, but I know just what would suit me, Aunt! I've seen—"

"Explain yourself without gestures. The moment you gesticulate you look common."

"I've seen a dress . . . oh, a dress created for Madame Lucy Gérard! Hundreds of tiny ruffles of pearl-grey silk muslin from top to bottom. And then a dress of lavender-blue cloth cut out on a black velvet foundation, the cut-out design making a sort of peacock's tail on the train."

The small hand with its precious stones flashed through the air.

"Enough! Enough! I see your fancy is to be dressed like a leading *comédienne* at the Théâtre Français,—and don't take that as a compliment! Come and pour out the coffee. And without jerking up the lip of the coffee-pot to prevent the drop from falling. I'd rather have a foot-bath in my saucer than see you juggling like a waiter in a café."

The next hour passed very quickly for Gilberte: Aunt Alicia had unlocked a casket of jewels to use for a lesson that dazzled her.

"What is that, Gigi?"

"A marquise diamond."

"We say, a marquise-shaped brilliant. And that?"

"A topaz."

Aunt Alicia threw up her hands and the sunlight, glancing off her rings, set off a myriad scintillations.

"A topaz! I have suffered many humiliations, but this surpasses them all. A topaz among my jewels! Why not an aquamarine or a chrysolite? It's a yellow diamond, little goose, and you won't often see its like. And this?"

Gilberte half opened her mouth, as if in a dream.

"Oh! That's an emerald. Oh, how beautiful it is!"

Aunt Alicia slipped the large square-cut emerald on one of her thin fingers and was lost in silence.

"Do you see," she said in a hushed voice "that almost blue flame darting about in the depths of the green light? Only the most beautiful emeralds contain that miracle of elusive blue."

"Who gave it to you, Aunt?" Gilberte dared to ask.

"A king," said Aunt Alicia simply.

"A great king?"

"No. A little one. Great kings do not give very fine stones."

"Why not?"

For a fleeting moment, Aunt Alicia proffered a glimpse of her tiny white teeth.

"If you want my opinion, it's because they don't want to. Between ourselves, the little ones don't either."

"Then who does give great big stones?"

"Who? The shy. The proud, too. And the bounders, because they think that to give a monster jewel is a sign of good breeding. Sometimes a woman does, to humiliate a man. Never wear second-rate jewels, wait till the really good ones come to you."

"And if they don't?"

"Well, then it can't be helped. Rather than a wretched little diamond full of flaws, wear a simple, plainly inexpensive ring. In that case you can say, 'It's a memento. I never part with it, day or night.' Don't ever wear artistic jewelry, it wrecks a woman's reputation."

"What is an artistic jewel?"

"It all depends. A mermaid in gold with eyes of chryso-
prase. An Egyptian scarab. A large engraved amethyst.
A not very heavy bracelet said to have been chased by a
master-hand. A lyre or star, mounted as a brooch. A stud-
ded tortoise. In a word, all of them, frightful. Never wear
baroque pearls, not even as hat-pins. Beware, above all
things, of family jewels!"

"But Grandmamma has a beautiful cameo, set as a
medallion."

"There are no beautiful cameos," said Alicia, with a toss
of the head. "There are precious stones and pearls. There
are white, yellow, blue, blue-white or pink diamonds. We
won't speak of black diamonds, they're not worth men-
tioning. Then there are rubies—when you can be sure of
them; sapphires, when they come from Kashmir; emeralds,
provided they have no fatal flaw, or are not too light in
color, or have a yellowish tint."

"Aunt, I'm very fond of opals, too."

"I am very sorry, but you are not to wear them. I won't
allow it."

Dumbfounded, Gilberte remained for a moment open-
mouthed.

"Oh! Do you too, Aunt, really believe that they bring
bad luck?"

"Why in the world not? You silly little creature," Alicia
went bubbling on, "you must pretend to believe in such
things. Believe in opals, believe—let's see, what can I sug-
gest—in turquoises that die, in the evil eye . . ."

"But," said Gigi, haltingly, "those are . . . are superstitions!"

"Of course they are, child. They also go by the name of weaknesses. A pretty little collection of weaknesses, and a terror of spiders, are indispensable stock-in-trade with men."

"Why, Aunt?"

The old lady closed the casket, and kept Gilberte kneeling before her.

"Because nine men out of ten are superstitious, nineteen out of twenty believe in the evil eye, and ninety-eight out of a hundred are afraid of spiders. They forgive us—oh! for many things, but not for the absence in us of their own failings," she said. "What makes you sigh?"

"I shall never remember all that!"

"The important thing is not for *you* to remember, but for me to know it."

"Aunt, what is a writing-set in . . . in malachite?"

"Always a calamity. But where on earth did you pick up such terms?"

"From the list of presents at grand weddings, Aunt, printed in the papers."

"Nice reading! But, at least you can gather from it what kind of presents you should never give, or accept."

While speaking, she began to touch here and there the young face on a level with her own, with the sharp pointed nail of her index finger. She lifted one slightly chapped lip, inspected the spotless enamel of the teeth.

"A fine jaw, my girl! With such teeth, I should have gobbled up Paris, and the rest of the world into the bargain. As it was, I had a good bite out of it. What's this you've got here? A small pimple? You shouldn't have a small pimple near your nose. And this? You've pinched a blackhead. You've no business to have such things, or to pinch them. I'll give you some of my astringent lotion. You musn't eat anything from the pork-butchers' except cooked ham. You don't put on powder?"

"Grandmamma won't let me."

"I should hope not. You go you-know-where regularly? Let me smell your breath. Not that it means anything at this hour, you've just had luncheon."

She laid her hands on Gigi's shoulders.

"Pay attention to what I'm going to say. You have it in your power to please. You have an impossible little nose, a nondescript mouth, cheeks rather like the wife of a moujik—"

"Oh, Aunt!" sighed Gilberte.

"But, with your eyes and eyelashes, your teeth, and your hair, you can get away with it, if you're not a perfect fool. As for the rest—"

She cupped her hands like conch-shells over Gigi's bosom and smiled.

"A promise, but a pretty promise, neatly moulded. Don't eat too many almonds, they add weight to the breasts. Ah! remind me to teach you how to choose cigars."

Gilberte opened her eyes so wide that the tips of her lashes touched her eyebrows.

"Why?"

She received a little tap on the cheek.

"Because—because I do nothing without good reason

If I take you in hand at all, I must do it thoroughly. Once a woman understands the tastes of a man, cigars included, and once a man knows what pleases a woman, they may be said to be well matched."

"And then they fight," concluded Gigi with a knowing air.

"What do you mean, they fight?"

The old lady looked at Gigi in consternation.

"Ah!" she added, "You certainly never invented the triple mirror! Come, you little psychologist! Let me give you a note for Madame Henriette at Béchoff."

While her aunt was writing at a miniature rose-pink escritoire, Gilberte breathed in the scent of the fastidiously furnished room. Without wanting them for herself, she examined the objects she knew so well but hardly appreciated: Cupid, the Archer, pointing to the hours on the mantel-piece; two rather daring pictures; a bed like the basin of a fountain and its chinchilla coverlet; a rosary of small seed pearls and the New Testament on the bedside table; two red Chinese vases fitted as lamps—a happy note against the grey of the walls.

"Run along, my little one. I shall send for you again quite soon. Don't forget to ask Victor for the cake you're to take home. Gently, don't disarrange my hair! And remember, I shall have my eye on you as you leave the house. Woe betide you if you march like a guardsman, or drag your feet behind you!"

The month of May fetched Gaston Lachaille back to Paris, and brought to Gilberte two well-cut dresses and a light-weight coat—"a sack-coat like Cléo de Mérode's" she called it—as well as hats and boots and shoes. To these she added, on her own account, a few curls over the forehead, which cheapened her appearance. She paraded in front of Gaston in a blue and white dress reaching almost to the ground. "A full seven and a half yards round, Tonton, my skirt measures!" She was more than proud of her slender waist, held in by a grosgrain sash with a silver buckle; but she tried every dodge to free her lovely strong neck from its whale-bone collar of "imitation Venetian point" which matched the tucks of the bodice. The full sleeves and wide flounced skirt of blue and white striped silk rustled deliciously, and Gilberte delighted in picking at the sleeves, to puff them out just below the shoulder.

"You remind me of a performing monkey," Lachaille said to her. "I liked you much better in your old tartan dress. In that uncomfortable collar you look just like a hen with a full crop. Take a peep at yourself!"

Feeling a little ruffled, Gilberte turned round to face the looking-glass. She had a lump in one of her cheeks caused by a large caramel, out of a box sent all the way from Nice at Gaston's order.

"I've heard a good deal about you, Tonton," she retorted, "but I've never heard it said that you had any taste in clothes."

He stared, almost choking, at this newly fledged young woman, then turned to Madame Alvarez.

"Charming manners you've taught her! I congratulate you!"

Whereupon he left the house without drinking his camomile tea, and Madame Alvarez wrung her hands.

"Look what you've done to us now, my poor Gigi!"

"I know," said Gigi, "but then why does he fly at me? He must know by now, I should think, that I can give as good as I get!"

Her grandmother shook her by the arm.

"But think what you've done, you wretched child! Good heavens! when will you learn to think? You've mortally offended the man, as likely as not. Just when we are doing our utmost to—"

"To do what, Grandmamma?"

"Why! to do everything, to make an elegant young lady of you, to show you off to advantage."

"For whose benefit, Grandmamma? You must admit that one doesn't have to turn oneself inside out for an old friend like Tonton!"

But Madame Alvarez admitted nothing; not even to her astonishment, when, the following day, Gaston Lachaille arrived in the best of spirits, wearing a light colored suit.

"Put on your hat, Gigi! I'm taking you out to tea."

"Where?" cried Gigi.

"To the *Réservoirs*, at Versailles!"

"Hurrah! Hurrah! Hurrah!" chanted Gilberte.

She turned towards the kitchen.

"Grandmamma, I'm having tea at the *Réservoirs*, with Tonton!"

Madame Alvarez appeared, and without stopping to untie the flowered satinette apron across her stomach, interposed her soft hand between Gilberte's arm and that of Gaston Lachaille.

"No, Gaston," she said simply.

"What do you mean, No?"

"Oh! Grandmamma!" wailed Gigi.

Madame Alvarez seemed not to hear her.

"Go to your room a minute, Gigi. I should like to talk to Monsieur Lachaille in private."

She watched Gilberte leave the room and close the door behind her; then, returning to Gaston, she met his dark, rather brutal stare without flinching.

"What is the meaning of all this, Mamita? Ever since yesterday, I find quite a change here. What's going on?"

"I shall be glad if you will sit down, Gaston, I'm tired," said Madame Alvarez. "Oh, my poor legs!"

She sighed, waited for a response that did not come, and then untied her apron, under which she was wearing a black dress with a large cameo pinned upon it. She motioned her guest to a high-backed chair, keeping the armchair for herself. Then she sat down heavily, smoothed her greying black coils, and folded her hands on her lap. The unhurried movement of her large dark lambent eyes, and the ease with which she remained motionless, were sure signs of her self-control.

"Gaston, you cannot doubt my friendship for you!" Lachaille emitted a short, businesslike laugh, and tugged at his moustache. "My friendship and my gratitude. Nevertheless, I must never forget that I have a soul entrusted to my care. Andrée, as you know, has neither the time nor the inclination to look after the girl. Our Gilberte has not got the gumption to make her own way in the world, like so many. She is just a child."

"Of sixteen," said Lachaille.

"Of nearly sixteen," consented Madame Alvarez. "For years you have been giving her sweets and playthings. She swears by Tonton, and by him alone. And now you want to take her out to tea, in your automobile, to the *Réservoirs!*"

Madame Alvarez placed a hand on her heart.

"Upon my soul and conscience, Gaston, if there were only you and me, I should say to you, 'Take Gilberte anywhere you like, I entrust her to you blindly.' But there are always the others. The eyes of the world are on you. To be seen tête-à-tête with you, is, for a woman—"

Gaston Lachaille lost patience.

"All right, all right, I understand. You want me to believe that once she is seen having tea with me, Gilberte is compromised! A slip of a girl, a flapper, a chit whom no one knows, whom no one notices!"

"Let us say, rather," interrupted Madame Alvarez gently, "that she will be labeled. No matter where you put in an appearance, Gaston, your presence is remarked upon. A young girl who goes out alone with you is no longer an ordinary girl, or even—to put it bluntly—a respectable girl. Now our little Gilberte must not, above all things, cease to be an ordinary young girl, at least not by that method. So far as it concerns you, it will simply end in one more story to be added to the long list already in existence but, personally, when I read of it in *Gil Blas*, I shall not be amused."

Gaston Lachaille rose, paced from the table to the door,

then from the door to the window, before replying.

"Very good, Mamita, I have no wish to vex you. I shan't argue," he said coldly. "Keep your precious child."

He turned round again to face Madame Alvarez, his chin held high.

"I can't help wondering, as a matter of interest, whom you are keeping her for! A clerk earning a hundred a year, who'll marry her and give her four children in three years?"

"I know the duty of a mother better than that," said Madame Alvarez composedly. "I shall do my best to entrust Gigi only to the care of a man capable of saying, 'I take charge of her and answer for her future.' May I have the pleasure of brewing you some camomile tea, Gaston?"

"No, thank you. I'm late already."

"Would you like Gigi to come and say goodbye?"

"Don't bother, I'll see her another time. I can't say when, I'm sure. I'm very much taken up these days."

"Never mind, Gaston, don't worry about her. Have a good time, Gaston."

Once alone, Madame Alvarez mopped her forehead, and went to open the door of Gilberte's room.

"You were listening at the door, Gigi!"

"No, Grandmamma."

"Yes, you had your ear to the key-hole. You must never listen at key-holes. You don't hear properly and so you get things all wrong. Monsieur Lachaille has gone."

"So I can see," said Gilberte.

"Now you must rub the new potatoes in a cloth. I'll sauté them when I come in."

"Are you going out, Grandmamma?"

"I'm going round to see Alicia."

"Again?"

"Is it your place to object?" said Madame Alvarez severely. "You had better bathe your eyes in cold water, since you have been silly enough to cry."

"Grandmamma!"

"What?"

"What difference could it make to you, if you'd let me go out with Tonton Gaston in my new dress?"

"Silence! If you can't understand anything about anything, at least let those who are capable of using their reason do so for you. And put on my rubber gloves before you touch the potatoes!"

Throughout the whole of the following week, silence reigned over the Alvarez household, except for a surprise visit, one day, from Aunt Alicia. She arrived in a hired brougham, all black lace and dull silk with a rose at her shoulder, and carried on an anxious conversation, strictly between themselves, with her younger sister. As she was leaving, she bestowed only a moment's attention on Gilberte, pecked at her cheek with a fleeting kiss, and was gone.

"What did she want?" Gilberte asked Madame Alvarez.

"Oh, nothing . . . the address of the heart specialist who treated Madame Buffetery."

Gilberte reflected for a moment.

"It was a long one," she said.

"What was long?"

"The address of the heart specialist. Grandmamma, I should like a *cachet*. I have a headache."

"But you had one yesterday. A headache doesn't last forty-eight hours!"

"Presumably my headaches are different from other people's," said Gilberte, offended.

She was losing some of her sweetness, and, on her return from school, would make some such remark as "My teacher has it in for me!" or complain of not being able to sleep. She was gradually slipping into a state of idleness, which her grandmother noticed, but did nothing to overcome.

One day Gigi was busy applying liquid chalk to her white canvas button boots, when Gaston Lachaille put in an appearance without ringing the bell. His hair was too long, his complexion sun-tanned, and he was wearing a broad check summer suit. He stopped short in front of Gilberte, who was perched high on a kitchen stool, her left hand shod with a boot.

"Oh! Grandmamma left the key in the door, that's just like her!"

As Gaston Lachaille looked at her without saying a word, she began to blush, put down the boot on the table and pulled her skirt down over her knees.

"So, Tonton, you slip in like a burglar! I believe you're thinner. Aren't you fed properly by that famous chef of yours who used to be with the Prince of Wales? Being thinner makes your eyes look larger, and at the same time makes your nose longer, and—"

"I have something to say to your grandmother," interrupted Gaston Lachaille. "Run into your room, Gigi."

For a moment she remained open-mouthed, then she jumped off her stool. The strong column of her neck, like an archangel's, swelled with anger as she advanced on Lachaille.

"Run into your room! Run into your room! And suppose I said the same to you? Who do you think you are here, ordering me to run into my room? All right, I'm going to my room! And I can tell you one thing; so long as you're in the house, I shan't come out of it!"

She slammed the door behind her, and there was a dramatic click of the bolt.

"Gaston," breathed Madame Alvarez, "I shall insist on the child apologising, yes, I shall insist; if necessary, I'll. . . . "

Gaston was not listening to her, and stood staring at the closed door.

"Now, Mamita," said he, "let us talk briefly and to the point."

"Let us go over it all once again," said Aunt Alicia. "To begin with, you are quite sure he said, 'She shall be spoiled, more than—' "

"Than any woman before her!"

"Yes, but that's the sort of vague phrase that every man comes out with. I like things cut and dried."

"Just what they were, Alicia, for he said that he would guarantee Gigi against every imaginable mishap, even against himself, by an insurance policy; and that he regarded himself more or less as her godfather."

"Yes, hmm . . . Not bad, not bad. But vague, vague as ever."

She was still in bed, her white hair arranged in curls against the pink pillow. She was absent-mindedly tying and untying the ribbon of her night-dress. Madame Alvarez, pale and wan under her morning hat as the moon behind passing clouds, was leaning cross-armed against the bedside.

"And he added, 'I don't wish to rush anything. Above all, I am Gigi's best pal. I shall give her all the time she wants to get used to me.' There were tears in his eyes. And he also said, 'After all, she won't have to deal with a savage.' A gentleman, in fact. A perfect gentleman."

"Yes, yes. Rather a vague gentleman. And the child, have you spoken frankly to her?"

"As was my duty, Alicia. This is no time for us to be treating her like a child from whom the cakes have to be hidden. Yes, I spoke frankly. I referred to Gaston as a miracle, as a god, as—"

"Tut, tut, tut," criticised Alicia, "I should have stressed the difficulties rather: the cards to be played, the fury of all those ladies, the conquest represented by so conspicuous a man."

Madame Alvarez wrung her hands.

"The difficulties! The cards to be played! Do you imagine she's like you? Don't you know her at all? She's very far from calculating, she's—"

"Thank you."

"I mean she has no ambition. I was even struck by the fact that she did not react either one way or the other. No cries of joy, no tears of emotion! All I got from her was, 'Oh, yes! Oh, it's very considerate of him.' Then, only at the very end, did she lay down, as her conditions—"

"Conditions, indeed!" murmured Alicia.

"—that she would answer Monsieur Lachaille's proposals herself, and discuss the matter alone with him. In other words, it was her business, and hers only."

"Let us be prepared for the worst! You've brought a nit-wit into the world. She will ask for the moon and, if I know him, she won't get it. He is coming at four o'clock?"

"Yes."

"Hasn't he sent anything? No flowers? No little present?"

"Nothing. Do you think that's a bad sign?"

"No. It's what one would expect. See that the child is nicely dressed. How is she looking?"

"Not too well, today. Poor little lamb—"

"Come, come!" said Alicia heartlessly. "You'll have time for tears another day—when she's succeeded in ruining the whole affair."

"You've eaten scarcely anything, Gigi."

"I wasn't too hungry, Grandmamma. May I have a little more coffee?"

"Of course."

"And a drop of Combier?"

"Why, yes. There's nothing in the world better than Combier for settling the stomach."

Through the open window rose the noise and heat from the street below. Gigi let the tip of her tongue lick round the bottom of her liqueur glass.

"If Aunt Alicia could see you, Gigi!" said Madame Alvarez light-heartedly.

Gigi's only reply was a disillusioned little smile. Her old plaid dress was too tight across the breast, and under the table she stretched out her long legs well beyond the limits of her skirt.

"What can Mamma be rehearsing today that's kept her from coming back to eat with us, Grandmamma? Do you think there really is a rehearsal going on at her Opéra-Comique?"

"She said so, didn't she?"

'Personally, I don't think she wanted to eat here."

"What makes you think that?"

Without taking her eyes off the sunny window, Gigi simply shrugged her shoulders.

"Oh, nothing, Grandmamma."

When she had drained the last drop of her Combier, she rose and began to clear the table.

"Leave all that, Gigi, I'll do it."

"Why, Grandmamma? I do it as a rule."

She looked Madame Alvarez straight in the face, with an expression the old lady could not meet.

"We began our meal late, it's almost three o'clock and you're not dressed yet; do pull yourself together, Gigi."

"It's never before taken me a whole hour to change my clothes."

"Won't you need my help? Are you satisfied your hair's all right?"

"It will do, Grandmamma. When the door bell rings, don't bother, I'll go and open it."

On the stroke of four, Gaston Lachaille rang three times. A childish, wistful face looked out from the bedroom door, listening. After three more impatient rings, Gilberte advanced as far as the middle of the hall. She still had on her old plaid dress and cotton stockings. She rubbed her cheeks with both fists, then ran to open the door.

"Good afternoon, Uncle Gaston."

"Didn't you want to let me in, you bad girl?"

They bumped shoulders in passing through the door, said "Oh, sorry!" a little too self-consciously, then laughed awkwardly.

"Please sit down, Tonton. D' you know, I didn't have time to change. Not like you! That navy blue serge couldn't look better!"

"You don't know what you're talking about! It's tweed."

"Of course. How silly of me!"

She sat down facing him, pulled her skirt over her knees, and they stared at each other. Gilberte's tomboy assurance deserted her; a strange woebegone look made her blue eyes seem twice their natural size.

"What's the matter with you, Gigi?" asked Lachaille softly. "Tell me something! Do you know why I'm here?"

She assented with an exaggerated nod.

"Do you want to, or don't you?" he asked, lowering his voice.

She pushed a curl behind her ear, and swallowed bravely.

"I don't want to."

Lachaille twirled the tips of his moustache between two fingers, and for a moment looked away from a pair of darkened blue eyes, a pink cheek with a single freckle, curved lashes, a mouth unaware of its power, a heavy mass of ash-gold hair, and a neck as straight as a column, strong, hardly feminine, all of a piece, innocent of jewelry.

"I don't want what you want," Gilberte began again. "You said to Grandmamma . . ."

He put out his hand to stop her. His mouth was slightly twisted to one side, as if he had the toothache.

"I know what I said to your grandmother. It's not worth repeating. Just tell me what it is you don't want. You can then tell me what you do want. I shall give it to you."

"You mean that?" cried Gilberte.

He nodded, letting his shoulders droop, as if tired out. She watched, with surprise, these signs of exhaustion and torment.

"Tonton, you told Grandmamma you wanted to make me my fortune."

"A very fine one," said Lachaille firmly.

"It will be fine if I like it," said Gilberte, no less firmly. "They've drummed into my ears that I am backward for my age, but all the same I know the meaning of words. 'Make me my fortune,' that means I should go away from here with you, and that I should sleep in your bed."

"Gigi, I beg of you!"

She stopped, because of the strong note of appeal in his voice.

"But, Tonton, why should I mind speaking of it to you? You didn't mind speaking of it to Grandmamma. Neither did Grandmamma mind speaking of it to me. Grandmamma wanted me to see nothing but the bright side. But I know more than she told me. I know very well that if you make me my fortune, then I must have my photograph in the papers, go to the Battle of Flowers and to the races at Deauville. When we quarrel, *Gil Blas* and *Paris en amour* will tell the whole story. When you throw me over once and for all, as you did Gentiane des Cevennes when you'd had enough of her—"

"What! You've heard about that? They've bothered you with all those old stories?"

She gave a solemn little nod.

"Grandmamma and Aunt Alicia. They've taught me that you're world-famous. I know too that Maryse Chuquet stole your letters, and you brought an action against her. I know that Countess Pariewsky was angry with you, because you didn't want to marry a *divorcée*, and she tried to shoot you. I know what all the world knows."

Lachaille put his hand on Gilberte's knee.

"Those are not the things we have to talk about together, Gigi. All that's in the past. All that's over and done with."

"Of course, Tonton, until it begins again. It's not your fault if you're world-famous. But I haven't got a world-famous sort of nature. So it won't do for me."

In pulling at the hem of her skirt, she caused Lachaille's hand to slip off her knee.

"Aunt Alicia and Grandmamma are on your side. But as it concerns me a little, after all, I think you must allow me to say a word on the subject. And my word is, that it won't do for me."

She got up and walked about the room. Gaston Lachaille's silence seemed to embarrass her. She punctuated her wanderings with, "After all, it's true, I suppose! No, it really won't do!"

"I should like to know," said Gaston at last, "whether you're not just trying to hide from me the fact that you dislike me. If you dislike me, you had better say so at once."

"Oh no, Tonton, I don't dislike you at all! I'm always delighted to see you! I'll prove it by making a suggestion in my turn. You could go on coming here as usual, even more often. No one would see any harm in it, since you're a friend of the family. You could go on bringing me liquor-ice, champagne on my birthdays, and on Sunday we should have an extra special game of piquet. Wouldn't that be a pleasant little life? A life without all this business of sleeping in your bed and everybody knowing about it, losing strings of pearls, being photographed all the time and having to be so careful."

She was absent-mindedly twisting a strand of hair round her nose, and pulled it so tight that she snuffled and the tip of her nose turned purple.

"A very pretty little life, as you say," interrupted Gaston Lachaille. "You're forgetting one thing only, Gigi, and that is, I'm in love with you."

"Oh!" she cried, "you never told me that."

"Well," he owned uneasily, "I'm telling you now."

She remained standing before him, silent and breathing fast. There was no concealing her embarrassment; the rise and fall of her bosom under the tight bodice, the hectic flush high on her cheeks, and the quivering of her close pressed lips—albeit ready to open again and taste of life.

"That's quite another thing!" she cried at last. "But then you are a terrible man! You're in love with me, and you want to drag me into a life where I'll have nothing but worries, where everyone gossips about everyone else, where the papers print nasty stories. You're in love with me, and you don't care a fig if you let me in for all sorts of horrible adventures, ending in separations, quarrels, Sandomirs, revolvers, and lau . . . and laudanum."

She burst into violent sobs, which made as much noise as a fit of coughing. Gaston put his arms round her to bend her towards him like a branch, but she escaped and took refuge between the wall and the piano.

"But listen, Gigi! Listen to me!"

"Never! I never want to see you again! I should never have believed it of you. You're not in love with me, you're a wicked man! Go away from here!"

She shut him out from sight by rubbing her eyes with closed fists. Gaston had moved over to her and was trying to discover some place on her well guarded face where he could kiss her. But his lips found only the point of a small chin wet with tears. At the sound of sobbing, Madame Alvarez had hurried in. Pale and circumspect, she had stopped in hesitation at the door to the kitchen.

"Good gracious, Gaston!" she said. "What on earth's the matter with her?"

"The matter!" said Lachaille. "The matter is that she doesn't want to."

"She doesn't want to!" repeated Madame Alvarez. "What do you mean, she doesn't want to?"

"No, she doesn't want to. I speak plainly enough, don't I?"

"No. I don't want to," whimpered Gigi.

Madame Alvarez looked at her granddaughter in a sort of terror.

"Gigi! It's enough to drive one raving mad! But I told you, Gigi. Gaston, as God is my witness, I told her—"

"You have told her too much!" cried Lachaille.

He turned his face towards the child, looking just a poor, sad, lovesick creature, but all he saw of her was a slim back shaken by sobs and a disheveled head of hair.

"Oh!" he exclaimed hoarsely, "I've had enough of this!" and he went out, banging the door.

The next day, at three o'clock, Aunt Alicia, summoned by *pneumatique,* stepped out from her hired brougham. She climbed the stairs up to the Alvarez' floor—pretending to the shortness of breath proper to someone with a weak heart—and noiselessly pushed open the door which her sister had left on the latch.

"Where's the child?"

"In her room. Do you want to see her?"

"There's plenty of time. How is she?"

"Very calm."

Alicia shook two angry little fists.

"Very calm! She has pulled the roof down about our heads, and she is very calm! These young people of today!"

Once again she raised her spotted veil and withered her sister with a single glance.

"And you, standing there, what do you propose doing?"

With a face like a crumpled rose, she sternly confronted the large pallid face of her sister, whose retort was mild in the extreme.

"What do I propose doing? How do you mean? I can't, after all, tie the child up!" Her burdened shoulders rose on a long sigh. "I surely have not deserved such children as these!"

"While you stand there wringing your hands, Lachaille has rushed away from here and in such a state that he may do something idiotic!"

"And even without his straw hat," said Madame Alvarez. "He got into his motor bare-headed! The whole street might have seen him!"

"If I were to be told that by this time he's already become engaged, or is busy making it up with Liane, it would not surprise me in the least!"

"It is a moment fraught with destiny," said Madame Alvarez lugubriously.

"And afterwards, how did you speak to that little brat?"

Madame Alvarez pursed her lips.

"Gigi may be a bit scatter-brained in certain things and backward for her age, but she's not what you say. A young girl who has held the attention of Monsieur Lachaille is not a little brat."

A furious shrug of the shoulders set Alicia's black lace quivering.

"All right, all right! With all due respect, then, how did you handle your precious princess?"

"I talked sense to her. I spoke to her of the family. I tried to make her understand that we sink or swim together. I enumerated all the things she could do for herself and for us."

"And what about nonsense? Did you talk nonsense to her? Didn't you talk to her of love, travel, moonlight, Italy? You must know how to harp on every string. Didn't you tell her that on the other side of the world the sea is phosphorescent, that there are humming-birds in all the flowers, and that you make love under gardenias in full bloom beside a moonlit fountain?"

Madame Alvarez looked at her spirited elder sister with sadness in her eyes.

"I couldn't tell her all that, Alicia, because I know nothing about it. I've never been further afield than Cabourg and Monte Carlo."

"Aren't you capable of inventing it?"

"No, Alicia."

Both fell silent. Alicia, with a gesture, made up her mind.

"Call the chit in to me. We shall see."

When Gilberte came in, Aunt Alicia had resumed all the airs and graces of a frivolous old lady and was smelling the tea-rose pinned near her chin.

"Good afternoon, my little Gigi."

"Good afternoon, Aunt Alicia."

"What is this Inez has been telling me? You have an admirer? And *what* an admirer! For your first attempt, it's a master-stroke!"

Gilberte acquiesced with a guarded, resigned little smile. She offered to Alicia's darting curiosity a fresh young face, to which the violet-blue shadow on her eyelids and the high color of her mouth gave an almost artificial effect. For coolness' sake, she had dragged back the hair off her temples with the help of two combs, and this drew up the corners of her eyes.

"And it seems you have been playing the naughty girl, and tried your claws on Monsieur Lachaille! Bravo, my brave little girl!"

Gilberte raised incredulous eyes to her aunt.

"Yes, indeed! Bravo! It will only make him all the happier when you are nice to him again."

"But I am nice to him, Aunt. Only, I don't want to, that's all."

"Yes, yes, we know. You've sent him packing to his sugar refinery, that's perfect. But don't send him to the Devil, he's quite capable of going. The fact is, you don't love him."

Gilberte gave a little childish shrug.

"Yes, Aunt, I'm very fond of him."

"Just what I said, you don't love him. Mind you, there's no harm in that, it leaves you free to act as you please. Ah, if you'd been head over heels in love with him, then I should have been a little anxious. Lachaille is a fine figure of a man. Well built—you've only to look at the photographs of him taken at Deauville in bathing costume. He's famous for that. Yes, I should feel sorry for you, my poor Gigi. To start by having a passionate love-affair—to go away all by your two selves to the other side of the world, forgetting everything in the arms of the man who adores you, listening to the song of love in an eternal spring—surely things of that sort must touch your heart! What does all that say to you?"

"It says to me that when the eternal spring is over Monsieur Lachaille will go off with another lady. Or else that the lady—me if you like—will leave Monsieur Lachaille, and Monsieur Lachaille will hurry off to blab the whole story. And then the lady, still me if you like, will have nothing else to do but get into another gentleman's bed. I don't want that. I'm not changeable by nature, indeed I'm not."

She crossed her arms over her breasts and shivered slightly.

"Grandmamma, may I have a *cachet faivre*? I want to go to bed, I feel cold."

"You great goose!" burst out Aunt Alicia, "a silly little milliner's shop is all you deserve! Be off, go and marry a bank clerk!"

"If you wish it, Aunt. But I want to go to bed."

Madame Alvarez put her hand on Gigi's forehead.

"Don't you feel well?"

"I'm all right, Grandmamma. Only I'm sad."

She leaned her head on Madame Alvarez' shoulder, and, for the first time in her life, closed her eyes pathetically like a grown woman. The two sisters exchanged glances.

"You must know, my Gigi," said Madame Alvarez, "that we won't torment you to that extent. If you say you really don't want to—"

"A failure is a failure," said Alicia caustically. "We can't go on discussing it for ever."

"You'll never be able to say you didn't have good advice and the very best at that," said Madame Alvarez.

"I know, Grandmamma, but I'm sad, all the same."

"Why?"

A tear trickled over Gilberte's downy cheek without wetting it, but she did not answer. A brisk peel of the door bell made her jump where she stood.

"Oh, it must be him," she said. "It is him! Grandmamma, I don't want to see him! Hide me, Grandmamma!"

At the low, passionate tone of her voice, Aunt Alicia raised an attentive head, and pricked an expert ear. Then she ran to open the door and came back a moment later. Gaston Lachaille, haggard, his eyes bloodshot, followed close behind her.

"Good afternoon, Mamita. Good afternoon, Gigi!" he said airily. "Please don't move, I've come to retrieve my straw hat."

None of the three women replied, and his assurance left him.

"Well, you might at least say a word to me, even if it's only How-d'you-do?"

Gilberte took a step towards him.

"No," she said, "You've not come to retrieve your straw hat. You have another one in your hand. And you would never bother about a hat. You've come to make me more miserable than ever."

"Really!" burst out Madame Alvarez. "This is more than I can stomach. How can you, Gigi! Here is a man who, out of the goodness of his generous heart—"

"If you please, Grandmamma, just a moment, and I shall have finished."

Instinctively she straightened her dress, adjusted the buckle of her sash, and marched up to Gaston.

"I've been thinking, Gaston. In fact, I've been thinking a great deal—"

He interrupted her, to stop her saying what he was afraid to hear.

"I swear to you, my darling—"

"No, don't swear to me. I've been thinking I would rather be miserable with you than without you. So . . ."

She tried twice to go on.

"So . . . There you are. How d'you do, Gaston, how d'you do?"

She offered him her cheek, in her usual way. He held her, a little longer than usual, until he felt her relax, and become calm and gentle in his arms. Madame Alvarez seemed about to hurry forward, but Alicia's impatient little hand restrained her.

"Leave well alone. Don't meddle any more. Can't you see she is far beyond us?"

She pointed to Gigi, who was resting a trusting head and the rich abundance of her hair on Lachaille's shoulder.

The happy man turned to Madame Alvarez.

"Mamita," he said, "will you do me the honor, the favor, give me the infinite joy of bestowing on me the hand. . . ."

Julie de Carneilhan

Translated by PATRICK LEIGH FERMOR

Julie de Carneilhan

Mme. de Carneilhan turned off the gas, leaving the earthen-ware saucepan on the stove. Beside the stove she laid out the Empire teacup, the Swedish spoon and the rye-bread folded in a rough silk Turkish napkin. The smell of hot chocolate made her yawn with hunger, for she had not eaten much for luncheon—a cold pork cutlet, a slice of bread and butter, half a pound of red currants and a cup of excellent coffee. During the meal she had worked away at a triangular cushion, cut out of an old pair of faded grey corduroy riding breeches. A fine-linked steel chain, which had once belonged, so Julie de Carneilhan said, to a monkey (though according to her brother the monkey had belonged to the chain) was to be sewn on one side of the cushion in the shape of a C, or possibly a J. "C would be easier to sew, but J is more decorative: it'll look terrific," she said to herself.

She put the lid on the steaming saucepan, mopped the kitchen slab with a cloth, and then filled the milk-can with water and shut the dust-bin. Feeling that she had lived up to her principles as the perfect housewife, she went into the studio. In front of a looking-glass in the hall, she put on a certain expression, a sort of contraction of the nostrils, to which she was specially attached. It accentuated, she maintained, the 'wild animal' side of her character.

Thinking that she heard voices on the stairs, Julie hurriedly put on her hat and a light overcoat the color of her ash-blonde hair, which she wore cut short and curled *a la Caracalla*. She threw down a pair of not quite clean gloves, and picked them up again—'Good enough to go to the pictures in'—then switched off two of the four lights, and sat down to wait in the best armchair. 'This is the last time,' she thought as she glanced round the studio, 'that I'll ever do up a room in red and blue. The color positively eats up the light, and costs the earth in electricity!'

One of the walls was red, one grey, and the other two were blue. The furniture was an odd mixture of style, the effect slightly too colonial, perhaps, but not unpleasing. The room was encumbered with a twelve-sided bronze tray-table from Indo-China, an armchair of South African ox-hide, bits of tooled leather from Fez, and basket work which had originally been plaited round English tobacco tins by the natives of the Gold Coast. The rest of the furniture was good eighteenth-century work, but it remained on its legs only because Mme. de Carneilhan's strong, deft hands were clever with glue-pot and pegs, and could even, when necessary, slide thin metal rods inside old bamboo and the broken chair-legs.

She waited ten minutes. Her patience came from fundamental humility. Her training and a superficial pride made her sit upright in her chair.

The studio gained depth from a long, unframed looking-glass. She looked with pleasure at the reflection of her well-set neck, at her bust which stubbornly retained its shape and firmness. A sheaf of dog whips and riding switches, valued as collector's pieces because they came from the Caucasus or Siberia, hung down in coils over the looking-glass.

Julie de Carneilhan resumed work on the cushion, boldly marking out the lines of the letter. And then suddenly she lost heart. 'It's no good,' she thought; 'it would be hideous.'

After ten minutes of waiting, Julie's proud and charming nose and her small well-defined mouth began to twitch nervously, and two large tears sparkled in the corners of her blue eyes. Her spirits revived at the sound of the bell, and she ran to the door.

"This is a fine time to come! It's no good trying to get round me, I loathe people who . . ."

She drew back and her voice changed.

"Oh, it's you."

"Yes, it's me. May I come in?"

"Have I ever kept you out?"

"Oh, once or twice—perhaps three times. Are you going out?"

"Yes. I'm waiting for some friends, that is, and they're disgustingly late."

"It's wretched weather, you know."

Léon de Carneilhan pulled off his gloves and rubbed his hands together. They were tanned by his open air life and polished by everyday contact with bridles. As he passed the looking-glass he contracted his nostrils like his sister, and, with his fair greying hair and blue eyes, this underlined the resemblance between them.

"What are you up to with those old breeches of mine?"

"Making a cushion. Do you mind?"

"It's too late to mind, seeing you've already cut them up."

His presence exuded an atmosphere of absent-minded distrust, and Julie scrutinised him with a similar look of suspicion. They lighted their cigarettes with the same match.

"Do you mind if I leave you?" Julie said. "I'm going to the pictures."

"I'm afraid I've come at an awkward time," Carneilhan said. Her only answer was a vague shrug. He then turned on his sister. Judging horseflesh had given his eyes a keen look, and her eyes, though softened by her make-up, wore an identical expression.

"Your husband is very ill."

"You don't say so!" said Julie in tones of mock horror. "Poor old Becker!"

"No, not Becker. Your second, Espivant."

For a moment she remained motionless, her mouth half open.

"How do you mean, Espivant?" she asked in a hesitant voice. "He was out and about yesterday, talking of a question he intended to ask in the *Chambre*. I heard that from one of the barmen at Maxim's who used to be my butler. What's wrong with him?"

"He suddenly collapsed, flat on his face, and had to be carried home."

"What about his wife? What's she got to say about it?"

"Nobody knows. It only happened at three this afternoon."

"She's probably letting down her long tresses and beseeching a last kiss while counting her rows of pearls with the other hand." They both gave a short laugh and continued smoking in silence. Julie blew the smoke out through her narrow and faultless nostrils.

"Do you think he'll die?"

Léon struck his bony knees with his hand. "How should I know? You might as well ask me to whom he'll leave the money that Marianne brought him in the marriage settlement."

"I bet it was the only way of getting him to make up his mind," said Julie with a grin.

"You may laugh, my dear. But think of Marianne's money and her looks! Herbert might well be tempted by less than that."

"Might be? He was," Julie said.

"You're too modest."

She lifted her smooth arrogant nose. "I'm not talking about me! I mean Galatée des Conches, and that idiot Béatrix."

Léon wagged his head with an experienced air. He was a fair haired, fierce and aging man, who had had great success with women.

"Béatrix is not bad, not bad at all."

"Do you know, I'm rather bored by the whole business," said Julie shortly.

She put on her gloves, and, straightening her little hat

of plaited felt, made it quite clear that she wished to see the last of her visitor.

"Tell me, Julie," Léon went on reflectively, "has Herbert been feeling friendly to you these last months?"

"Friendly? Yes. As with all the women he drops. He's always one move behind in his friendliness."

"Much more so with you than with the others. Didn't he pay your debts when he remarried?"

"What nonsense. I only had about twenty-two thousand francs' worth. One can't run up debts any more. Everything's cash nowadays."

"Supposing he leaves you a token of his friendship, a really solid one, when he dies!"

Julie's blue eyes assumed an expression of childish credulity.

"No? Do you really think he might die?"

"Of course I don't! I only said supposing when he died, he left you . . ."

Julie had stopped listening. She was running through her furniture in her mind, banishing her Colonial freaks and her Louis XIV relics, planning a change of house, a bathroom in yellow and black. She was not really grasping, only improvident and rather careless.

"Listen, my dear, I'm going out, as my young friends haven't put in an appearance. I'm going to the pictures."

"Do you really think you should? The news of Herbert's illness is already in the later edition of the evening papers. *'The physicians have so far issued no statement as to the gravity of the sudden illness which at five o'clock overcame the Comte d'Espivant, right-wing Deputy. . . .'"*

"What about it? Am I expected to put on mourning in advance for a man who was unfaithful to me for eight years and has been married again for another three?"

"It makes no difference. You were the wife people talked about. You can bet that everyone to-night has forgotten Marianne and is asking how Julie de Carneilhan is taking it."

"Do you really think so? You may be right."

Flattered by the thought, she smiled and brushed back a pretty little lock of hair that half covered her ear. But at the sound of a footfall on the stairs and loud laughter she at once became nervous and flustered.

"Do you hear that? They were supposed to pick me up at a quarter past eight. It's turned nine, and there they are kicking up a row on the stairs. Aren't people awful nowadays? What a crew!"

"Who are they?"

Julie shrugged her shoulders.

"Nobody. Some young friends of mine."

"Our sort of age?"

She gave him a long, challenging look.

"My dear, would you expect them to be!"

"Well for Heaven's sake, drop them for this evening."

She blushed, and tears came to her eyes.

"No, no, I won't! Why should I remain all alone when everybody else is having fun? There is a very good film at the Marbœuf and the program changes to-morrow."

She protested as though she were struggling against some violent danger, and flogged the arm of her chair with her gloves. Her brother contemplated her with a kind of bad-tempered patience. He was used to dealing with mares that were far more intractable.

"Listen to me. Don't behave like an idiot. It's only for this evening, and who knows if Herbert . . ."

"But I don't *care* about Herbert. I don't see why I should in any way concern myself each time he catches a chill! I forbid you to mention it in front of my friends."

"What do you bet they don't already know? There goes the bell. Shall I let them in?"

"No, no. I'll go."

She ran to the door like a little girl. Léon de Carneilhan, pricking his ears, could hear only his sister's voice.

"Ah! So there you are, only an hour late! Come on in; we can't stand talking here."

Two women and a young man came in without a word.

"My brother, the Comte de Carneilhan, Madame Encelade, Mademoiselle Lucie Albert, Monsieur Vatard, my brother, the Comte de Carneilhan. No, don't sit down. What have you got to say for yourselves?"

M. Vatard and Mme. Encelade tacitly delegated the spokesmanship to Mlle. Lucie Albert, who seemed the shyest of the three, her eyes were so enormous.

"We weren't going to come. I said we ought to telephone. . . . We read in the papers that . . . that the Count was ill. . . ."

Julie, unwillingly admitting defeat, shot a glance at her brother, and the three newcomers did the same. In answer to these deferential glances, Léon de Carneilhan put on the expression that his sister called "the mask of a fox that has betrayed its king by hunting with humans." But Julie gave up the struggle.

"My dears, it can't be helped," she declared. "Herbert and I got ourselves talked about far too much for his illness not to draw a certain amount of attention to me. So . . ."

"I understand," said Coco Vatard.

"You're not the only one who understands," said Mme. Encelade tartly. "Lucie and I understand too."

"I'll give you a ring to-morrow."

"Is there anything I can do to help?" asked Lucie Albert.

"Nothing, darling. You're an angel. Let's all meet again soon, dears. I'll see you out."

From the studio Carneilhan could hear the four of them laughing and talking in low voices. One of the three women called Coco Vatard a crackpot, and then the door closed.

Her brother displayed no surprise when Julie returned. He knew of old the sudden weaknesses of this beautiful creature: she flouted public opinion, emerged cool and serene from conjugal disasters and put up with the makeshift existence of a woman living without money or help, but was unable to miss a treat, to which she'd been looking forward, without crying a little and bowing her shoulders and suddenly looking her age.

"My poor Julie, won't you ever change?"

She sat upright. Her eyes were wet but furious.

"I'm not 'your poor Julie' for a start! You stick to selling old hacks and young pigs and leave me alone!"

"Shall I take you out to dinner somewhere?"

"No!"

"Have you got anything in the flat?"

"I've got some chocolate. . . ."

"To eat?"

"What a horrid thought! No; to drink. I was going to have it when I came home. You know, young people are quite capable of dropping you at your door after the pictures without so much as giving you a drink. They're like that. There are some plums, and three eggs . . . yes, and some tinned tunny and a lettuce."

"Any whisky?"

"Of course. That's one thing I've always got."

"It's started raining. Would you like me to go?"

She caught at her brother with a gesture of alarm.

"No; please don't!"

"Well, let's try and soften the shock we've had! I'll lend you a hand. How do you want the eggs?"

"Don't care."

"I'll do you a tunny omelette. Put the chocolate on the stove for afterwards."

Gaily, as though armed against the worst by a frivolity that closely resembled courage (and which frequently promoted it), they forgot everything except getting their meal ready. They set about it with the skill and competitiveness of overgrown Boy Scouts. Léon de Carneilhan discovered the remains of some crème d'Isigny, and poured it into the salad. He tied a red-striped towel round his waist under his coat, and Julie took off her dress and put on a dressing-gown. They escaped all trace of absurdity by the deftness of their movements, their long and unself-conscious practice in handling humble everyday objects. While Leon was beating the eggs for the omelette, Julie laid the card table with two blue and two red plates, a handsome decanter and a rather ugly jug, and, then, putting a small pot of bright blue lobelias between the places, cried, "That looks grand!"

The gusto with which they ate had its roots in their indestructible appetites and digestions. In their friendship they were like two of a litter that can never play together without leaving traces of tooth and claw, wounding each other in the most sensitive places. Neither of them complained about their frugal supper; they rose nourished, but without having eaten their fill. The plates were replaced by ash trays and cards. Relaxed at last, Julie answered all her brother's questions with a good grace. A rainy draught from the window stirred her ringlets; and from her brother's 'traitor-fox' look, she perceived that the arrogant carriage of her head, her blue eyes, so prompt to sparkle with tears, and the radiance of her downy complexion and her hair, made her still the beautiful Julie de Carneilhan. Julie de Carneilhan, as people, in spite of a couple of marriages and divorces, still called her.

Lèon had taken off his coat. He never wore a waistcoat and he felt stifled the moment he was confined in a room. The body under the shirt was lean and hard—all table corners, Julie called it—a body almost numb to feeling and pitilessly ill-treated by its owner.

"How are the ducks going, Lèon?"

"Badly. If only I hadn't got those wretched little pigs on my hands! I've sent one of the brood-mares back to Père Carneilhan. Henrietta, the bay."

"Sent it back? By train?"

"No fear. By road. Gayant rode her."

"Lucky chap! I'd have loved to have ridden her there for you."

"You're too busy," said Carneilhan, not without irony. "It took him twelve days. He and the mare slept in the fields, a blanket apiece. She stuffed herself with all the oats she came across on the way! They'd have been in the soup if anybody'd caught them. Gayant's fodder was bread and cheese and garlic. She was so fat when they arrived that Père Carneilhan thought she was in foal, and Gayant had to disillusion him."

"When was all this?"

"In June."

Without more words, they both fell into a day-dream of roads in June running through the green oat-fields. Thinking of the lulling gait of the mare, the cool freshness between four and eight o'clock in the morning, the little rhythmical creak of the saddle and the first red streak of sunlight over the squat towers of Carneilhan, Julie felt her eyes growing moist once again. She flung a quick malevolent glance at her brother.

"It's very odd, when you're in shirt-sleeves, you look like a cavalry lieutenant who's taken to the bottle."

"Thanks."

"Don't mention it, dear."

"I mean thanks for 'lieutenant.' Who on earth's that chap you call Coco Vatard?"

"Nothing. Just somebody with a motor-car."

"A flame?"

"No."

"What about the girl, the one you called an angel? Is she your fancy?"

"Heavens no," sighed Julie. "I'm absolutely heart-whole. I think my life's heading for a big change. She's a very interesting little thing; a pianist and cashier in a night club, and to-day's her night off."

"It's none of my business, Julie, but what exactly would you do if you had any money?"

"Oh, thousands of idiotic things," said Julie haughtily. "Why?"

"Well, this Herbert affair. I can't help thinking about it, that's all."

She put her hand on her brother's arm, and he looked at it as though taken unawares by the fraternal gesture.

"It's not worth worrying about. That flighty line of his took us all in. If he dies, he dies. No one will see the color of any money that he has."

"You're talking like a fortune-teller."

Julie's eyes lit up.

"Oh, my dear, I know one! It's priceless. She tells your fortune in melted candlewax! She told me, all in one sitting, that another war would break out, that I should have a sensational meeting and that Marianne would die of cancer."

"Marianne? How did you know she was talking about Marianne?"

The blood flowed into Julie's cheeks. She was splendid in attack, but inclined to lose her head when she was on the defensive.

"Why, I understood perfectly well from her description. It's the kind of thing you feel."

"How did you know she was talking about Marianne?" repeated Léon. "Tell me, or I'll tickle you up and down your spine!"

"Pax! I'll tell you, I promise!" Julie cried in haste. "Well, it was Toni. . . ."

"Toni? Marianne's son?"

"Yes. I asked him, my dear—we're on the best of terms —I asked him to pinch one of his mother's silk stockings, when she took them off before going to bed. You see, the candle woman has to have something worn by the person concerned."

"And did he bring it?"

Julie nodded.

"What a queer family," said Carneilhan. "It's all rather comic," he went on lightly. "It's getting late, and I must be on my way, old girl. It's an hour past midnight."

"How small . . ." said Julie.

"How do you mean, small?"

"Only that people always talk about 'the small hours.' Ha! ha ha!"

She burst out laughing, and he realised that she was slightly tipsy. But she managed to walk steadily as far as the window.

"There's still a taxi on the rank. Shall I whistle for it?"

"Don't bother. I'll walk back. It's not raining."

She did not insist. Her brother often walked back to Saint Cloud, crossing the Bois de Boulogne with a tireless stride. One night, at the approach of an ugly-looking customer, he had jumped straight into a thicket with a leap of such length and swiftness that the stranger, frightened out of his wits, had taken to his heels. He loved the hours of the night as day began to break, always got home before six, and his horses started to whinny expectantly while he was still a long way off.

He shook Julie's hand in a vague manner and made off towards the thing he cared for most in the world; the shrill whinny of his faithful mares, and the friendly language of their great affectionate lips close to their master's expert ear.

"It must be Friday," thought Mme. de Carneilhan, still half asleep. "I can smell fish."

There was a large general grocer's shop at the corner of the street. When Julie had taken the lease of the "studio with every modern comfort" she had sacrificed smartness to convenience, a bargain she never ceased regretting, especially on fish days, cabbage days and melon days.

The presence of the daily cleaning woman washing up in the kitchen-bathroom indicated that it was only about half-past nine, so Julie went to sleep again; but not without twinges of guilt dating from her earliest childhood, when she had been used to sharp little cuts with a riding-crop from her father's stern but equitable hand. In those days Julie and Léon, barefoot and in silence, used to fight in front of the door (which opened ineluctably at seven in winter and six in summer) to avoid being beaten the first. Well warmed up and still tingling, they put on their sole-

worn shoes without an atom of rancor, and threw them-
selves upon the backs of their ponies and galloped to catch
up with the Comte de Carneilhan. Their father would be
mounted on a Breton nag with a back like a basket, or on a
bag of bones as high as a church, or even on a saddled cow.
She was a light-colored animal, as fair as himself, oat-fed
and fiery-eyed, and she cocked up her tail when she took
the jumps with her teats swinging to and fro like bell-clap-
pers. He used to ride her just to demonstrate what he could
get out of anything with hooves and flat teeth, and to draw
attention to himself at the horse-fairs and important market
days in Périgord.

On such days he lent Julie and Léon the pick of his
stable. Having set out from Carneilhan on horseback, the
children often had to trudge home with their saddles on
their shoulders or get a lift in a peasant's cart, their smart
appearance and good seats having helped to sell the ponies
on the spot. For a time they would remain obdurate and
embittered, shedding secret tears for the little horse they
had loved. But, as they grew up, they developed a taste
for these frequent changes of mount. And when, at the
age of seventeen, Julie de Carneilhan married a rich man
from Holland called Julius Becker, she was not particularly
worried. "I'll change him," she thought vaguely to herself,
"next market day."

As other people dream longingly of university degrees or
legal briefs, Julie would often dream that she was on horse-
back. Mme. Encelade, who was given to interpreting
dreams, declared: "That means that you ought to go to
bed with somebody."

"No it doesn't," Julie insisted. "It simply means that I want to be on horseback."

And she would plan to borrow her brother's mare, Hirondelle. But the next morning she would wake up late, and fall into a brown study. Léon, what's more, refused to lend her Hirondelle, and suggested Tullia—a quiet, uninteresting, sure-footed animal, compact of all the virtues of a nursery governess. Julie was on her dignity at once.

"My dear boy, you don't expect me to appear in the Bois on a dappled mare?"

The water, as it gurgled into the bath in the kitchen next to the studio, set the narrow partition shaking musically. "Ten o'clock!" Julie got out of bed and pulled her pyjama belt tight. Feeling well and sprightly, with a clean taste on her tongue and throat, she remembered that she had been drinking the night before. Spirits treated her mercifully, as they did Père Carneilhan. They cleared her complexion and her brain. She could boast without lying that never a drop of syrupy liqueur had been allowed to pass the barrier of her mouth. Her teeth were healthy and unevenly set, the two middle incisors being on the large side and the two others smaller and slanting slightly backwards.

"I'm going to dip my teeth in a glass of water," she would say in the morning, and then go and drink a tumblerful at the kitchen tap. This family catch-phrase, she was in the habit of telling her friends, had cost her the affections of a good-looking lieutenant she had hardly got to work on; failing to catch the joke, he had assumed that she wore a set of false teeth.

She stopped in front of the looking-glass and screwed up

her nose. Sleep had put all her ringlets out of curl: they stood out stiffly all over her head like bits of straw.

"I look as though I'd been sleeping in the stables," she observed to herself. She stopped again to telephone, and listened motionlessly to the prolonged ringing tone at the other end. "Hello? Hello? . . . Really, what a bore this is! What? M. Vatard had gone out? Already? Good, thank you." Grimacing scornfully, she pulled a stray slipper towards her with her big toe. "Oh dear, oh dear, that boy and his beastly factory . . ." and made for the part of the kitchen curtained off by a waterproof hanging fitted to a rod, and known as the bathroom.

An electric stove with two rings was fitted to the top of a cupboard beside the bath. When the cleaning woman was out, Mme. de Carneilhan could have her bath and keep an eye on her breakafst at the same time. She had retained, from a childhood steeped in assured if penurious family pride, a profound lack of bashfulness and a total disregard for the presence of servants. "Stir up the water for me, Peyre," she used to shout to the kitchen gardener at Carneilhan when she was thirteen, fourteen, fifteen years old. The man would then beat the surface of the fish pond by the spring, for Julie could not bear the sinuous, invisible creatures that haunted its depths. Then she would shout: "Turn round and look the other way!" and throwing off her dress, slip into the water—it was warm on top, but ice-cold lower down—swim round a bit and then get out, as oblivious of the man who beat the water for her as she was of her own beauty.

"Good morning to you, Madame du Sabrier," she called

to her daily woman in tones of mock ceremony as she pulled off her crumpled pyjamas.

Before getting into the bath, she did some deep breathing exercises and a few knee-bends like a dancer. Disapproving of naked beauty, Mme. Sabrier turned the other way.

"Are you having lunch in, Madame? What would you like to eat?"

"I'd like—let me see—cream cheese and skate in black butter. The black and white together would look particularly smart."

She laughed under a helmet of lather. When she was in her bath, Julie soaped herself all over, including her head, like a man.

Mme. Sabrier heaved a deep sigh.

"It's not fair. There's no justice in the world," she said. "You were up drinking last night, weren't you? I saw the glasses. And there you are, spry as a goldfish. And I've never drunk a drop, and here am I all doubled up. And you are forty-four, too. . . . It's not fair. . . ."

"I don't want to seem inquisitive, but I'd like to know the name of the pig who told you how old I was?"

Mme. Sabrier smiled at last.

"Well now! I've got my little ways and means, Madame. It was the chauffeur who brought a letter for you one day. A chauffeur from the left bank of the river."

"So that's how they behave on the left bank? They'll catch it when I get at them. Give me my dressing-gown."

"Now don't you go making wet footmarks all over my

clean floor, please. He told me he got it from your first husband."

'It's Herbert's chauffeur,' thought Julie as she went out. She stopped at the doorway—she made 'good exits' through force of habit—and said "My second, Madame Sabrier. My second husband. And not the last either!"

"It's not fair," sighed Mme. Sabrier. "Here are your newspapers."

'Dead? Or not? If he's dead, it'll be on the front page.' Clutching the papers in her wct hand, she went and sat on her bed. 'Nobody on the front page. He must be just ill on page two: What did I say? *We are happy to announce that the sudden illness of the Comte d'Espivant appears to offer no cause for alarm.*' "There," Julie cried out loud, "I was sure of it! I could have gone to the pictures after all! The dirty dog! And Professors Hattoutant and Giscard at his bedside, if you please! Marianne must be getting worried about her source of . . ."

She threw the paper aside and opened the only cupboard in the studio, which she had lined with looking-glass as a make-up cabinet and fitted with electric light. She was clever with her fingers and impulsively attacked any job in hand; but she soon grew bored and her unfinished handiwork would remain as a series of little monuments to her skill and her inconstancy.

'A chauffeur from the left bank,' she thought. 'That must have been my old Beaupied bringing a letter from Toni. It's Toni's fault. . . . What a nuisance boys of that age are! He decided he wanted to see me, and who does he send with the letter. His stepfather's chauffeur! Herbert has a mania for keeping on his chauffeurs till they fall to bits. He thinks that what was 'aristocratic' where coachmen were concerned now applies to mechanics."

She brushed her wet hair back till it lay flat against her scalp. Taken unawares like this, with nothing on her face and plunged in disgruntled thoughts, Julie resembled her brother in certain characteristics—a wild look, with narrowing temples and the chin and jawbone fining down into a muzzle. But everything was redeemed by her nose and a rosy coloring that could stand up to anything. She dabbed a patch of face-cream on her delicious nose, and spread it on with her forefinger. She made herself up with skill, plucked a couple of hairs from her upper lip, curled her hair with lively twists of the hand. "I'll walk in the Bois for a bit," she said to herself. "I won't put on my lizard-skin shoes, or they won't last out the year."

She ran to answer the telephone, cursing jubilantly to herself. She did this whenever her restless indolence and over-encumbered solitude were forced into action.

"Hello? Is that you, Coco? Does that mean that it's past twelve and you've got away from the office? Oh! What rotten luck. . . . I wanted to go for a tremendous walk. What? No, I wanted to go to-day. To-morrow's not the same thing at all. What? Herbert? He's better, of course. All he cares about is being a nuisance to other people. All right, to-night then, but I loathe having to wait for anything I enjoy. What? My dear boy, who on earth do you think you're talking to? See you this evening." She put the receiver back and broke into a little urchin-like smile that put years on her all at once. She quickly resumed her serious expression and became once more a tempestuous and masterful blonde. In five minutes' time she was dressed in a white tailored shirt, a skirt with a pattern of black and white birds' feet and a black jacket that flouted every current fashion. Her slightly overdone trimness betrayed the fact that Julie de Carneilhan was approaching the age when women decide to sacrifice their faces to their figures.

'I ought to have a purple carnation. Ten francs . . . no joke at the moment.' She rummaged among her handkerchiefs and found a small one of mauve crepe which she twisted into the shape of a flower. She snipped at it deftly with her scissors and then frilled it out in her buttonhole. 'Marvellous!' Then her face clouded over with the same alacrity. 'What an idiot I am! The handkerchief cost a whole *louis*.' She always reckoned in louis out of smartness and what she called 'good form.' A cloud drifted across the sky and chased away all desire to go for a walk. 'Shall I ring up Lucie? Or find out when the sales begin at Hermés? Or . . .'

She trembled at the sound of the telephone, which started to ring just as she was stretching out her hand for the receiver. Like many creatures leading an unprotected life, she regarded the telephone as her only source of help.

"Hello! Yes, speaking. What? I can't hear. Would you say it again? Who did you say was speaking?" The tone of her voice altered and her shoulders fell into a slight stoop.

"Is . . . is that you, Herbert? Yes, of course, I read it in the papers like everybody else. So it wasn't anything serious?" She saw herself across the room in the looking-glass and sat up straight. "Frightening us all like that! What?

Well, *us* means the whole of Paris, my dear, half of France, and a good hunk of abroad."

She laughed, listened for a moment and then stopped laughing.

"Where are you telephoning from? What? Come there, to your house? Oh, nothing. I was going to have luncheon alone. No, nobody. No, of course I'm not saying no, but . . . what about Marianne? All right. Yes. But it's nothing. Don't be absurd. Yes; I'll keep an eye out of the window."

Julie replaced the receiver slowly. She put on a black straw hat that reminded her of her early childhood, and opened the door into the kitchen.

"Madame Sabrier," she said, in an uncertain voice. Then she was suddenly on the alert with her nostrils wide.

"What's that awful stink of fish?"

"Why, it's the skate, Madame. Madame told me. White cheese and black butter."

"But it's frightful. You didn't really think . . ."

The corners of her mouth sank, and she said, in piteous tones: "I only thought I was saying something funny. You can eat your wretched skate. But leave me the cream cheese. I'll buy . . . well, we'll see. . . ."

She sank back into uncertainty, fiddling idly with some oddments on the chimney-piece, and then she went to lean on the window-sill, with one foot resting on top of the other. When a long black motor drew up among the delivery-tricycles outside the grocers', Julie pulled herself together and ran downstairs like a girl, feeling all the exhilaration of her firm, slim legs, her light breasts and her freedom from a single ounce of extra flesh.

"Why, of course, it's Beaupied. How are you, Beaupied? You never change a bit."

"Madame la Comtesse flatters me."

"No, Beaupied, really. You're always the same, specially since I can't turn my back on you for five minutes without your telling my charwomen that I'm forty-four!"

"Me? Oh! I can promise your Ladyship . . . ."

"Anyway, I'm not forty-four, Beaupied. I'm forty-five. Drive home, would you."

"Er—home," repeated the grey-haired chauffeur. "Which . . ."

"Yours," said Mme. de Carneilhan kindly. "Ours, I mean the same one, in the Rue Saint-Sabas."

Once the door was shut, she brought the stern and critical eye of the impecunious to bear on the car. 'A real bounder's turn-out! They bought it at a motor show. It must have been left over by a Maharajah. Herbert always did have a tendency to buy motor-hearses. And all upholstered in pearl-grey! Why not mauve satin? And a chauffeur rigged up in summer livery. I suppose one can't have everything—millions and taste as well. . . .' Her critical sense was equally hard upon the cut-out flower in her buttonhole. She took it off and threw it out of the window as they drove into the flower-planted courtyard.

Julie had not foreseen the evocative power of the surroundings which she herself had once chosen and loved. Her pulse was thumping in her eardrums, and before shaking her head to the chauffeur when he asked if her ladyship would like to be driven back later, she raised her eyes to the first floor. Her second husband, drawn to the window by the sound of the motor-car, was leaning out and shouting "Two o'clock sharp!" to Beaupied.

'Two o'clock sharp,' she repeated to herself, 'and the car used to hang about till four! Unless, of course, Herbert slunk off in a taxi to see some wretched girl-friend.' She ascended the little flight of steps and went through the door of the hall almost without being aware of it, guided unerringly by the memory of her foot on the stone stairs, her hand on the door knob. The moment she crossed the threshold, a heavy atmosphere of feminine scent pulled her together. 'Marianne's scent .   . too much of it, too much money, too many diamonds, too much hair. . . .' An unexpected irritation sharpened her faculties. On the first floor she thought she caught, through a half-open door, the thread of a brilliant glance, an intake of breath; and the door closed. Her room! A footman paced along in front of her. She expected him to open the door of the study next to Espivant's room, but he asked her to wait in a little room that she could not remember. She could hear Espivant's voice somewhere behind the thin walls, and for a moment she lost all sense of time. The present became meaningless, as if lost in the heart of a dream, yet she was aware that she was dreaming. The footman came back and she followed him.

'Where on earth does Herbert sleep?' she wondered, counting the closed doors. 'My room . . . the linen cupboard . . . his room . . . the room we used to call the nursery . . .' She stopped dead all at once with a gesture of despair. 'I forgot to change my old shoes!' She almost turned right about and took to her heels. Her calm was restored by a second's consideration. 'After all, what does it matter? Well I never, he's gone and settled in the nursery. How very odd!' Her guide vanished and Julie made a fine entrance with her charming nose in the air, her eyes feigning short sight, her small mouth half open in an agreeable but unaffectionate smile, and her gaze focused straight ahead at the level of her eyes. But Herbert's voice rose from a little bed much lower down.

"So I'm reduced to sending for you? It never occurred to you to come and ask how I was?"

His voice was young and cheerful and pitched in a key that Julie was still unable to hear without anger and pain. She lowered her eyes and saw Herbert in bed. She took him in at a glance. 'Oh!' she said to herself. 'He's done for.' The smell of ether, well-known to Julie from many a disreputable haunt, suddenly assumed a terrible significance. It gave her the cue for her words and behaviour.

"Herbert," she said, a little too fulsomely. "What's this new stunt of yours, and all this publicity in the papers? And are those pale grey silk pyjamas for my benefit? What sort of opinion do you expect me to carry away of a man who interviews me in pale grey silk?"

The hand that Herbert stretched out to her seemed to have thickened. It waved her into a little armchair close to the bed.

"Would you like to smoke?" he said. "You can."

"What about you?"

"Not this morning, my dear. I don't even want to."

She was unable to single out any definite sign of deterioration in Espivant's face. He was 'switching on the charm' for her, as he did for everybody, from pure force of habit. But a mysterious process seemed imperceptibly to have puffed up all that had been hollow the day before, and conversely, to have scooped out the convexities of the slim brown Gascon mask. Julie had long realised that his handsome face was merely, under its masculine brow, a collection of slightly effeminate features. But the fire in the light brown eyes, the mouth retaining all its youthful delicacy and the deliberately unfashionable moustache, there they all were before her eyes again, and once again she bit the edge of her tongue to punish herself for still being hurt by them.

"Have you had luncheon yet, Youlka? Do have something with me! Just to please me!"

'"Just to please me" . . . D, E flat, E natural, A flat. Same phrase on the same notes,' thought Julie.

"But . . ." she began, turning towards the door.

"I'm having my tiny luncheon all alone. Marianne, who was up all night—there was not the slightest need for it—is having a rest."

"Just anything, then. Some fruit. . . . It's my day for fruit."

"Lovely. Darling, I'm going to ring. Nobody will disturb us once they've brought the food. I'll tell you all about my tiresome attack, if you'd like to hear it. But perhaps it would be a bore. Youlka, does being here mean anything to you?"

Julie understood, from the caressing tone of his voice, that he still enjoyed hurting her.

"No," she said coldly.

In came a male nurse, in white, followed by a secretary with a handful of telegrams. Espivant began speaking before the latter could get a word out.

"No, no, Cousteix. Nothing for the moment. You just see to them all, there's a good chap. After all, I *am* ill!" he said with a laugh. "I'll have a look at my letters this evening. Perhaps . . . !"

He propped himself on his fists to hoist himself into a sitting position. The effort lasted only a moment, but his mouth gaped strangely open, and Julie perceived genuine anxiety rather than mere officiousness in the haste with which the nurse ran to help him.

"What a ridiculously narrow bed," Julie reproached him. "It's only about eighty centimetres wide, like a house-maid's!"

The nurse glanced at her approvingly as he left the room. "Sh!" whispered Espivant. "It's all part of my plan! It's my self-defence bed!"

They were still laughing with spiteful complicity when two tables laden with fruit were wheeled in. Julie found it all faultless: late cherries, rose-colored peaches, thin-skinned Marseilles figs, cloudy hot-house grapes that had been carefully protected from the wasps. Iced water and champagne trembled in thick cut-glass jugs, chiselled with a pattern of nail-heads. Julie's nostrils opened wide to the fumes of the coffee and the smell of the yellow rose standing next to a pot of fresh cream. She carefully concealed the pleasure she derived from all this luxury.

"Who asked for this ham, Herbert? Nobody wants it."

Espivant made a careless gesture.

"Marianne, I expect. Anything else you want?"

"No, thanks. So Marianne knew that I . . . ?"

"What are you worrying about? Please don't tire me!"

A ray of sunshine fell across the gleaming silver. Herbert chose the best of the peaches, still adorned with its living green leaf, and let it rest in the palm of his hand.

"How lovely it is . . ." he sighed. "Take this one. Do you still drink your coffee while you're eating fruit?"

This reminder of their old life together caught Julie unawares. She flushed, and steadied herself by drinking a glass of champagne.

"How pretty the table looks," she said. "Cherries too! Let me play with all this for a bit; don't you worry about me. Is there some medicine or other you ought to take?"

Espivant, who had cut one of the peaches, left it on his plate. He took a handful of cherries and held them up to the full light.

"Look, they're so clear you can almost see the stones inside! What have I ever had of my own after all? All I'll have to say goodbye to amounts to just about this."

He dropped the cherries and waved towards the little sunlit table. His gesture did not exclude the tall fair-haired woman sitting slant-wise in her chair, facing the light, and feeling as happy as a wasp in the sun. She wiped her lips, wrinkling her brows as she did so.

"Goodbye? How do you mean?"

Espivant leaned towards her. As he emerged from the shadow, the strange almost vegetable color of his face became at once apparent, the greenish white of his forehead and temples and of the skin round his mouth.

Round his brown eyes were dark circles; so many women, too many women, had painted them there and loved them.

"It's all up with me, Youlka," he said with affected lightness. "No, do let me talk about it! Pour out the coffee. Yes, yes, I'm allowed coffee. Aren't you surprised to see so few doctors 'at my bedside,' as they say? No? What a brute you are; you never notice anything! You don't even notice what a man looks like unless you've got him face to face. And, when I use the expression 'face to face,' it's only because I respect the precincts of a dwelling that matrimony has doubly sanctified."

He laughed, and made Julie laugh too. This she did with constraint at first; then she gave way to a helpless fit of laughing as easily as she might have burst into tears.

"Suppose she heard us . . ." she said.

"Who? Marianne? She's bound to, a bit."

"You behave like a cad to her, Herbert."

"No, I lie to her. I . . . I was a cad to you because I used to tell you the truth."

Her nostrils stiffened as she tore open a fig with her teeth.

"You've got to admit I paid you back in the same coin."

"Only because I wrung your neck until you owned up."

He threw her one of those deep and slanting glances that he had employed when he was still her unfaithful and jealous husband. He even stuck his fist on his hip. Some divine intervention had stripped him forever of the most effectual elements of his attractiveness, and all the violence aroused in Julie by these accents of a bygone day melted in pity. 'Poor man . . .' And since, through lack of vocation or from habit, she was prone to confuse pity with boredom, she felt herself practically a prisoner between the bedridden Herbert, the elaborate silver and the various knick-knacks that were calling her. She longed for her street full of shops and for Coco Vatard and Lucie Albert with all their youth and naïve intentness on their work and amusements. She looked about her and began to criticise the furniture.

"Herbert, are you really attached to that chintz? Has nobody ever told you that the pink-and-black chintz suited you about as well as a rope of pearls would a bulldog? Haven't you got any real friends?"

"Very few."

"And what on earth are you doing, all tucked up here in the nursery? Is it an attempt to make yourself seem younger? That's *too* much."

Espivant, leaning on the pillow, was drinking his coffee.

"Shove the table to one side, would you?" he asked her without answering her question. "Put your coffee on top of mine, and bring the cigarettes over. I want to talk to you."

Julie obeyed quickly lest he should catch sight of her old shoes and went on pulling the furniture to pieces in order to distract his attention.

"Lovely lemon-wood. But surely a bit chichi for a man's room?"

The secretary came back holding a telephone with a

long trailing wire. "It's the President of the Republic asking for news."

"How well all those spirals of telephone wire suit you, Cousteix! You look like a vine. This is my friend Cousteix, who is kind enough to be my secretary: the Comtesse de Carneilhan. Thank the President, Cousteix. Say I'm ill. Not very ill. Just fairly ill—anything you like. Oh, and while you're there, Cousteix—— Julie, will you excuse me a moment?"

'It's very odd,' Julie was thinking, Herbert has never been able to talk naturally to a secretary or an inferior. The authority of the Espivants is just about as recent as their title. Saint-Simon saw them moving in, and Viel-Castel made fun of them. And now, there's Herbert bitching about in the hopes of putting his secretary into an ecstasy.'

She cried "Oh!" and leapt forward. For, the moment the door was closed behind Cousteix, Espivant fell back with his eyes shut. Julie found a bottle, opened it, damped a napkin with sal volatile, and fanned Herbert's nostrils so vigorously that his fainting fit lasted less than sixty seconds.

"Don't call anyone; it's nothing," Herbert said in a clear voice. "I'm getting used to it. Any coffee left? Do give me some. You were so quick. I didn't have time to lose consciousness. Thank you."

He sat up without any help and breathed deeply. The whole of his greenish face was smiling.

"It's queer, you know, the feeling of well-being, of optimism, that accompanies each of these, what shall I call them—little deaths. Would you like some brandy, Youlka? I've got some here that dates from—oh, from Pepin the Short."

He was slightly out of breath and overcome by a sudden gloom. She could not take her eyes off his pale face and deep eye-sockets.

"Thanks, I won't. I drank too much last night."

"Ah? Who with? Where? Was it fun? Go on, tell!"

He leant forward and the blood returned to his cheeks. Julie recognised his mode of speech, his veiled eyes, the wild hope of widening the range of his senses, and began to hate him again.

"No, it was nothing. I sat up drinking whisky with Léon, that's all. Pure hygiene! Do you want to talk to me, or shall I let you rest? I can always come back."

"Yes, but perhaps I shan't always be able to. Do stay! Even if it bores you. You're so easily bored."

He smiled at her without a trace of goodwill, but went on holding her hand. 'We know each other too well,' thought Julie. 'We're still quite capable of playing dirty tricks on each other, but we can no longer deceive each other.' She shook her head in token of denial, sat down opposite Espivant and poured cream into a second cup of coffee. A young male voice shouted a few words in the courtyard below.

"It's Toni," Espivant explained.

Julie lowered her eyes to conceal a smile. 'If you really think I need you,' she thought, 'to tell me that it's Toni . . .'

"My darling pet," Herbert began, "we were saying that I was going to die. You can't always be there to intervene. . . . Oh, I remember one day, when you'd got a saucepan of milk on the stove, the telephone began ringing, the milk was rising and you dealt with the telephone and the milk at the same time, turning off the gas with your elbow without letting go of the saucepan or the receiver. You were superb. We were poor then."

'I still am,' she thought to herself and hid her feet under the chair. But, as Espivant grew less pale and vague and more animated, she felt strangely happy and proud that he owed his present well-being to her.

"How's Becker, by the way?"

"All right. He's in Amsterdam."

"Does he still give you an allowance? How much?"

Julie blushed, and did not answer. She was hesitating between the truth and a lie, and finally voted for the truth.

"Four thousand a month."

"Not what you'd call royal."

"Why should it be royal? He's only a baron, and then only if you don't look too close."

"Including rent?"

"Yes."

"He hasn't cancelled the insurance in his own favor?"

"No."

Espivant gazed at her with what she always called his 'small look'; pointed, expert, and pressed tight between his eyelids. She knew that his attention had alighted at last on her slightly faded black jacket and her white shirt, spotless, but so often laundered. His eyes came to rest on her feet. 'That's done it. He's seen them.' She heaved a breath of deliverance, ate the last of the cherries, and slowly powdered her nose. Her bag was almost new.

"You never told me," Espivant coldly reproached her.

"It's against all my principles," she answered in the same tone. He made his voice still harder.

"Of course, your way of life has got nothing to do with me."

"No, nothing at all."

She lowered her forehead, arming herself against whatever blows were coming; but Espivant remained calm. 'He's sparing himself, not me,' thought Julie.

"Idiot," he said gently, "let's talk. I've announced my impending dissolution to you three times, and all you do is talk about furniture and interior decoration because you don't like this sexless room. Give me a cigarette. You haven't grasped the fact that I 'happen' to sleep here at least three times a week: 'No, no, don't change a thing in this ugly room, my darling, you know I only want your—our—room. But I've got to work late this evening, and I'm feeling tired and ugly.'"

He imitated himself talking to his second wife, and Julie could not help admiring so much langour and amorous authoritativeness. 'He's a past master in treachery,' she thought.

"Do you call her *vous* like that?"

"Not always. She likes contrasts. So you see, that's how I'm able to wriggle out of it."

"Wriggle out of it?" Julie repeated thoughtfully.

"Well," Herbert said crossly, "you don't need a translation, do you?"

"Oh, no . . . only I say it in a different way. Go on,

though. I'd never have thought that Marianne was so——— It's true she's only thirty-five: the age when a woman doesn't know that, once out of twice, she ought to say 'No' to a man of . . . our age. A respectable spouse will finish off a man of fifty twice as quickly as a clever tart who knows better than to wear out her own property."

"Here, I'm not fifty!"

"I know. Not for another six months. I was talking in general terms."

She gazed at Espivant with a look that derived nearly all its kindness from the blue make-up round her eyes. 'Perhaps,' she thought, 'he will never be fifty.'

"Well," she resumed, "you've got a wife who stands no nonsense. Go on."

He absent-mindedly crushed out his half-smoked cigarette.

"Go on? There's nothing more to say. You've just told my entire story . . . and my wife's."

"Rich wives are expensive."

"So are beautiful ones. Oh, I realize now what an idiot I was! I've tried all sorts of things, gadgets, pills."

"Like the Duc de Morny?"

"Like the Duc de Morny. We'll not come to much good copying the Napoleonic nobility."

'We? How does he mean "we"?'—malicious gaiety suddenly overcame her at the thought—'Once "we" no longer means Herbert and Julie. He's surely not lumping together the Carneilhans and the Espivants?' She was careful to conceal the pride that bound her to the name of her family, to its ragged antiquity and to the remains of the massive-walled castle, half manor and half farmhouse, which, for the last nine hundred years, had never been called anything but Carneilhan.

"Don't be rude to the Second Empire," she said. "I'm having my boudoir all quilted and buttoned like the Comtesse de Teba's. But, seriously, Herbert, why don't you just go away? Surely you've had enough of this house and its dismal little box-hedges? Go away. Take your pale grey pyjamas . . . and your dowry."

"Ah! My dowry!"

He gazed dreamily at the chintz-covered ceiling and seemed on the point of a decision.

"How they talked about the 'dowry' that fixed my election! Five millions? Four millions? How much, Julie?"

"Some people said five. Some two."

She wanted to please and insult him at the same time. She stroked his lip and his small musketeer's moustache.

"Five or two, you were cheap at the price."

He caught her hand, the hand so skilful at every task it touched, and kissed it vaguely as she withdrew it.

"Did you hear that? There have been at least four rings at the door since you arrived. I bet Marianne's been entertaining in my place and that she's already promised since this morning to build a bridge, a school, a wash-house and an orphanage."

"And will she really do it?"

"They'll bring her the estimates, and she'll have them looked into. All that takes time."

He sat up and undid the button of the pale grey py-jamas at his thick neck.

"She pays for things; she doesn't give. Do you get the idea, Youlka?"

"American style?"

"I don't know. I haven't married any American so far. My dowry! She's put 'all her worldly goods' at my disposal. You see the difference?"

"Of course I do. You've been had."

They went on smoking in silence. Espivant, from tiredness and perhaps from chronic flirtatiousness, lowered his dark eyelids. Julie listened to light feminine footsteps in the corridor. 'Perhaps that's her. I've been here over an hour,' she thought. 'Is that all he wanted to tell me?'

"Actually, why *did* you marry her?"

Herbert opened his eyes again and looked at her like a reproachful schoolmaster.

"My dear child, what a question! Four months to run an election campaign, a widowed beauty paying me her *devoirs*, a . . . an extremely embarrassed financial situation. That was my position."

"Nobody quite knows what's going on, even in a very dicky financial situation. But a marriage like yours makes everything as clear as daylight."

"Yes, but supposing I'd only been Marianne's lover, just think of the massed howling going up from my old friends and political enemies. *'Where does the money come from?'*"

"Nobody asks where the money comes from once the candidate's elected."

Espivant sat up laughing.

"You seem to know a lot all at once! Who told you all this?"

"You did. I'm just dishing up what you told me about Puylamere's candidature."

Herbert gave her an attentive look from between his lashes, and she met it without embarrassment.

"It seems you're always destined to fill me with admiration, Youlka."

"Yes; like a racehorse that starts winning the moment it's been sold. You're simply a child with a moustache. You thought you'd be rich because Marianne was; that's your excuse. You were desperately in need of a lot of useless odds and ends, you wanted motor-cars like the Argyropoulos; you wanted to throw Venetian parties like the Fauchier-Magnans; you even wanted a more beautiful wife than anyone else."

She was talking airily, knitting round her eyes the network of wrinkles blurred by her grey-blue make-up. Herbert let her run on, greedy for flattery and insult. He made a gesture of protest, and the sunlight on his bloated white hand for an instant robbed Julie of speech.

"I wanted," Herbert went on plaintively, "I wanted a sheaf of Corneille's unpublished manuscripts enough to fill a great book . . . and then I wanted a château. Oh! how I wanted a château!"

He jerked himself into a sitting position with the agility of a healthy young man.

"Just imagine it, Julie. It was called Maucombe. The whole castle lies reflected in a magnificent lake. It looks as if it doesn't take itself quite seriously, as if it felt almost too fifteenth-century with all those corner-towers and pinnacles and gateways and gothic arches! And the look-ing-glass it is built in the middle of! I wanted things I'd been dreaming of for so long!"

He looked at Julie and went on. ". . . That we'd been dreaming of for so long!"

She smiled at him generously.

"Oh, I'm quicker than you at forgetting what I want. I do think Marianne might have . . . ."

The swollen white hand reappeared in the sunbeam, and made a gesture of indecision. 'I'd have given it him, in the old days, if I'd been Marianne,' she went on think-ing. 'He's never more irresistible than when he wants something for entirely selfish reasons!'

"So you didn't get your fairy-tale Robida castle in the end? Why not?"

"Oh, it's most involved. It meant draining a swamp that had formed because they'd allowed the dykes to go to pot. Too dear; not a healthy enough region. Too iso-lated. People like that have got two passwords that crop up the whole time—'too much,' and 'not enough.' "

"Who have?"

Espivant looked for a moment like a man who is being spied on. "I really don't know, to tell you the truth. You don't tumble bang into the *middle* of a fortune like Marianne's; you fall *alongside* it, somewhere in the neigh-borhood. You arrive there. . . . I'm not boring you, Julie?"

"Don't be silly."

"Well, you arrive there like a chap who has been forced by a motor accident to spend half a day with a strange family that live by the roadside, and whose new hosts will keep on repeating, 'This is Uncle Reveillaud, and that lady is my sister-in-law, Charlotte's aunt, and that tall boy over there is George, who is going to Saint-Cyr next term.' As if the poor wretch could remember any of it after five minutes!"

He was interrupted by a fit of coughing.

"Herbert, you're tiring yourself. Shall I give you something to drink?"

He made a gesture of refusal.

"I'm not coughing from my throat, but from my heart. Never mind. Marianne's fortune is a . . . a huge foreign body, something fearful, enormous and secretive, talking every known language and always having something wrong with it, just as I might feel sick or you'd have a pain in the back."

"I *beg* your pardon, I never have a pain in the back," said Julie proudly.

"Yes, yes, we all know it's made of solid steel!" Espivant said, raising his shoulders. "Unlike the mineral resources of Marianne. Whenever you want . . . well, I don't know."

"The moon?" Julie suggested.

"Let's say the moon—you suddenly discover that copper has got chlorosis that year, weevils have got at the diamonds, and the swallows have gobbled up all the ground-nuts from the trees."

Julie burst into one of her real laughs, with tears in her eyes and her mouth wide open. She thought she heard a rustle outside the door, and laughed a bit louder, while Espivant dropped his voice.

"Reams and reams of paper, portfolios, calculating machines, arctically cold offices in impossible parts of the town, hideous malformed little brats carting piles of documents about, and lawyers better dressed than I am, who say: 'The Comte d'Espivant is no concern of ours. Our business is direct with the lady, called Anfredi Marianne-Hélène, widow of Hortiz Ludovic-Ramon. . . .' That's Marianne's fortune for you, that and lots of other things; but it's not what you would call 'money.' It's a board of directors. It's a labyrinth. At last, at the end of a corridor, you bump up against a tiny old man called Saillard, who is racked with asthma, and whose name is always just mentioned like that. Just Saillard. Marianne's always going to see Saillard, or coming back from seeing Saillard. She *often* comes back with a face as long as your arm, saying, 'It's no good. Saillard was against it!' "

"Against what?"

"Against immobilising four millions for the purchase of a country estate, against advancing eighteen hundred thousand francs to buy a ravishing little Fragonard, an extraordinary bargain. Saillard would like to point out to Madame la Comtesse d'Espivant that her diamonds were reset in the modern fashion at the time of her marriage, and besides there is that new set of emeralds which was recently acquired. That, as guardian of her son, who is still a minor, Hortiz Antoine-René, she is obliged to . . . Oh! I'm fed up with it all!" cried Espivant, stretching his arms. "It's a funny thing, when I open my arms wide, there's a place here where . . ."

He pricked his ears towards the garden. "Oh, I know

who that is. Professor Giscard. Oh dear, I can't just put him off like an office-boy. Julie, you must come again. We've only had time to talk nonsense. Tell me, would you like to? Would it amuse you in the slightest to come again?"

"Of course, I'm quite ready to."

"Quite ready to! You'd catch it, you condescending bitch, if only I were better!"

Julie thought he was making a sort of heavy joke, but she was astounded to see that he was heading for one of those sharp, unpredictable outbursts that used to rock their conjugal household, and reach a resounding climax that died away only in the dust and ashes of broken plates. Oh really,' she thought, 'he's too tiresome. . . .' But she hastened to laugh as though she were still afraid of him, and promised to come again.

"You know, a bus brings me straight to your door. I'd prefer it to Beaupied. The back of his neck wobbles and it looks beastly if you're sitting behind him. Your servants' hall always looks like an almshouse for old age pensioners. And that motor! Do you think I like bowling about in an archbishop's car all done up in pearl-grey? And you might tell the Countess—I mean the second of the name—that in Paris, in a motor-car like that, one doesn't dress up one's chauffeur in white linen."

"If you don't go, you'll have to tell her yourself," Espivant interrupted, "because she'll be coming upstairs with Giscard. Off you go, my darling. I'll give you a ring. God, what a lovely figure you've got! Indestructible monster!"

He looked at her enviously and then turned away to

fix his eyes on the door through which could come help and condemnation.

On the landing Julie realised that she had lost some of the self-assurance which, two hours earlier, had lightened her step and predisposed her for adventure. All the closed doors along the gallery, which she had slyly scrutinised on the way up, now seemed suspicious. Downstairs she manhandled the old iron latch that had been swinging on the glass-panelled door since Louis XV's day, and almost sprained her ankle on the gravel. 'Ah,' she sighed when she was on the pavement at last, 'that's better. I'm sure Marianne watched me leaving. She was watching me from all those doorways. She hoped I'd break my leg in the garden. And, with all that fuss, what did I have for lunch? I don't feel an ounce heavier! A peach, some cherries, a few figs. And, I must say, wonderful coffee.'

Cheered by having turned her back on what she most abhorred, a sick-bed, she breathed in the brief Parisian summer. The yellow rose-bud pinned to her lapel was beginning to droop. 'One of Marianne's roses.' Far from wishing to throw it away, she pressed it tight in her hand like plundered treasure. Two or three times her thoughts returned, almost gluttonously, to the two hours she had just spent in the forbidden zone. But she wisely postponed analysing them. She would pull everything to pieces when she got home. The men who passed her ran their eyes from the ash-blonde nape of her neck down to her shabby shoes, and she stopped a moment in front of all the shoe-shops. 'It'll be time to start thinking about gloves next,' she sighed. And she sought sanctuary from temptation inside a bus.

She felt a spasm of affection, as though she were just returning after a long absence, at the sight of the quavering little lift and the ramshackle staircase with its peeling plaster. On a sudden impulse she changed the position of several bits of furniture in the studio. Then, plugging in the electric iron, she spread a cloth over the kitchen table, and set to work. A black marocain crepe dress, that had been overworked for both evening and afternoon wear, was attacked with the iron and diluted ammonia. Water mixed with glycerine was dabbed on to elbows and hips that were threatening to turn shiny. A navy-blue tailor-made, whose four little pockets were covered with dull blue and red sequins, received the same careful treatment, and Julie was busy soaping a blouse, two pairs of camiknickers and some silk stockings when she was disturbed by three rings on the bell. She kept her overall on while she answered the door and brought her visitor back into the kitchen.

"What's the time, Coco? I wasn't expecting you yet!"

"Five o'clock."

"Already!"

"You might say 'at last.' "

"I was busy, as you see. The day seems to have flown."

"Lucky you!"

"Me?"

She surveyed the young man with cheerful derision. How odd that anyone should call her 'lucky.'

"You can wait in the studio, if you like."

"May I stay here?"

"You won't be in my way. Sit down on Madame Sabrier's stool. I'll only be another ten minutes."

She went on with her work, rolled her washing up in a damp towel, ironed the pleats of a skirt, changed her shoes and stitched up a hem. Coco Vatard followed her every movement since his arrival. Julie had devoted a slightly insulting attention to her various tasks, spreading cream on the heels of her shoes and plying the velvet polishing-rag with rapid strokes of her forearm.

"Is it fun watching?" she asked him.

His light-colored eyes remained fixed upon her. "Yes," he said in an earnest voice. "Nobody works like you. If only my dyers at the factory worked like that! You've such a deft and easy knack of doing things. I could watch you forever."

"Wouldn't you care to help me? Or for me to have a rest?"

Sitting on the edge of the bath-tub, she unfastened her overall and whisked it off with an aggressive gesture. She splashed cold water on her downy arms, on her shoulders and throat, barely distinguishable in color from her hair. Her one concession to modesty was to tie a little Tyrolean scarf round her neck. Only under her chin could she detect the least sign of flabbiness.

"No," Coco said after a moment's reflection. "I haven't got your knack of doing things so well. And why should you want to rest? You're always bored when you're not busy."

"That's not true!" she exclaimed.

Anger could bring tears to her eyes as promptly as laughter. But Coco showed no feeling other than admiration. He lifted the edge of his jacket and punctiliously pulled up the knees of his trousers. He was so near to being impeccably dressed that Julie hoped that she might actually make him so by putting a finishing touch to the knot of his tie. But she gave up the attempt almost at once, and drew back as he was about to take her into his arms.

"How good you smell," he said, with a sincerity which never deserted him. "You smell of under the arms and polish. Won't you be kind to me to-day?"

She gave him a distant look, her head tilted to one side. 'He really is rather nice,' she thought, 'in spite of his Sunday-best look on every day of the week. A decent young industrialist with big childish eyes and a turned-up nose. But as for . . .'

She sighed, and said, "I'm hungry."

"Hungry? Why on earth?"

She dilated her nostrils and raised her chin.

"Because, my dear boy, I had no time for luncheon. The Comte d'Espivant sent his car for me, and I sat by his bed for three or four hours, perhaps longer."

"Is he better?" asked Coco carelessly.

"No. Worse."

As she wanted to dine out and go to the cinema afterwards, she added, in a business-like way, "Professor Giscard is pessimistic, that's to say, but there is no immediate danger."

"And what does his wife think of your going to see your—her husband?"

"Nothing. She wasn't present at our meeting."

"Ah," said Coco reflectively, before he finally made up his mind. "It's disgusting!"

"What's disgusting?"

"Calling on each other like that. It's disgusting of him to have sent for you, disgusting of you to have gone, and disgusting of the other woman to have stood for it."

Julie did not react, and went on soaping her hands under the kitchen tap, looking at Coco's reflection in the small looking-glass over the sink. 'A lot he knows about it,' she thought. 'A first-rate executive in the cleaning and dyeing industry, no doubt, and treats himself to a mild binge at regular intervals. I bet he's got a faded photograph of his father in his wallet, dressed as a private. He's a nice boy.'

"You poor wretch," she said out loud. "What do you suppose you and I have got in common?"

"What?"

"I suppose that we both want to go out. Where are we going to dine? Are you meeting Lucie Albert? But not old Encelade, I presume?"

"No," Coco said. "Neither. You gave me no marching orders. Will it bore you if there's just the two of us?"

She smoothed out the three little vertical lines that the slightest vexation incised between her eyebrows.

"Of course not. But make me swallow something before dinner, or I'll eat one of your cheeks off."

Julie gently touched with her painted lips the clean-shaven cheek he proffered.

She was still in bed at ten o'clock next morning. She listened through her sleep to the familiar sounds of activity in the kitchen. When Mme. Sabrier half opened the studio door, Julie allowed her no time for her usual grievances.

"A glass of cold water, and some cocoa made with water, not milk. No breakfast or luncheon. No electric cleaner. See to my shoes and my tailor-made suit, and then off you go. I'm asleep. No letters? See you to-morrow, Madame Sabrier. Don't brush the sequins on the little pockets; they might come off."

She rolled over like a gun-dog and lay with her forehead against the wall. But she was unable to slip back into the pleasant, slumbrous condition that usually followed her brief and tumultuous nights of imbibing mixed drinks. 'It's the fault of the champagne,' she thought. 'Anyway, to be good at all, champagne must be marvellous. Nowadays, night clubs are all supplied with a standard champagne that tastes metallic. Give me brandy every time, with or without water, or a decent whisky that leaves you with a clean tongue.' The smell of cold tobacco smoke still lingered in her hair. 'My mouth and nose feel positively poisonous this morning. What on earth's the matter with me?'

A glass of cold water swept away the morning fog.

"Of course!" she cried aloud, "I had a row with Coco Vatard!"

She got back into bed and carefully pulled up the single sheet; it was worn, but made of linen and large enough to double over and tuck into her narrow divan bed. Gazing at the ceiling, she went back over the course of her evening. Shadow Number One had been the *tête-à-tête* dinner in the outskirts of Paris. When they left, in spite of Coco's misgivings, she had sat at the steering-wheel. "Do be careful," he begged her. "It's Papa's car; mine's being re-lined. If Papa saw you taking corners like that!"

"We ought to have brought Papa along too," she had said at length. "You'd have been happier then."

Her harmless little remark transformed Coco. He became mute and pompous and unready to accept any joke against his family. In other circumstances, the restaurant and the dinner would have met with Julie's approval. The dusk was darkening into night, the lights were reflected in the diminutive lake, the soft damp air carried the smell of geraniums and there was music which set her humming. But all this was too much for Coco.

"Why is it all so sad, Julie?"

She surveyed him with what remained of her benevolence, still humming softly to avoid having to say: 'It's so sad, because you're the wrong person to be here with me. And nothing here is really meant for you. You're not made for drinking or for dining with a woman who doesn't love you, somebody who comes from far away and remains there even when you hold her to your heart. You're really cut out for family dinners at home, for having a night out on Saturdays, for pretending to have outstripped your father when you are barely able to follow in his tracks or even to respect him as he deserves. It makes me sad to be here, too. But then I've been here often enough with other men, so it's not so serious in my case. I share out the sadness between Becker and Espivant and Puylamare, and others you've never heard of. Or perhaps you have, and it makes no difference. Once, for instance, I had dinner at that table down there with my first husband. I was called Baroness

Becker then. At another table sat a lieutenant in uniform, with a civilian. I couldn't take my eyes off the lieutenant. It's a funny thing, nowadays one no longer sees those really fair-haired lieutenants. This one got up all of a sudden, came straight over to our table, apologised, and then stated his name, adding, "Your humble cousin, Madame!" Then up he climbed into a genealogical tree, reeling off strings of names and marriages and kinships. Becker kept nodding his head and saying, "Of course . . . yes, yes, I see. . . . Quite right. It's true there is quite a family likeness between my wife and you." And there wasn't a shred of truth in it, except the lieutenant's spun-gold hair and certain other qualities, very authentic ones, that he revealed later. But I can't tell that sort of story to someone like you. You're only sitting beside me because we went home together after supper—two? three months ago?—I've forgotten. I must say, we both had a wonderful time. But why should we begin all over again? You're like one of those old-fashioned French girls, who say "Mama, I'm engaged to be married, a gentleman kissed me in the garden!" Yes, that's the way, order some more champagne. Two hundred and sixty francs are my entire fortune at the moment, and there are still several days till Becker's cheque turns up. After all, I can't soak you for anything, my-poor-boy-who-is-not-yet-rich! I've never liked taking money from men. Treat the Comtesse de Carneilhan to food and drink. She's not really a Countess, anyway, but only, this evening, disgustingly Carneilhan, and a bad lot like all of them!'

But she knew that with her flat dark blue felt hat tilted over one eye, and her yellow rose-petal skin toning with her hair, both the time of night and the lighting were becoming to her.

Others dining there had recognised her, and Coco found her ravishing. It was just about then that her young companion had tried to snatch her hand and kiss it under the table, and she had slapped his face. As bad luck would have it, this gesture, applied to Coco's flat compact cheek, was as clear and resounding as a stage-smack, and everyone who did not see it heard it.

They laughed, and Coco had the sense to do the same. So Julie wrinkling up her nose 'like a wild animal' was the only one to be cross, and she had trouble in recovering her temper.

'Going on to the Bal Tabarin was my idea. The drive back. Oh yes! He didn't want me to drive Papa's car. He wanted us to pull up by the side of the road in the Bois des Fausses-Reposes and make love. A regular picnic! A charming idea, really, and I can't think why I put a stop to it. Just my luck, I'm hungry again!'

Getting out of bed, she hunted through the food locker, which did its best to look like a frigidaire, and found a triangle of white cheese left over from the day before. Sprinkling a slice of bread with salt and pepper, most of her optimism returned to her as she munched away. But she always dreaded, during these difficult last days of the month, her punctual and ineluctable yearnings for food. Spurned and postponed by endless cigarettes on an empty stomach, these yearnings came back again to torment her digestion. Julie had broken herself in to every kind of diet and could cope with anything except hunger. 'Too early for oysters, but there are all sorts of little things I could swallow piping hot. I could do myself proud on ten francs, on the terrace of the little café. With a glass of muscadot to wash it down!' As she ate her bread and cheese, she sniffed the warm, damp noon-day. 'If only we could have two more months of this weather, two months without having to think about a warm coat!'

Without looking at the time, she went and smoked her first cigarette on her bed. All the details of the night before came back to her, from the gloomy dinner to the floor-show at the Tabarin, and the encounter with Beatrix de la Roche-Tannoy. She was an ex-society woman turned cabaret singer. 'Third star on the posters of the Ba-Ta-Clan! Poor Beatrix imagines a scandal in high life remains exciting for ever! We all went to see her when she first appeared on the stage at the Casino. But it didn't take long to see that the big la Roche-Tannoy nose, under all those paste tiaras and ostrich feathers, was even more tiresome than in ordinary life. So we all forgot about it.'

Julie was still bored, despite the castles of naked flesh piled up on the stage and dance floor of the Tabarin, so she made room for her friend. She was on the plump side and dressed in a little conical mediaeval head-dress covered with sequins. Julie introduced Coco Vatard.

"Coco, order some more champagne for Madame de la Roche-Tannoy."

"Here we go," said Coco with a sort of polite familiarity. "Are you alone, Beatrix?"

"Yes. I came on business. I've got to see Sandrini after the show. He wants to sign me up for the winter Revue."

"Are you . . . happy about it?"

"Delighted. Goodness, if only I'd known, I'd have dropped that gang of stuck-up idiots ten years sooner!"

"You didn't lose much time as it was," said Julie with a certain ferocity.

"And what about you? How is your father keeping?"

"My dear, he's amazing. He's still training a few colts at Carneilhan."

"No, really?" said Coco. "I say, I never knew you had a father."

Julie looked at him without saying a word, and then exchanged smiles with Beatrix.

"You never told me you had a father. Why didn't you tell me?"

"Haven't had time," Julie said.

With a pointed laugh, she made clear to Beatrix the recent date and the unimportance of her relationship with Coco Vatard. Beatrix, amused, buried her big nose in her big glass.

"And how's your mother?" Julie asked her.

"Married again, my dear, just to spite me. At seventy-one!"

"Well, I must say!" said Coco Vatard. "That's going it."

"Coco," Julie said, "pour out some champagne for Madame de la Roche-Tannoy. But what did Volodia say about her marrying again?"

"Volodia? He wanted to commit suicide. Just imagine, he'd been officially engaged to my mother for thirty years!"

"Good God!" said Coco Vatard. "Do you mean to say he wanted to commit suicide because of the old ha——I mean, because of a person of seventy-one? I must be dreaming!"

Neither of the two women appeared to have heard. Julie pushed the plate of little sandwiches to one side and put her elbows on the table so that she could lean closer to Beatrix, who followed her lead.

"Do you still see your sister Castelbeluze?" Julie asked.

Beatrix sat up straight and opened her fur coat, revealing breasts pressed tightly together by her low-cut dress.

"Her? most certainly I don't! She took sides the moment I changed my way of living, and stirred up my whole family against me." The huge, historical nose was lowered confidentially. "But, I must say, my brother-in-law behaved very well. He didn't chime in with the rest of the pack. He gets nicer the more you know him," Beatrix whispered. "And talking of that, do tell me how things are between you and Espivant?"

"Much the same! We dote on each other as long as we're not married. I spent at least three hours with him to-day! So you see."

"At his house?"

"At his house, of course. He's still laid up."

"But, Julie! What about his wife all this time?"

"Marianne? Nothing to do with me, darling. She was minding her own business, I expect."

Beatrix's close-set eyes and long nose registered such utter if belated astonishment that Julie, relishing its full flavor, blushed and then laughed exultantly. 'She'll repeat that to the whole of Christendom!' she thought.

"Is it true that Espivant is going to die?"

"Of course it isn't! His pulse is violently irregular; that's all due to the strain of parliamentary life, and so on. . . ."

"You told me," interrupted Coco, "that the Comte d'Espivant was in a really bad way."

"Your lighter, Coco. Thanks."

"I asked you," Madame de la Roche-Tannoy went on, "because Espivant, after all, has got no relations."

"Don't I know it, my dear! None at all."

A prolonged glance, fanned into flame by the champagne, passed between them. No alcoholic languor, however, loosened the fibre of these two steady drinkers or made their intimacy less cautious.

"Of course, you know the rumor that has been going round for the last few days? About Espivant's divorce?"

"I know something even more interesting," Julie answered smoothly. "Not an immediate divorce, perhaps, but a separation. It seems that Marianne is suffering from some very serious illness."

Beatrix whinnied with laughter.

"A serious illness is a promise people very seldom keep."

"Pure gossip," Julie said.

"If you aren't certain," said Coco, "why do you talk about it? What business is it of yours?"

Julie pushed the young man's glass and ash-tray to one side, and leaning forward, covered half of the little table with her bust. Her sleeves were once again beside Beatrix's bare arms and bracelets. They both gave way to the need, which they would have denied hotly if they had had nothing to drink, of stealing back, like burglars, into the world they had abandoned with such pointless ostentation. Their conversation became an exchange of scandals and mendacious confidences, of slanders and boasts which they only half believed. Dates were quoted and, above all, names usually qualified by outrageous epithets. A *rinforzando* of the orchestra wrenched them back from this passionate preoccupation.

"My dear," cried Beatrix, "it's the end. The Apotheosis of Woman! Where's your young friend got to?"

"Powdering his nose, I suppose."

"Will you excuse me if I leave you now? I don't want to miss Sandrini. Do let's meet soon."

"Darling, do let's."

Julie, left alone, watched the lights going out one by one while the crowd thronged towards the exit, stirring up, as they went, a nimbus of hanging dust. She made a sign to the barman, and he came up to her table.

"The gentleman apologised for not being able to wait. Everything is paid for."

"Splendid," said Julie.

She went down as far as the church of Saint-Augustin on foot. The cool night air played about her coatless shoulders, her face, whose warm colors were lost in the gloaming. She felt acutely aware of her solitude all of a sudden, and at once lost the sense of well-being she had felt after hours in the open air, the good dinner and the abundance of wine. 'Ah, why isn't that young idiot here?' As it was long past midnight, she climbed into a *fiacre* to save money, bewailing, in a confused fashion, the lot of the old broken-down cab-horse, Espivant's inconsequent greed and the taciturn mood of the cabby who refused, as they drove from the eighth to the sixteenth *arrondissement,* to tell his life story to Julie de Carneilhan.

Once she was out of her bath and had made up her face, she planned to lie down for an hour on her newly made bed; but she was summoned by the ring of the telephone. She ran into the studio stark naked, with muttered objurations and an assumed bad temper that changed tone as soon as she heard the voice of Lucie Albert.

"Is that you, my pet? Did you have a nice evening? Oh, of course, it was Saturday. It's no use, I'll never get used to Saturday."

In the looking-glass opposite, a tall, naked woman was watching her. From her feet to her small head with its golden-beige hair she was the color of a yellow tea-rose, with the rather spare, flat belly of a barren woman, a pretty navel placed high at her middle and breasts that had lost none of their fineness, except in her own severely critical eyes. 'Just a shade more like jelly-fish than apples cut in half these days,' was her verdict. Reiterated squeaks of "Hello! Hello!" were calling her, and she realised that she was not listening.

"Yes, my pet, we were cut off. What? Oh! A procession of Beauty Queens! Yes, yes, it would be great fun, the prize-winners are always so wonderfully inadequate, aren't they? What, tea thrown in? What a Saturnalia! I said, 'What a Saturnalia!' No, 'Saturnalia'. . . . . It doesn't matter, darling. All right, I'll meet you here about four."

She remained standing there naked, with her hand on

the telephone, overcome with gloom at the thought of the emptiness of the day ahead, though it was no different from most of her days. 'It's Beatrix's fault. That great nose of hers brings me bad luck. To be quite fair, it's also because it's the eighth of the month. From the eighth to the fifteenth, my morale varies with the state of my finances.' She struck a few becoming attitudes with her feet together and her arms above her head, and then stopped because the need for food was gnawing the pit of her stomach. 'How I loathe eating alone, but I suppose I'd better resign myself to doing so till the Becker check turns up!'

The telephone sounded once more and for a moment she stood in nervous immobility, thinking that Espivant might be calling her. But it was only Coco Vatard, for whose benefit she quite pointlessly raised her eyebrows, dilated her nostrils, and rested a hand on her hip. She spoke to him in the second person plural.

"What? You're phenomenally ignorant of how to behave, my dear boy. Angry? Me? But you're merely grotesque! What did you say? You needn't bother about me. Besides, Beatrix had her car and very kindly drove me home."

Far away, in an echoing atmosphere where Julie could hear a typewriter at work and the slower rhythm of some kind of motor, Coco was obstinately and sincerely attempting to explain. "You don't understand. Do let me speak, Julie. No, I didn't mean to play you a dirty trick, but I had Papa's car, and I saw that it was past one o'clock, and the cleaners turn up at home at five and always tackle the cars first. I get up at six-thirty on Sundays and weekdays alike, and I said to myself, 'Those two with their interminable mutterings have dropped me flat as if I wasn't there, and then supposing I strike lucky and Julie is kind to me, I know I'll be out till half-past five in the morning. I'll cut my losses and go home, at least I'll have a full working day and no rows with Papa.' Julie, no, do listen. Julie, I'll come and collect you. We'll have lunch in the Bois. Listen, Julie. I was only doing everything for the best."

All of a sudden Mme. de Carneilhan renounced her dignity and the pompous *vous*, and burst out laughing as she sized herself up in the looking-glass.

"Come here now, you idiot! Didn't I take you in beautifully? See you in a moment."

She looked fiercely at the telephone, believing she hated the person to whom, without appearing to, she had just surrendered. From Becker to Coco Vatard, how many men had she given in to on a tone of command?

She had to answer the telephone yet a third time, and listen to a grating, constricted voice that she did not recognise at first.

"Oh!" she said. "It's you, Toni? Have you got a sore throat? Good morning. I didn't recognise your voice. Is everybody well?"

"You went to the Rue Saint-Sabas."

"Yes. I even heard you talking in the garden."

"You went to the Rue Saint-Sabas," the voice grated. "You went and saw your—my stepfather. I don't want you to go and see that man. I forbid you to see him. Yes, that's it. I forbid you. No, it's *not* because of my mother. I don't want you to see him again, nor him to see you. Yes, I forbid you."

Julie put the receiver gently back on its hook without listening further. She heard another ring, and a second explosion of the broken voice punctuated by tears. 'As for that one,' she thought, 'he's the most difficult of the lot.'

She dressed with automatic deftness, putting on her black-and-white dress. Don't talk to me about boys in their 'teens,' she thought. 'What business is it of his? Young boys are a real pest. It's lucky I don't like them. A kiss on the forehead and a couple of dabs of my scent behind his ears, and he thinks he's my lover, if you please! All the same, I've a feeling he may turn out to be most tiresome. I might get rid of him by seeing Espivant only very rarely.' She knew, as she looked at her reflection, that she would do nothing so reasonable.

A moment later, she was completely taken up with Coco's arrival, and with the only too well known pleasure she derived from the presence of a man. 'A tree in the desert,' she thought, looking at Coco. However, she listened to Coco's version of the night before with an expression of supreme mockery.

"You see, Julie . . ." As he spoke he bumped into the twelve-sided table and almost upset the pot of lobelias. ". . . I've got my dignity as well, Julie."

To punish him for the word she tweaked the ends of his bow tie, rucked up his hair and pulled him about in all directions, like a sharp-toothed bitch that pretends to play so that she can bite. He only just managed to laugh, and tried to protect himself. "Julie, it's my new suit! I hate anyone touching my tie!" She kissed him absent-mindedly, and at the touch of her strong, cold, painted lips, he stopped speaking in devout expectancy. But Julie rewarded him no further and led the way downstairs.

They both took trouble to be pleasant while they ate their luncheon. In front of some worried-looking business-men and a few young women destined for a cinema career and a Deputy who greeted her a shade too famil-iarly, Julie posed as a woman indifferent to her reputation, calling Coco *tu* in a loud voice. Coco automatically slipped into the part of an adored young man. He plunged his honest grey eyes into Julie's, where they struck shallow bottom on a spangled, cold and unconfiding blue sand.

"Who was the chap you said 'Hello' to, Julie, over there in the corner?"

"A Deputy called Puylamare."

"Do you know him well?"

"Enough not to want to know him better."

"So you don't mind him seeing us together?"

"My dear infant, please get it into your head that I don't care a damn. Not only Puylamare, I mean, but everybody."

"How nice you are!"

But, even as he spoke he did not seem sure that she was so nice after all. Near the muddy little lake a swarm of starlings, about a hundred strong, settled among the branches where the leaves were already turning to gold. They were plump and heavy, and their whistling sounded like a winter wind.

"What are you doing to-day, Julie?"

"It all depends. What is to-day?"

"Don't you ever know what day it is, Julie?"

"Yes, whenever the fifteenth turns out to be a Saturday or Sunday."

"Why?"

"Because then I can't get my . . . my allowance till Monday."

"Julie," he said kindly, "it's the ninth to-day. You wouldn't be needing any money, would you?"

Julie turned to him in surprise.

'It's usually women,' she thought, 'who make these offers so diffidently.' She said "No" with her head, preferring not to speak. 'I should only say something silly,' she pondered, 'or rather I couldn't help saying "Yes," that I've got to pay Madame Sabrier for the week, that I've only got two hundred and forty francs left, that . . . yes, that I do need some money.'

Leaning on the table, she kept brushing Coco's hand with a rose she had been given by the *maître d'hôtel*. She felt a faint wave of friendship towards the hand with its thumb deformed by an accident with some piece of machinery: the manicurist did not always succeed in removing a line of vivid green round the edge of the nail, the acid stain of some color test.

"Once," she said, "I tried to dye a blouse by myself. Oh, my dear, for a month I could never take my gloves off, except at home."

"Of course you couldn't manage it; you're only a beginner," said Coco. "Julie, please be kind and tell me—wouldn't you like a little money?"

She shook her head once more. 'If I start talking about it I'll let myself go, and admit I'm gnawed all of a sudden by a longing for all kinds of things I need; I'd say I'd like some stockings, gloves, a fur coat, two new tailor-mades, scent by the litre and cakes of soap by the dozen. I haven't been like this for ages. What's got into me? If I don't hold myself back, if this blessed innocent gives me some of his salary and then thinks I'm in his debt, life will again be a hell.'

She shook herself, smiled, and began powdering her nose.

"You're an angel. Send me a little bottle of *Fairyland.* And take me home. I've got to change my suit. I've got a date with Lucie. We're going to have a great time at the procession of Beauty Queens in the banqueting hall of *Le Journal.*"

"What about me?" Coco begged.

Julie put on her faraway look, and glanced at Coco between her darkened lashes.

"If you'd like to . . . if you're free."

"Free as air. But only till half-past seven. We've got a dinner to-night for the anniversary of my parents' wedding."

"Really? You haven't talked about them for ages. Come on, then; it's three o'clock! It's absurd, sitting on at a table as though we were at a wedding breakfast. Just look at Puylamare on the job! He arrived long before us, and there he is still, drinking *Franciscaine.* He's not fifty yet, and he looks old enough to be my grandfather!"

As they crossed the room, she vaguely acknowledged an inquisitive and familiar greeting from the Deputy, who looked Coco up and down.

They drove back to Paris the long way round, and Coco's grey eyes made it clear to Julie how much he longed for her to be 'kind' to him. With a glance and a dilation of the nostrils, she promised she would, and he began driving the car like a taxi-man at the outset of his career.

Feeling relaxed and faintly perturbed and at the mercy of a melancholy she forbade herself to explore, Julie laughed at the speed of his driving and the rash way he took the corners. 'He's not a clumsy lover by any means,' she thought. 'He's full of instinct and warmth. I am too. We've got lots of time before Lucie comes to pick me up. I won't take the cover off the divan. I've only got one sheet on the bed, and it's a turned one with a seam down the middle. We'll carry on just as if we were on the grass.'

In the hall Julie saw that Coco Vatard's face had turned into the very picture of carnal desire—foolish-featured, and lilac-colored, as if bruised, under the eyes. She had to push him aside and say, "Wait, wait a minute," in a low voice, feeling an access of indulgence for this healthy and uncomplicated young male in all the confusion of his impatience.

But, before the elevator began to move, the *concierge* ran up and pushed an envelope through the bars.

"A chauffeur brought this for you."

"When?" shouted Julie, sailing up into the air.

"Just a moment ago!" squeaked the concierge. "No message!"

In spite of the half-darkness, Julie recognised Espivant's writing—sharp, incisive writing which often cut into the paper. Coco Vatard's hand pressed hers softly.

"Do leave me alone, you!" she said crossly.

He recoiled as far as the narrow elevator would allow.

"Why 'me'?" he asked in an offended voice.

"Really, Coco, you might at least behave in the elevator."

When they were in her flat, she left him standing while she read the letter. He walked up and down the studio, and, of course, banged into the twelve-sided table, to which he said "Sorry." When he saw Julie folding the letter up, he risked a question.

"Nothing nasty?"

"No, no," said Julie quickly. Then she added, more slowly, "Only it's rather a bore. I shan't be able to go with Lucie to the Beauty Queens at five. . . . Quick. Go and open the door. That's Lucie ringing. She's early for once."

Coco Vatard came back, followed by Lucie.

"Julie can't come with us to the Beauty Queens at five," he repeated in a gloomy voice.

"Why?" asked Lucie Albert.

At the slightest provocation she would open her anxious eyes wide: eyes which a year before had taken the first prize as 'the largest in Paris.' But everybody had forgotten that by now, although she would still unveil those vast orbs —beyond the bounds of decency or tact—till they seemed the size of a mare's; swamped by dark irises and equally devoid of intelligence.

"You might at least say good afternoon, Julie!"

"Good afternoon, my angel. You look very pretty to-day," Julie added without thinking.

"But why can't you come? Why did you tell me you could come, then? What shall I do if you don't come?"

'She's awful,' thought Julie. 'When she opens her eyes like that, it makes my head ache. And that little purple hat!' She turned to Coco, as though in search of help.

"Coco can tell you that a letter I've just received has upset all my plans for the afternoon, can't you, Coco?"

"Yes," said Coco impassively. "Julie's not coming with us because she wants to go and see Monsieur d'Espivant."

"How do you mean? Nobody said anything about Monsieur d'Espivant that I know?"

"That's got nothing to do with it. I say you want to go and see him. And that this is rotten for us. And also that you're wrong to go. If you want my advice, you oughtn't to."

'What on earth is he talking about? Advising me not to go . . . He offers me his good advice. It's grotesque, it's . . .' She had grown so red in the face that the down on her cheeks and close to her ears veiled her skin like silver gauze.

"That's quite right," said Lucie Albert. "You oughtn't to go. Anyway, what did the Count say in his letter? Probably lies. Just think, after the way he treated you!"

"Oh, she knows all right," said Coco Vatard.

"And we'd have a lovely time at *Le Journal*. Maurice de Waleffe told me he'd put us in the very best places and that he'd keep some chocolate for us, whatever happens.

Because you know how people carry on when the refreshments are free, the chocolate's always the first to go."

Coco frowned.

"No need to bother about free refreshments if I'm coming with you."

Julie emerged painfully from her silence, lifted her nose in the air and adopted her thin head-voice.

"When you've quite finished, may I say something? I'm not compelled to account for my actions to either of you. But I admit it is a question of Monsieur d'Espivant's health, which is in a bad enough condition . . ."

"To have you on toast," said Coco.

"What exactly does that mean?"

He became very young and contrite: "Oh! Nothing, Julie. You know, you hurt my feelings, and then I get spiteful. Julie, anybody else in my place. . . ."

She calmed down, smiled at his grey eyes and turned-up nose, and thought, vaguely, 'I'd have done much better to let him have a few moments of fun and, incidentally, enjoyed myself too into the bargain. It's too late now. Also, they're bound to be right, he and that little idiot. Probably all lies.' Four strokes chimed from the clock of the neighboring school. Julie picked Coco's gloves up from the table and Lucie's bag and tossed them over to their owners.

"Off you go. Quick."

"Oh!" Lucie was outraged.

"And supposing I don't come back?" ventured Coco in a challenging tone.

Julie gazed at him from a long way off.

"You're a good boy," she said.

She went up to him and diplomatically stroked his clear cheek.

"And very good-looking . . . very. Lucie, my love, do excuse me."

She pushed them both out and shot the bolt in order to feel more definitely separated from them, free to remain standing with her arms hanging at her sides and listen to their footsteps dying away down the staircase. She dressed herself with her usual speed and efficiency, and, when she was ready, wondered why she was going. 'Probably lies,' as Lucie says, 'nothing but lies.'

She had lived a great deal among lies, before plumping for a small life of her own, a sincere and restricted life from which all pretence, even in matters sensual, was banished. How many crazy decisions and allegiances to successive aspects of the truth! Had she not, one day when her costume for a fancy dress had demanded short hair, cut off the great chestnut mane that fell below her waist when she let it down? 'I could have hired a wig,' she thought. 'I might also, at a pinch, have passed the rest of my life with Becker, or with Espivant. If it comes to that, I could also have gone on stirring puddings in an old saucepan at Carneilhan. The things "one might have done" are, in fact, the things one could not do. Lies? After all, why not?' She had not always taken sides against the fascination of destroying truth and confidence. 'The man who wrote this knew what he was about!'

When she had found a seat in the bus, she unfolded the letter, thinking she might have read it too hastily. But she remembered the most important words: "Please come," that is to say, and "darling Youlka."

Julie was not particularly surprised to find Herbert d'Espivant up and dressed and in his study. 'But why, oh why,' she thought, 'that maroon-colored velvet jacket?' No trace remained of the exhilarated mood in which she had stepped on to the bus, with the letter crackling in her bag like a new bank-note. She felt absent-minded, aware of her surroundings, sharply critical and rather coarse-grained, and she had the bad taste to go and lean, for a moment, on the open window-sill.

"Did I introduce my friend Cousteix?"

"Of course," she said, and she stretched out her hand with the gracious gesture of a hostess, to a young man slightly aged by a beard. 'Model secretary for a pretentious politician. Young tutor for an adolescent prince. Herbert always knew how to choose his secretaries.' Cousteix vanished like a shadow and Herbert took Julie by the elbow and led her into the sunlight by the window.

"What if they see us from the garden?" she said. "You're not interesting any more, now you're well on the road to recovery."

"I thought," Herbert said, "you were only interested in men in full possession of their powers. No, I'm not well yet. But I almost look it, don't I?"

He confronted the daylight, and she observed his clean-shaven cheek, his short hair, the moustache skilfully clipped and trimmed. 'It's a disaster,' thought Julie and her eyes grew moist, not with pity, but with regret for the past, for this faithless musketeer of hers, with his delicate beauty and his faintly martial pose. Espivant's smile died away. He became hard, businesslike and preoccupied once more.

"Sit down. Get it into your head that I'm lonely here. Lonely as I suppose everybody is. Are you? You wouldn't tell me. I'm absolutely alone, living beside a woman who's in love with me, and ill now that I'm faced with a political life I started too late. Anyway, there's going to be a war."

"A war?" said Julie.

"Does that surprise you? You read the papers, don't you?"

"The illustrated ones, now and then. But I only looked surprised because a fortune-teller told me we were going to have a war."

"Is that all you care?"

"Yes," Julie said. "All I know about wars is how to be glad if we win, and how to die if I have to."

Espivant looked at her with envy.

"But don't you realise what a terrible war it would be? Worse than the last one?"

She made a gesture of indifference.

"I don't bother my head about it. After all, it's nothing to do with women." She reflected a moment and then went on: "But you're fifty. And you're not—not at the moment—outstandingly fit. . . ."

"My dear, I know I'm not up to much," said Espivant bitterly, "and I don't need reassuring."

"It's not you I'm reassuring," said Julie, "but me."

Espivant fixed his whole attention on her. He seemed to believe her. He kissed her hand and then put an arm round her shoulders. She disengaged herself, cleverly pivoting away from him.

"Palace furniture, Herbert?"

"Yes. Kept, as one might say, in Boulle."

"Are you the culprit?"

"I had accomplices. But don't start on interior decorating again. I haven't the time."

"Nor have I."

Julie stared him in the face with studied insolence, for she was feeling inferior to her normal self—dry-skinned, less rose-complexioned than usual, small-eyed—and she hated it. Espivant shrugged his shoulders.

"It's no day for rows, Youlka. I've only been up a couple of hours."

"But you haven't had any more of those attacks since my visit, have you?"

"Only one. Let's forget about it. My house gets on my nerves. Oh, don't keep listening towards the gallery; nobody's there. Do you know where Marianne is?"

"No."

"She's gone in search of her son."

"In search . . . ? What did you say?"

"Of her son. I wish you'd listen, Youlka! Toni didn't come home last night. My opinion is, he's with some woman. But his mother's off her head with anxiety. After all, seventeen is young to stay out all night, especially without warning. And then, he's too good-looking, much too good-looking. Are you listening? What are you thinking about?"

"What you're saying. Didn't he leave any clue?"

"Yes, an idiotic note for his mother: 'I'll never set foot in this house again,' or something of the kind. Marianne swears nothing had gone wrong between them, but I simply can't believe it."

"Did he take any money with him?"

"Very little. Marianne doesn't give him much. Only in driblets."

"Why?"

"She says that that's the right thing. I slip him five louis now and then."

"Are you on good terms with your stepson?"

"Very good terms. He's not specially communicative, but he's very sweet-tempered, rather difficult to size up—the least troublesome child in the world. He's got a little flat, two and a half rooms on the second floor, and I haven't seen him for . . . let me see, for forty-eight hours. Do you know him?"

"I've caught glimpses of him. You're on good terms with him, but you don't like him. Is that right? No, you don't like him. Of course you don't like him. You've got your hands full with one Marianne; a pair of them would be too much. She and the boy look so much alike that you can hardly stand it. Is that it? Go on, do tell. Surely you can tell *me*?"

She advanced, pushing Espivant with her forefinger, and putting her face close to his, which was exactly on a level with her own; and attacking the hazel of his eyes with the blue of hers, hardening their expression and harassing him as she used to in the old days when she wanted to make him own up to an infidelity in thought or deed. Caught by surprise, he gave way, and took refuge in cynicism.

"Well, as far as that goes, I don't really care a damn one way or the other. If he had been my own son . . . But I've neither the years nor the temperament for an adoptive father. But I'm worried about this business, for Marianne's sake. Anything that interferes with her normal course of life makes her . . . how shall I put it? When something tiresome happens to either of us, you or me, we just call it tiresome."

"Or even worse."

"While Marianne calls it an unheard-of event, an unimaginable catastrophe."

"She's the sensitive sort."

"No; but she's fundamentally gloomy. And actually, nothing but the most fortunate things ever happen to her."

"Herbert, you're forgetting yourself!"

They both burst out laughing, when the bell of the private telephone interrupted them.

"What is it, Cousteix? They' found the boy? No? But that's too much of a good thing! No; don't go there now. Stay here, and take all incoming calls, but only tell me when there's something urgent. I want to be left in peace. Hang on to Mademoiselle Billecoq and get her to take down anything important from the foreign wireless stations. Thank you. Oh, and Cousteix—give me Billecoq—I want to dictate. There are one or two odds and ends."

While he was dictating, Julie made a tour of the room. 'Herbert and I never managed to furnish this study. I'd worked out a rather Balzacian decoration, the furnishings all imaginary, the name of the nonexistent picture written up on the walls. And now it's much too full. That huge Panini! And those Guardis, thirteen to the dozen. And that array of telephones! It's a funny thing, all those symbols of activity; I can never quite believe that Herbert really needs them.'

She was striving to distract her mind from an awkward fact. 'Toni refuses to set foot here again. Toni has disappeared. It's no business of mine. Really none.' Then she remembered the telephone conversation, the tearful and discordant voice, the childish threats. 'Toni didn't sleep at home. And he wrote that he *refused* to come back.'

Julie wandered about the room, peered at a little picture entirely filled with Venice, stroked with disgusted hands the brass and tortoiseshell of the Boulle while she listened to Espivant's voice dictating into the mouthpiece ". . . *the points, my dear colleague, that you have kindly brought to my notice by no means imply that I must consider. . . .* Are you following, Mademoiselle Billecoq? For Heaven's sake try and keep up."

'Toni stayed out all night. He doesn't want to set foot in his stepfather's house.' She frowned, ferociously calling to mind the faint adolescent face so like Marianne's. 'If only he were dead,' she exclaimed to herself, 'we should be well rid of him!' It escaped her notice that her thoughts had been expressed as 'We should' instead of 'I should.'

"That's all. Take me off the office line, Billecoq. Tell

Monsieur Cousteix to put me on only if Madame d'Espivant telephones. Come, Youlka. I'm so sorry."

He pulled up a great, unfriendly crimson armchair for Julie. 'Venetian Louis XIV,' she thought; 'the nastiest style in the world. The whole room stinks of Venice. I loathe rooms furnished according to a single idea. If I know anything of Herbert, he's probably very proud of it.' She made her wild-animal grimace and sat down gingerly. Espivant cast a slow glance over her crossed legs and her shoes. His look put her in a good mood at once.

"I've got my pretty shoes on to-day," she said with a laugh.

"And your pretty legs every day," Herbert answered. "How do you find me, Youlka?"

"Dangerous."

He leant back in his chair, beaming. "That's the right sort of talk, but it would not be the right sort of behavior."

"Would you like to tie my hands, for safety?"

"You've got so many other weapons."

He contemplated her thoughtfully and without desire.

"Youlka, I want to go to the country."

"I give you my full permission."

"I need some money."

"I've got two hundred and forty francs."

"What did you do with that receipt I gave you, for fun —and also because I was furious—when you sold your diamond necklace during your divorce suit? Before we were married. You remember. . . . *I hereby testify that I have received from Madame Julius Becker, Baroness of the early pink Dutch variety, the exorbitant sum of . . .*"

"What a memory."

". . . the exorbitant sum of a million, Youlka!"

"That's it. A million that didn't last long, to give it its due."

"What's a million?"

"It was tiny, done up in two rubber bands. . . ."

"Had no staying-power, eh?"

They laughed, rubbing shoulders and cold-heartedly provoking each other.

"Did you throw the paper away? Because, my dear child, that comic document is an absolutely genuine receipt. Do you remember I mentioned—idiotically!—that the sum was 'in the nature of a loan.' And I can still see the beautiful sheet of paper, all stamped and engraved, that I consecrated to that masterpiece of prose."

He was consulting his extraordinary memory, which never played him false. 'He's like a starling. Léon's right,' thought Julie. 'When Herbert makes an effort to remember anything he squints a bit.'

"You put the paper away in . . ."

"In that lovely box inlaid with mother-o'-pearl, a chocolate box, with your other letters and your love-letters. I've still got the box, even if I haven't got the stamped paper."

On the alert, she lied in exactly the level and sociable tones she had used in former contests: fencing-matches that used to end in sudden sharp squalls. But to-day, talking as he was only of money, Julie was frightened, not of his violence, but of his diplomacy.

"Have a good hunt for it," he said in a cajoling voice. "I owe you a million, Julie, do you realise?"

"No," Julie said in all sincerity.

"But I do, really. I'd like to pay it back to you. Why don't you claim it? Because I wouldn't give it back? Wrong for once! Marianne can't bear debts, especially mine. Do you get me?"

Julie blushed so much that there was no need to answer.

"Well, don't let's say any more about it. I was only saying . . ."

She bowed her head.

"I quite realise why you said it. But I shouldn't think Marianne's the sort of woman to believe, on the strength of a mere affirmation . . ."

Herbert interrupted her as though he had his answer pat.

"Marianne's the sort of woman who believes what she sees," he said.

He lowered his glance from her eyes the instant he felt that she was about to bridle, and began stroking her shoulders. "You're the only person I enjoy playing dangerous games with, Youlka. I forgot to tell you that the two medical big-wigs, Hattoutant and Giscard, have given me an ultimatum. I've got to quit Paris and political life. The country—and do you see me in the country?"

"I've seen you there. But you don't like it."

He gave her a melancholy smile that had all the appearance of being genuine.

"When we used to go riding at Carneilhan, you used to have your great mane of hair knotted up tight like the tail of a cart-horse. It was in a terrible mess sometimes when you got home. . . ."

She thrust the glowing evocation from her with a wave of the hand.

"No, please. Can't you go to the country alone?"

He lowered his head.

"Politics aren't the only thing I've been warned off. You know, in Paris, somehow, the intimacy of married life seems to be a very small part of the twenty-four hours."

"You don't say so!"

"And Deauville wouldn't be too bad either. Everybody goes to bed late. But the country . . ."

Listening reflectively, Julie repressed an awkward temptation to burst out laughing.

"Did they tell your wife there would be . . . certain restrictions?"

"Heavens, no. I put a stop to that. That's the sort of commission I undertake myself."

"What will she say?"

"Oh, nothing. She'll settle in a different room, quite straightforwardly. On nights when there is a full moon or a smell of new-mown hay, she'll get as far away as possible, but not quickly enough for me not to see what her feelings are. Stop laughing, you beast, or I'll chuck the Regent's ink-pot at your head. It's a fake, anyhow," he went on coldly.

"And . . . what about divorce?"

"Too soon. I've got absolutely nothing of my own."

He grew angry again and shouted, "Good heavens! After all, I'm not demanding anything extraordinary. That million francs was Becker's money, the proceeds of Becker's presents. You gave it to me, and a fine shindy there would have been if I'd refused it!"

"I agree. But it was my money as well. I had a right to give that. But how can I give Marianne's?"

"Oh, we'd share it," he said naïvely. "I mean . . . I'd give you some."

Julie smiled in spite of herself.

Espivant, certain now that she would consent, pressed his point home.

"Marianne's money is—ought to be—everybody's. It's gloomy, mysterious money with a sombre, Mexican face, and it makes a sound like metal held prisoner underground. A million is only a tiny spangle of all those remote minerals."

She listened, trembling and overswept by a breath from former times. Her practised ear could single out the spurious anger, the incurable gaiety, the knack of seduction in the very avowal of unworthiness, the gusts of marital hatred and, above all, the positive refusal to be poor again. 'I've never hesitated,' she thought, 'almost flinging myself headlong into poverty, if it was a question of escape. What's he saying? He's still going on about Marianne?'

She saw him break off and press the region of his heart with both hands.

"I swear to you, when I first found myself with that rose-colored body—it was the color of pink wax—in my arms, and that endless mass of hair, so long and thick I was almost frightened when it was all spread out in my bed, I thought I'd overturned the statue barring the entrance—you know, Youlka, it comes in the *Arabian Nights*—the entrance of the underworld with a cave full of emeralds, a cave full of rubies, a cave full of sapphires. And as the statue was fond of me into the bargain—fond, much too fond really—the whole thing seemed easy, agreeable, intoxicating, lasting, and I thought myself an astonishing fellow."

He sat on the arm of Youlka's chair and leaned up against her.

"My poor beautiful darling, my poor, poor beautiful darling. These are things that I ought never to tell you! My poor beautiful darling, if you only knew how cheated of everything I feel. And then I go and send for *you*."

Leaning against Julie, he tipped up her little black straw boater. She believed not a word he was saying; but, spurred by an overmastering curiosity, she laid her cheek against his velvet jacket. Herbert froze into immobility and Julie knew that he was expecting and fearing one of those gentle but imperious advances—so friendly and so amorous —which he used to call 'the Youlka manner.' 'Always on the look-out for sensuality,' she thought, 'pleasure-blackmail, pleasure-panacea, pleasure-deathblow. Is that all he knows about or understands?'

Through the cloth of his suit she felt the irregular beating of Herbert's damaged heart, and thenceforward it dominated every other sound. She was scared all of a sudden by the broken rhythm, scared lest the unequal beats should stop, and she sat up straight. A voice that was studiedly, miraculously deep and precise, floated down to her.

"Didn't you like it there, Youlka darling?"

She shook her head to avoid answering and took Herbert by the arm. "Don't sit perched like that on the arm of the chair!"

"Like a bird on a branch!" he said. "By the way, Youlka, has Becker's remittance turned up?"

"No. It comes on the fifteenth. Three notches in the girth, as Léon would say."

"What's Léon's rank in the Army?"

"Captain. The dried-up remains of one, that's to say. Why?"

"Because of the war."

"Oh, really . . ." Julie said with a sigh of boredom.

"Yes, really, just as you say; what does Léon think about it?"

"Well, if war breaks out he's going to sell his pigs. Kill his mare Hirondelle, and join up again."

"How do you mean, kill his mare? Poor wretch! What a brute Léon is. Why?"

Julie looked at him disdainfully.

"If you don't understand, it's no use explaining."

"You Carneilhans are very lucky. You never see further than your noses."

He glanced furtively at his reflection in the brass and tortoiseshell looking-glass. Julie realised that he was thinking about his illness and the uncertainty of his life.

"Here, Youlka. I wish you'd have this."

He unclasped from his wrist a watch attached to a platinum curb-chain, and handed it to her.

"Is it eatable, Herbert?"

"Yes; when one's got teeth like yours. It's too heavy for

me. Everything seems to tire me now. The bracelet presses just where a vein is beating, or an artery. Sell it or pawn it. . . . I'd like it to be a sort of link between us, a sort of something . . ."

"Something on account," said Julie.

He slid the warm chain into her hand.

"Oh, my poor old darling, don't pretend to be tougher than you really are! It doesn't fool me. Let's each of us do what we can for the other. It would be our only virtue! If only I had some money! It's pretty odd, you'll admit, that I never do have any. Would you like to carry off one of the Guardis for breakfast to-morrow? Or would you prefer a Panini three metres by five?"

"Oh, a little slice of the Panini would be ample, thanks! Do they all belong to you?"

"Nothing here belongs to me. It was a decision I made at the time of my marriage. I stuck to it afterwards out of good manners, and now I have to go on, because I've no option. But . . ."

He leaned over Julie, making his brown eyes shine with a more brilliant lustre and bringing his sinuous moustached mouth close to her ear. "But I can steal," he said archly.

Julie shook her head.

"You're flattering yourself," she said. "That's what one thinks. But after all, what *can* one carry away from a luxurious marital establishment? I know something about it! It boils down to three trunks full of clothes, some books you don't really care about, a few knick-knacks, a necklace, a couple of clips and three rings. And a pair of hideous cuff-links left lying about in a bowl, that you take on principle. Pictures, yes. But rich people haven't owned pictures for very long"—she raised her eyes to the Panini—"and what pictures!"

She opened her hand and looked at the warm chain.

"It certainly looks a very good watch," she said.

"But you must certainly keep the watch!" Espivant cried. "There are two little platinum prongs that fit on to a link of the chain; you press them and the watch comes off. Let's have it a moment. It's beautifully made."

They both sat down, leaning over the watch. A sunbeam turned the nape of Julie's neck into a solid pillar of silver. Herbert's over-silky hair, surrounding a small and carefully hidden tonsure, curled like a woman's. Both of them, quite oblivious of their age, were as fascinated as children with a mechanical toy.

"Marvellous!" said Julie. "What are they called, these sort of fat links, more or less square? They're like a convict's chains."

"I'll give another in exchange," said Espivant.

"Who to?"

"To Marianne, of course, when she's found her lost chick. Hello, that's her. Idiot," he said, laughing. "That's her, calling I mean—that little wooden buzzer ringing under the desk. Hello, Cousteix? Put her through, quick. Hello? Darling, at last! Where are you? Where? But that's miles away! I can't hear at all well."

Julie had withdrawn to the end of the room, and watched him going through the motions of love and concern; questioning with raised eyebrows, pursing his lips into a heart-shape and sticking his chin out to underline 'very badly' with a note of plaintiveness. 'Anyone else would come to bits under the ludicrousness of it all,' she thought! 'Yet he gets away with it. It's a star turn.'

"Found him? Alive? Ah! But why is your voice so tragic, then, my Black Rose?"

He threw Julie a gay little kiss across the telephone with the tips of his fingers. 'A star turn with all its execrable taste and all its bounderishness. If he thinks I like it . . .' The mask of the caressing musketeer froze under her eyes and the seductive voice stumbled over the words: "With . . . with what? Veronal? But . . . but is he out of danger? Oh, the idiot child! Neuilly Hospital? Of *course* I understand it's not your fault in any way. But try and talk more clearly, for God's sake. I beg your pardon, darling, but you can imagine that your emotion and mine don't make things easier."

He fell silent and listened for a long time without interrupting. Holding a pencil in his free hand, he began to draw little rabbits, traced in a single outline, on the blotting paper. Julie's piercing eyes counted them automatically. But she gave up counting after the word 'veronal' and lay in wait for some unknown and vaguely threatening event. She breathed in deeply and felt ready for what was to come. 'It will be the moment when he stops drawing those little rabbits.' He stopped drawing, threw down his pencil and raised his eyes to Julie.

"All right," he said. "The rest isn't particularly important; you'll tell me when you get here," he said into the telephone. "To-morrow, the whole business will seem no more than a bad dream for both of us. Of course you must leave him there. It's the wisest thing to do. Don't . . . don't hurry, darling; the urgent thing was for me to know where you were. Me too, darling, me too."

He hung up the receiver without lowering his eyes from Julie and lit a cigarette.

"Well, Youlka," he said at last, "so you've developed a taste for young boys."

As she did not answer, he went on:

"To clear up anything that remains obscure, I'd like to inform you that Toni was discovered unconscious at the Hotel Continental. A photograph of you was found beside his bed. Also, a letter saying that he was taking his life voluntarily, and a note from you putting off a rendezvous. That's all. What have you got to say to all that?"

"Nothing," Julie said.

He stood up with violence.

"What do you mean, nothing?"

"Ah yes, of course! I'd like to know if you'd have preferred the note from me to have been an acceptance of the rendezvous, instead of a refusal. I *didn't put it off*. I *refused* it."

She felt at the top of her form, a condition of which her moral solitude had for a long time robbed her. Once again she was deep in the atmosphere where women, the permanent objects of men's rivalry, bear all their suspicions light-heartedly, listen to their insults, yield under varied assaults and hold their own against masculine presumption and derive from it all a simple and lively pleasure. Her horse-woman's muscles twitched in her thighs and she felt in her breast the rhythm of her full and regular heart-beats. 'He's got no idea what to say or do,' she thought. 'In point of fact, men scarcely ever have. But what's this particular one looking so cross about?'

She was disturbed by her feeling of jubilation. Besides, the presence of several former Julies was blinding her to the implications of the moment. One of her vanished selves was in full flight from good old Becker and flinging herself at the head of a poor but very handsome young officer who was almost demolished by so splendid a catastrophe. Another Julie, naked and golden this time, shivered with cold and impatience between two men who were on the point of coming to blows, but they finally thought better of it. A credulous Julie followed, blindly absorbed by her passion for Espivant, then betrayed, desperate, and, in the end, consoled. They were Julies ready for any drama, provided they were dramas of love. Julies who were only capable of triumph, subtlety, kindness, ferocity or stoicism if these were the byproducts of love. These and the easy chastity and the physical passion that it engendered were the fruits of Julie's faithful and unflagging appetite for love.

"And when, if I'm not being indiscreet, did this story begin?"

She fixed on Espivant a tenacious blue gaze that overflowed with the spirit of hazard and defiance. 'So he's made up his mind,' she thought. 'Men are not very quick thinkers.'

"Your question would be extremely indiscreet if there *were* any story. But there isn't."

"As if I'd believe that!"

"Young Mr. Hortiz wanted to behave like his step-papa. Yes, you don't like that name, do you? I think it's rather fun. It was perfectly natural for him to fall in love with me, at his age and mine. And that's the whole story, as you call it. I've just learnt the rest from you. A bit more and it would have been the end."

"I shouldn't advise you to laugh about it!"

"Thanks, I've never needed your advice or permission to laugh. After all, nobody's been killed by the business. And who on earth doesn't commit suicide, more or less, between fifteen and twenty?" She walked up to the desk and took a cigarette from a vase as she would have drawn an arrow from a quiver.

"A light, please, Espivant."

He held out his lighter without a word. The blood was in her cheeks, and she carried herself like a figure-head. Her lips trembled slightly. She surrounded herself with smoke and went on.

"A little fellow less than eighteen years old! A sort of delicate little Borgia! I agree, he's very beautiful. But pff! you ought to know, unless you've quite forgotten what I think of the Italian statuette kind of beauty. I bet he's got two lilac-colored buttons on his chest and a dismal little——"

"That's enough!" Espivant said.

"Enough of what?" Julie innocently asked.

"Enough of all that . . . of all that filth."

"But what filth, Herbert? Here am I cudgelling my brains to tell the truth: I clear myself of the slur of corrupting children—whom I hold, anyway, in holy abomination. I can't bear veal, lamb or kid, and I can't bear adolescents. If there's anybody who knows my amorous proclivities, surely that person is not very far from here, at this very moment?"

She was longing to overstep the mark, to hear insulting words and slamming doors, to twist her wrists free from somebody's hands again—either a lover's or a stranger's—to measure her strength against that of another, voluptuously, or in a struggle. But Espivant, she saw, was holding himself back and breathing with difficulty. A generous impulse overcame her. "Here we are with only this scrap of nonsense between us," she went on, "and he's not worth all this fuss! You're not really cross, are you?"

"Yes," said Herbert.

"Cross-*cross*, or just cross?"

He answered with a gesture and avoided looking at her.

"Seriously? But really, Herbert, why?"

Herbert remained standing, his eyes lowered. Julie saw that he was rumpling with one hand under his jacket the place where his heart lay. She shoved a chair from behind into the hollow of his knees, briskly enough to jerk him into the seat by surprise.

"Herbert, will you please tell me how I'm to blame in all this business? Because I really don't see . . ."

"Leave me alone," he cried in a low voice. "I don't see either! But I'm not going to stand your—that in front of me, talking to me—I'm not going to have you discussing any male creature as if you were deciding to use it or not to use it! You're free and I'm married. I quite realise all that. But your liberty doesn't extend to coming here and then, under my very nose, appraising the Hortiz boy's physique."

As Julie merely shrugged her shoulders, he struck the desk with his fist.

"The Hortiz boy or anyone else! You are the field that I've mown and trampled! But I swear that if others have done the same after me, you're not going to come here and shove the marks they've left on you under my nose!"

He looked her up and down, trying to master his irregular breathing, and Julie admired him with a growing anxiety. She felt a danger swelling inside her that she would be unwilling to escape. But Espivant made a gesture of affliction, and only said: "Go away."

"What do you mean, go away?"

"What I say. Go away!"

She pivoted round on her heel, went out and slammed the door behind her. Strangers gazed at her as she crossed the garden, but she did not even see them.

She plunged into the warm street as into a bath. Then, mastering her passion, she called Espivant a cad and a fool. But, deep down in herself, she went over and over the insulting words, weighing up all they contained of promise or of threat. Towards the south, a storm hung heavy over the city. Paris waited for it supinely with all her *concierges* out of doors on the watered and steaming pavements. 'This kind of weather,' grinned Julie, 'must make Marianne curse herself for being a redhead!' For she knew that the strange purplish hair of Mme. d'Espivant owed nothing to dye.

Now and then she accorded a thought, a 'poor kid' to

Toni Hortiz, coldly summoning up the loosened, prostrate body, the inanimate beauty of the child who had wished to sleep for ever. 'It was his right. But it was idiotic. At that age, luckily, one's as clumsy at dying as at living. It's hot. A cold river to swim in, that's what I want.' She noticed that her bag seemed heavier on her arm. 'Of course, the chain. I've got it. I'll sell it tomorrow morning.'

She took a cab to *Le Journal*. Under irregular raindrops, each the size of a flower petal, the curiosity aroused by the Beauty Queens had filled the streets. Lucie Albert, in her joy at seeing Julie, made her signs as though she had been shipwrecked, to which Julie gave cold response. But she was determined to enjoy herself to the full. They sat side by side in the hottest part of the room. Bereft of all pity for the exhausted Beauties, Julie sized them up with a whip-like glance, which lashed them from head to heel: she commented on hair falling out of curl, on the delicacy or coarseness of wrist or ankle, the stoop of a shoulder-blade, the little constellations of freckles at the top of young arms, the dress from a foreign capital. This cannibal feast only ended when she saw that Lucie Albert was on the point of fainting or being sick.

The storm, lightened by the shower, had drifted by without a downpour and now it was sailing up and away, opening its lips of fire across a pale yellow sunset.

"Come on, my angel. I'll take you out to dinner," Julie said.

The girl looked at her with her enormous eyes—vast globes unaccustomed to the light of day—and said, "Oh no, Julie. I'm feeling sick . . . and it's too expensive."

"Come on. I'm rich. We'll dance afterwards to cool ourselves down!"

"And what about Coco Vatard?" suggested Lucie Albert. "You've no idea what the poor fellow said to me when we were going downstairs."

"No," said Julie. "No Coco to-day, thanks. That'll do."

She made the usual grimace with her nostrils. Her cheeks were hot under their silver down and her blue eyes sombre and aggressive. She rubbed the make-up even over her eyelids in a shop-window looking-glass.

She fed her little slave in the Place du Tertre. She filled her up with Asti-Spumante, but only drank iced water and coffee herself.

"But you're eating nothing, Julie. What's the matter? Julie, you haven't told me anything about this afternoon. Did you have words with that gentleman?"

"No, my love. He was very nice. But when I'm not hungry I don't eat, that's all."

She went on listening in a vague way to the childish chatter of the simple little creature. Gay and downcast by turns, Lucie would willingly have joined her solitude in all docility to Julie's, had she been given the chance. But this Julie refused to give. She had always scorned the help that one woman gives to another.

"The other night," Lucie was saying, "one of the clients paid his bill with a thousand-franc note, and Gaston brought it to me at the cash desk. It was about three in the morning. It was a new note, but it didn't seem quite smooth enough between the fingers. I didn't want to make a fuss, but . . ."

Julie breathed in the air of the Parisian night, a pleasure costing little, and reserved for people who refuse to stay indoors. A shooting star streaked briefly across the upper sky and soon lost itself in the vaporous zone hanging over Paris.

"Are you sure it's not later than ten, Julie? You know, I've got to be in the night club at ten forty-five."

They danced for a few minutes to the accordion, but Julie, still dreaming of violence and free fights, grew tired if leading all the time a partner who was too fragile and submissive.

"You look as though you're on the warpath to-night, Julie! Who have you got your knife into?"

"I'm wondering," Julie said. "Come on. I'll drop you at your night club by taxi."

Julie went home, although it was hardly eleven. A little family café next door supplied her with half a bottle of water, which she swallowed at a draught on the deserted terrace, under the reddened leaves of a chestnut tree. The late passers-by turned round to look at this fair-haired woman, as she sat smoking all by herself. Her legs were crossed, her face was lost in shadow and a silver reflection played over the nape of her neck and her silk stockings. She allowed herself to be gazed at without displeasure. Her evening, already half over, no longer held any terrors for her.

She undressed slowly, and created a breath of air between the studio and the kitchen before going straight to a little mother-of-pearl fitted box, without a lock, which was hidden in the hanging-cupboard. She undid a bundle of letters, picked out a sheet of paper bearing a sixty-centime stamp, and re-read it. *"I hereby testify that I have received, in the nature of a loan, from Madame Julius Becker . . ."* She folded it up at once, and put back everything in good order.

She scattered her remaining hundred and forty francs and the platinum chain over her bedside table. Then she put on her damp bath-robe and sat down to make out a list. 'Two tailor-made suits. Four blouses. Two v. pretty pullovers. A long overcoat. An afternoon dress. Stockings, gloves, shoes, hats (two only). Underclothes. A very smart mackintosh.' She took the chain solemnly into the kitchen to weigh it on the scales; but she could not find the weights. She lay listening to the wind sweeping across the sheet-zinc of the roof, and then turned the lamp on again and picked up the list. Opposite 'underclothes' she wrote 'For whose benefit?' and then crossed it out and went back to bed.

The days following were measured out to Julie in equal doses of disappointment and intoxication. She went to a Dressmaking House where she unearthed an elderly and rebellious saleswoman, who wore a bang of carrot-colored tow on her forehead, told horrifying tales about the days of vitriol-throwing, and smoked in the w.c. But she made the clumsy mistake of saying to Julie, "Ah, in our day,

Countess . . . ," and Julie squandered eight out of her ten thousand francs at another dressmaker's.

"But what are you doing?" Lucie Albert complained into the telephone. "Nobody seems to see you anymore."

"I'm working," Julie answered importantly. "Come round if you like and I'll teach you how to knit washable sports-gloves."

Her experimental bent and her skill with her hands had returned to her. She gilded a pair of mules, and tried painting a solution of *vernis-Martin* over an old biscuit box, which turned out like an enormous caramel. Finally, she knitted some gloves and a scarf out of very thick pink string, over which Lucie Albert was lost in admiration. The huge, nocturnal eyes of the little pianist-cashier blinked sleepily as she tried to follow the needles, for she could only manage to relax when sitting at a table in a bar or outside of a café.

"I've seen some lovely washable gloves in the Rue Fontaine," she said. "They've even got some sky-blue ones."

"Knitted by machinery," said Lucie.

"Yes. And what if they are? They're just as good."

Brand-new, dashing, self-centered, dressed up in grey and black, smartly gloved and wearing a pink scarf, Julie went out one morning at eleven o'clock. There was a yellow, end-of-August sun, and she stopped in front of the glass between two shop windows. 'A woman like that,' she thought, 'can still look a knock-out if she's properly dressed. That little felt hat with the wood-pigeon's feather is a pure marvel. All the outfit needs is a dark grey man. But that's an expensive accessory.'

She was surprised to discover that her new wardrobe filled her with melancholy and a thirst for further luxuries. She found herself standing absent-mindedly on the kerb and waiting, not for *a* motor-car, but *the* motor-car, *her* motor-car. Only half awake, she would reach out for the cool contact of another body asleep outside the discarded sheets. She fingered the old place of the wedding ring on her fourth finger. Then she remembered that, in her impetuosity and unreason, she had lost the sleeper with the cold knees, the motor-car, the tiresome but charming house, the ring and the trace of the ring. All that she had frittered away became almost tangible, and she opened her lovely nostrils to the memory of the tonic smell exhaled, when they grew warm to each other's contact, by the copper-red mare she used to ride and her Russia-leather saddle. 'A Russia-leather saddle! Heavens, how flash I must have been! A saddle that must have cost—God knows how much! The mare, too. After the mare, I had a little car. Then I had the old Encelade woman instead of my Carneilhan Rocquencourt cousins and my Espivant sister-in-law, and Coco Vatard instead of Puylamare. And anybody who came and told me I had lost on the deal would have caught it hot!' But so far there had been only Julie de Carneilhan to reproach her with the social status of Mme. Encelade (expert in massage and removing tattoo marks and threading pearl necklaces), with the opinionated youth of Coco Vatard and the transparent emptiness of Lucie Albert.

A little later, she thought she had fallen ill. But, inexperienced as she was in illnesses, she thought it might be something to do with the change of life. 'Already?' she thought, 'And for a sou I should have said I was going strong.' But when she questioned her bodily state, she was rewarded with neither instruction nor blame. She thought about Espivant every day, and about Marianne and young Toni, and in all sincerity said to herself, 'It's odd how little I think of those people!'

Coco Vatard was the beneficiary of this sudden access of superficial democracy. Recalled and amnestied, he duly admired the hats and the dresses, the bronze-colored stockings stretched tight on legs with small, well-placed muscles. In token of her new gentle disposition, Julie was 'kind' to him, at last, one silent afternoon in the half-darkness of the studio. But he had no chance of putting into words the overwhelming gratitude he felt for the long, fair and faintly luminous reef lying beside him. At the first word, the tip of a cigarette reddened in the shadows and Julie's muffled voice reached his ears.

"No. I hate talking about it afterwards."

Julie could not help noticing that, apart from his effusiveness, Coco was becoming gloomy in the extreme. One day she tried to make him laugh by telling him how, in order to fit herself out with new clothes, she had sold a wristwatch. But he failed to laugh.

"Oh! I was sure you must have done something silly. You never consult me about anything. That wrist-watch —which, by the way, I never saw you wearing—you may need it some day. You ought to have sold it only in the event of war. God knows what will happen to you when I'm gone."

"You think a lot about the war, Coco."

"I'm twenty-eight, Julie."

They were just finishing luncheon in the Bois. Julie powdered her nose and strengthened the red on a mouth which was the same pink color inside as her scarf and her cord gloves. The melancholy that she discerned in Coco's wide-open eyes did not disturb her, for she knew that love seldom finds expression in gaiety.

"I'll be recalled to the infantry. But I'll wangle to get into a motorised unit."

As he was talking only about himself and a hypothetical war, she interrupted him without hesitation.

"By the way, Coco. I've fallen out with Monsieur d'Espivant."

"Oh," Coco said. "I don't like that."

She laughed in his face and opened her jacket, showing her grey and pink-edged blouse drawn tight across her bosom.

"Well, I don't want to argue. But may one know why you're so keen, all of a sudden, that my relationship with Monsieur d'Espivant should be marked by cordiality?"

"That's easy. Your falling out, as you say, with that gentleman means that something pretty—well, pretty tough—must have occurred between you."

"We'll admit that. And then?"

"Well, something pretty tough could only be the result of something intimate, so I wonder . . . But you'll jump down my throat again."

"What do you think?"

Coco did not turn his eyes away, although Julie was searching them with a blue, unloving gaze.

"I wonder what you can both have been up to that was so intimate, in your past or your present, for the conversation to turn nasty. Quarrelling with a man so 'gravely ill,' as you call it . . . weren't you afraid that it might have done for him?"

She avoided answering him. Her one desire was to be elsewhere, far away from him. Sooner begin the last three years all over again! Three years that had destroyed her bit by bit, with every hour worsening the last hour's work and each month evoking a more facile surrender than the month before, leading to a life that she was too frivolous and too proud to consider vain, a life to which her physical health, like the optimism of strong children, alone gave any value. Haphazard months, needy periods of waiting. Does all this, then, happen in a woman's life because of certain definite infractions and disobediences, through individual omissions, the breach of a companionship with one man, the choice of another, and then the fact of being chosen by yet a third? The long sequence of household cares, of toil with the needle, of turned skirts—"My dear, I swear it's better than right-side out!"—of ingenuities which one pretends are so many little triumphs, are not, then, the result of pure hazard, but of a hostile, of an almost fatalistic power? She thought without gratitude of good old Becker's gratuitous alms-giving. She called to mind those little festivities of the flesh, swiftly conducted and swiftly forgotten, exasperated moments from which a broken masculine voice seemed to rise to Julie's ears. 'It's not their real voice,' thought Julie, 'but the voice of an instant.' Three, four years of improvised meals on a card-table—"Delicious, these radishes with mustard. Julie's really *full* of ideas!"—and restaurants where one went with one's lips properly made up and a dazzling complexion and a smile that pretended to be short-sighted, but revealed the authentic lady; champagne and caviar, or, perhaps, oysters, and *pâté de foie de porc*. Forty—forty-two—forty-five years old. "Who is that? Why it's the beautiful Madame de Carneilhan. Do you mean to say that name means nothing to you?"

The wind, blowing up the corners of the tablecloth, announced the fact that rain was gathering in the sky, and that the bottom of the shallow lower lake was only mud.

"Julie, you're not feeling ill, are you?"

She shook her head and smiled patiently. 'No,' she answered within herself. 'I'm just waiting for the moment when you are no longer there. Because you're something I've never come across, and something I shan't be able to put up with much longer: a really clear-sighted man. You read through me into another man, and you treat him as an enemy. One would really think that Herbert has no secrets for you. You hate him and understand him. When I think of Espivant you ask me if I'm feeling ill. What good advice you could give me from the height of your twenty-eight years! An honest little counsellor, one of those little plebeian marvels that chance sometimes placed at the elbows of queens. But the bitches of queens go to bed with the marvel and turn him into a trumpery duke, an embittered lover and a misunderstood statesman. With you as my adviser I'd never do "anything silly," as you so nicely put it.'

She emptied her glass of brandy at a gulp, though it was a very old brandy and worth serious attention, a smooth and civilised brandy.

"Alley-oop!" said Julie, putting her glass down.

"Bravo!" said Coco Vatard.

'If he only knew what he was applauding! Nothing silly any more—that's tantamount to saying I'll never be any use to anyone again—not even to myself. He'd keep me from ruining myself, or from being taken in. People can always ruin themselves again, even when they've got nothing. The clever ones pick them out a mile off. And he is full of scruples. Coco would never try to turn a receipt written as a joke into ready money, for instance. Chance has fortunately placed a good seventeen years between us; to mention only *that* particular distance.'

"The brandy makes your eyes shine, Julie. They're so blue—a frightening blue," Coco said in a low voice. "But you don't say a word to me. Won't you talk to me at least with your eyes?"

By half closing her eyelids, she softened the blue that he found so terrible.

'The clear-sighted little wretch!' she thought. 'It makes his company intolerable.'

"It's the Carneilhan blue," she said. "My father used to scare us with that blue when we were children. And then my brother and I discovered that we'd inherited it. Léon maintains that that particular blue tames horses."

"Really?" said Coco sarcastically. "And what color does he break in his pigs with?"

Julie did not flicker an eyelid, for Coco's fate was sealed.

'He's impossible,' her thoughts continued. 'He suspects everything with any likeness to me. I hope he'll soon detest me too.'

"You'd much prefer me to have no family, wouldn't you, Coco?"

"I don't wish anybody's death," Coco said.

She looked at him prudently, well aware of the profound distrust that a man feels after a recent act of possession.

"Take me home, my dear, will you? I'm in a bit of a hurry to-day."

Her companion had the unwisdom to look surprised, a fact that she attributed to his clandestine espionage. The tired summer all round their luncheon table was cruel to her skin, thirsting as it was for the touch of salt water and deprived of the wind which, in the country round Carneilhan, would be ruffling the aspens and scattering the chaff in the threshing-yard. The smell of the yawning melon on a neighbor's dessert plate suddenly ruined the smell of her coffee.

'He spies on me. He keeps a check on how I spend my hours and days. He knows I've got nothing to do, apart from all that soaping and darning he finds so reassuring, and knows that Espivant is forbidden fruit for me at the moment. Had I realised that myself?'

She became playful, as if she had some crime to conceal, throwing crumbs to the sparrows, exclaiming in front of a great barrier of red geraniums. On the way back to the car she picked up a tomtit's feather with a silver tip and stuck it into Coco's buttonhole.

"You should never give feathers away, or birds. It brings bad luck to friendships."

"Throw it away, then."

He laid his hand flat on the little feather as though to protect it.

"No," he said. "What's given is given."

But she put an arm round his shoulders, and, letting her fingers fall, sought and plucked out the tit's feather and abandoned it to the stormy wind. She turned her head away from his grateful glance. '*I* know, I know, you're humbly thankful. But you won't be humble for long. That was the very last thing I shall do for you,' she thought. She hummed a tune. She went on humming inside the car so that he shouldn't dare to speak.

"Drop me there, Coco, in front of the chemist's. I've got to pick something up."

She jumped out nimbly before the car had stopped. Taken unawares, Coco bumped against the pavement with the near-side front wheel.

"Your driving's become hopeless these days, my child."

"I know," Coco admitted.

He got out, and touched a scratch on the rim with his finger.

"I'll wait, Julie. Be quick."

"No, no!" she cried. "I'm almost at home."

But at that moment the downpour turned the pavement blue, and Julie ran and bought the first tube of tooth-paste she saw, went back to the car, and let herself be driven home. She seemed to hear, resounding through her whole body, the warning drone of a terrible intolerance. Already she was unable to bear Coco approaching her refuge and drawing up outside her door.

"Till this evening . . ." Coco began.

"This evening," Julie said, "I've got my brother coming."

Coco raised his eyebrows and opened his eyes wide.

"Your brother?"

"My brother. Don't ask which. I've only got one. We're dining together."

She thrust the lower part of her face forward, in imitation of Léon, sucking in her cheeks and pulling down over her eyes brows as yellow, under the brown pencil strokes, as the flowers of a willow, and clamped on her features a disfiguring and specifically Carneilhan mask, as if she were loosing dogs on a trespasser.

"All right," Coco said. "You needn't make faces at me like that. We'll telephone each other, then. Wait a moment, Julie! You'll spoil your lovely suit."

But she opened the door and ran across the pavement under the warm lash of the rain. She hid behind the second door in the hall, and only went up in the lift after she had seen the car drive off. Tears and rain-drops were running down her cheeks, relaxing the almost convulsive tension of her intolerance.

She allowed the last slanting arrows of the downpour to come into the studio. A pure blue, harbinger of clear skies, was rising in the west. She looked after her wet clothes before telephoning Léon de Carneilhan. As she waited beside the instrument, well-known sounds penetrated the wide and murmurous enclosure at the other end —a sharp whinny, and then the grave bell-note of a wooden bucket striking the flagstones. She recalled the stables opening on to the yard, the terrible little office on ground-floor level and the room on the first floor. This was the habitat of the bachelor Léon de Carneilhan; and that was all Julie knew about it. She suspected that her brother had a leaning toward adventures in deserted lanes and open-air village laundries; a tendency that sprang from a certain grossness of appetite and the pride of a man bereft of fortune. Their particular brand of fraternal relationship shied away from any exchange of confidences. "We're too much relations to be friends," Julie would say. But because she was the younger in age and strength, something deep-rooted in Julie compelled her to respect Léon de Carneilhan and his capacity for living alone.

With her first glance that evening, she noticed his drawn muzzle, his tanned and hollow cheeks, and said nothing. But she asked him about his mare Hirondelle. Carneilhan lowered his eyes.

"I've changed all my ideas," he said. "I don't think we'll be able to avoid war much longer, but I've decided to take Hirondelle to Carneilhan. After all, she's entitled to live out her life in peace. She's nineteen, and still a beauty."

Julie stopped beating the vinaigrette sauce.

"You're taking her? Taking her yourself?"

"Yes. Gayant will ride La Grosse and lead Tullia. They're all I've got left. I've sold out. I couldn't carry on."

"Well done!" Julie said at a venture.

She looked him furtively up and down for any sign of

prosperity. But he was not even wearing a new tie. Nothing he wore ever seemed quite able to rise above a certain level of threadbare cleanliness.

"But," Julie asked, "will Hirondelle be able to do the journey?"

He smiled gently, as though the mare were looking at him.

"She'll do it slowly, at her ease. I'm quitting the high road after Le Mans, it's too hard on her feet. She'll be wild with delight. What are you giving us to eat?"

"Beef the way—you know—they used to do it in Périgord. Then salad, cheese and fruit. Go down and get the rolls, would you? I clean forgot."

She followed him out with her eye. 'There's white pack thread showing in his moustache and his nose is getting bigger. That's how the end starts, even with Carneilhans.'

After a few short and regulation questions, they began their meal, without talking.

"Has selling out made things any easier?" Julie asked.

"It's given me breathing space," Léon answered. He went and put the beef back in the oven and returned the compliment with another question.

"And Espivant, still at death's door?"

"He's not so bad," Julie said. "Remind me to tell you about him after dinner."

Carneilhan, with Julie's permission, dined in his shirt-sleeves, drinking away serenely at a nondescript red wine that showed black in the lamplight.

"But," Julie said all of a sudden, "if you're taking the

whole lot to Carneilhan—does that mean you're going to stay there?"

"Not that I know."

The ambiguous answer was not enough for Julie. The deep mauvish night closing over Paris warned her of summer's end and made her dread the disappearance of this long-faced, fair-haired man out of the same mold as herself; sitting with grim eyes on his plate, eating with peasant's hands and the movements of a gentleman.

"These are real greengages," he said. "They're excellent."

"Tell me, Léon, when do you think you'll start?"

"Why do you want to know? A week to-day."

"As soon as that?"

He surveyed his sister through the smoke of a mediocre cigar that lit unevenly.

"It's not as soon as all that. The nights are getting longer. But it'll be cooler in the daytime."

"Yes. Do you remember when we went to Cabourg with my lovely chestnut mare?"

"Yes. And Espivant too, don't forget! He soon packed up."

"Yes. So your mind's made up?"

"Unless it comes down in buckets that day, of course."

"Yes. Have you any news from Carneilhan? What's the weather like down there?"

"Magnificent."

Julie was afraid of insisting. Nevertheless, there were twenty questions on the tip of her tongue about the downstairs room, the 'blue room,' three poultry-yard pheasants, the brood-mares and even old Father Carneilhan. She felt a strange weakness in her that sighed for somewhere cut in the rick's side, to lie down in the hay, for the afternoon torpor of that pale and shingly soil. She got up suddenly.

"Stay where you are. I'll go and make the coffee. Will you clear the table?"

When she came back with the brown coffee-pot, the cloth had been straightened on the card-table, the whisky and brandy, glasses and cigarettes and the cups laid out. Julie gave a whistle of approval. Before sitting down she took the stamped sheet of paper out of the box of love-letters and laid it down in front of her brother.

"What do you think of that?"

He read it slowly, and, before putting it down, verified the watermark by holding it up to the light.

"I understand your keeping it. It's your affair. But apart from that, I don't think it's specially interesting. Why did you show it to me?"

"But it was you who . . . who told me that you felt there might be a lot of money that Espivant . . ."

Carneilhan interrupted her.

"I meant if he died, and not what advantage might be got out of him during his lifetime. This paper dates from before that ridiculous marriage of yours. Who would dream of stirring up that ugly old story and spattering everyone with mud?"

"Oh, all right," said Julie disconcertedly. "Let's pretend I never mentioned it."

"Once and for all, nothing that puts you in touch with Espivant can do you any good."

"Why, pray?"

"Because you're so weak."

He kept his eyes fixed on his sister. She merely lowered hers, started shelling almonds and burnt her lips with the boiling coffee, while keeping well out of range of his blue irises and their pinhead black pupils.

"But who can have been putting that into your head?"

"Only me, really."

"Or one of your little pals who thought he might get something out of it."

Julie straightened up with a jerk and assumed a lofty tone of voice.

"Really, my dear boy, I may have all sorts of nonsense with 'my little pals,' but not to the extent of telling them my family affairs!"

"Espivant's not part of your family," Carneilhan observed.

"No. But don't let's split hairs. Let's drop the whole thing. My idea was no good. Yours wasn't any better, as Herbert's well again now. Do you know, by the way, that he never saw a penny of that famous dowry? He told me so himself."

"I can quite believe it," grunted Carneilhan. "He's such a fool."

"I agree that he's not a genius, but a fool? . . ."

"Yes. Don't you see that he's done nothing but idiotic things all his life—always in a bright and intelligent manner? That stroke of genius, his last marriage, let's take a look at that! If I married a rich woman, I'd have her cleaning my boots."

"It's always so nice to be at your feet."

"You can always get out of anything," Carneilhan went on. "Anyway, I'd never marry a rich woman." He thought for a moment, and then jerked up his lean head. "If he failed to get hold of 'his' dowry, how can you have thought of asking for all or part of the million back?"

Julie went purple, and feigned stupidity.

"Oh, as for me, you know there's not a single blunder I don't make! But you must give me credit for consulting you first."

"Delighted to do so."

She felt uneasy at his suspicions and tried to put him off the scent by dragging him away from Espivant. She managed to do so by telling him, with exaggerated abandon, the tale of Toni's attempted suicide, and Carneilhan emitted a hard laugh when he learnt that Espivant had flown off the handle.

"You know how he is," Julie elaborated, "when he hears that a man is after a woman he has known! He feels ever so slightly a cuckold."

When Léon swept the crumbs off the table with the edge of his hand—a gesture that seemed to say, 'None of this is of any use to anyone'—Julie breathed again and poured herself out a middling drink. Her stiffness fell away, she beamed in the lamplight and felt the warmth of the alcohol rise to her temples. She felt that her efforts had been crowned with success when she heard Carneilhan, in good spirits at last, say, "I don't know how you manage it, but you don't look a day over thirty to-night." She longed to become even more deserving of this praise and its undertow of silent, fraternal jealousy; so, like a bird trailing a supposedly broken wing, she had to direct attention away from the truth. She burst out with her ringing laugh, shed two tears, and told Carneilhan that she wanted to "ditch Coco Vatard," who was getting on her nerves.

Then she seemed to lose her head, and, with it, all discrimination between what she should and should not confide to a Carneilhan very much on the alert. She pulled to shreds poor harmless little Coco, brandished his scalp, plunged it into dye-steeped vats. "Can you see me, my dear, waking up beside a chap with a violet stomach and a green nose!" Carneilhan did not allow himself to be blinded all at once. While Julie, her lips shining with brandy and her straw-colored hair all uncurled by the rain, deliberately stripped her cast-off playmate down to the skin and beyond, Carneilhan risked, in a level tone of voice, a harmless question: "Didn't Herbert impress you as being rather a sham? And don't you find it slightly odd that Herbert seems to need you so much all of a sudden?" He tired of it in the end, and Julie no longer noticed the name that he kept dropping between her snippets of chatter in the hope of tripping her up. The conversation became a confused noise in her ears, and Julie was suddenly struck down by the need for sleep. She rolled herself up in the blanket of her divan-bed and stopped talking. Léon de Carneilhan pushed the leaves of the french window to, switched off all the lights except the one beside the bed and turned out the gas in the kitchen. When he left, Julie was asleep under the dark red cover, and the short locks of her hair shone with the same pallor as her skin. She did not so much as tremble at the slam of the hall door.

Next morning she determined to take action, and laid her plans. By 'plans' she always meant a series of decisions which seemed quite incoherent to other people, often earning censure from her friends and ridicule from her acquaintances, for she acted in defiance of what either would have advised. On this occasion, she took one precaution—which was to consult the candlewoman. With a new candle tucked into her breast next to the skin, she went and woke up Lucie Albert, to drag her off, pale from fatigue, with gaping eyes and a body in the throes of a kind of walking hypnosis. But that little creature of the night did not forget to take a candle from the piano for herself, one of two pink and faded spirals, which she slipped inside her blouse.

"What, Julie, another taxi?"

"Another taxi. And that's not all. Jump in, and go to sleep until we get to the Avenue Junot."

When the open taxi drove past a looking-glass, Julie passed stern judgment on the slender, rocking silhouette, the pallor and the drowsiness of her companion, which made her all the more satisfied with her own upright reflection, her old black-and-white tailor-made (which had just been cleaned yet again), and the pink-and-yellow color of the nosegay formed by her face and her short froth of curly hair. Her secret state of mind and body was patent in her determined expression, her nostrils particularly open to the wind, and her mouth at its largest, painted a challenging red.

At the candlewoman's, an unchanging temperature not unlike the chill of the inside of a church prevailed in the little parlor. Cane-bottomed chairs stood against the wall, and the only decoration was a kind of diploma framed in black.

"*I certify,*" Julie read out loud, "*that Madame Elena did everything in her power to prevent my late lamented daughter Géneviève from leaving on the yacht, having told her that she would be going to her death.* I say, this is a scream."

"Oh, Julie! There's nothing to laugh at! Think of that poor young woman being drowned! It's not funny at all!"

Julie gazed at her little friend.

"How on earth could you know, my poor darling, what's funny or not?"

Mme. Elena came in yawning, wagging her head over the arduous duties of her profession and complaining that she did not get enough sleep: apparently she did not qualify as sleep the sort of permanently torpid state that smeared her eyes with a vague blue haze. The rest of her, from the check apron to the loaf-like bun of hair, might have belonged to a self-respecting charwoman. She started on the lighted candle with a knife as though she were scraping a carrot, and mumbled darkly to excite her two consultants. She spelt out, in the pools of hardened wax, that Julie would become involved with a rather unreliable man, that she would go on a journey and, finally, that she would climb a spiral staircase. With Lucie she became even more sibylline, and pronounced, as she pressed the old twisted candle on a sham Rouen plate, vague sentences about a hidden child. But what did the untrustworthy man and the clandestine child matter to Julie and Lucie Albert?

All they wanted was to give themselves up to the enjoyment of a mystery that would never be elucidated. Lucie kept on saying, "Yes, yes," nodding her head as though she were memorising an order. Julie took refuge behind an expression of mute Carneilhan aloofness. She left Mme. Elena's as though she had just been to a masseuse, and settled down outside a café. Lucie Albert managed to wake up at last when faced with a coffee and cream.

"I feel as hungry as I used to be after High Mass at Carneilhan," cried Julie.

"I'm feeling ever so peckish, too!" cried Lucie Albert. "Julie, just think! A hidden baby! It's amazing!"

"But have you got one?"

"Oh no, Julie! But everybody I meet now will make me think of hidden babies; it's fascinating. And do you see yourself in what she told you?"

Julie smiled as she buttered her *croissant*.

"Not at all! So you see how much easier I feel about things! I mean about what I'm going to do."

"But what things?"

Julie buried her teeth in the *croissant*, and swept the Place Clichy with an optimistic glance. Now, in the August heat, it was as dusty and deserted as a cross-roads in the provinces.

"Anything, any nonsense. But, you know, *sensible* nonsense for once."

"Julie, you're not going to marry Coco?"

"What did you say?"

Lucie Albert retreated scared to the back of her chair.

"It wasn't *my* idea, Julie. Coco's the one who's always

saying, 'I'm very much afraid that woman is the woman of my life.' Don't curl your lip up like that; it looks awful. But do you believe what she foretells, Julie?"

"For five minutes. Then I hardly think about it."

She thought it wiser to lie no further. She was gauging the length of the next few days, swept clean of any observant intruder. Even Toni Hortiz, packed off by Marianne to the top of some wretched Alp, was recovering from his first suicide, and Mme. Elena had only read into her destiny those jumbled images of staircases and journeys. Far away from indiscreet surveillance, she was breathing in deeply a new atmosphere of freedom, through which, when the moment came, she could advance alone, and select her blunder, and cherish her last fling of folly. 'But why should it be the last?' her pride whispered. Whenever she was in the throes of activity or impatience, she tensed the muscles in her thighs as though she were on horse-back.

"You go and sleep," she told Lucie Albert. "When can you sleep till?"

"Four, five o'clock. Specially after having eaten. I only have to dress and make up."

Julie's over-sensitive nostrils suspected the little thing of not washing much; her hair had gone lack-lustre from long hours, night after night, in a fog of cigar and cigarette smoke. Her skin, she thought, looked as pale and damp as chicory.

"Poor kid," she said. "I'll drop you."

The enormous eyes, which betrayed only the signs of accumulated sleepless nights, grew larger still.

"Oh, Julie, Julie! You'll end up by sleeping on straw!"

"On straw? But you've no idea of the price of straw. It's terrible!" Julie laughed. "Goodbye. I might drop in for a glass of something this evening."

"O *do*! *Do* Julie! I'll play that pretty little tune out of *Les Biches* for you in the *entr'acte*! Do you promise?"

Between eleven and one in the morning, Julie made her way down to the night club. Alone, dressed in a new black tailor-made, she sat down in front of a gin-fizz at a table smaller than a tea-tray, attracting attention by her fine stature, the sulphur-colored carnation echoing the shade of her hair, and her blue eyes as unabashed as those of the blind. She exchanged smiles now and then with her little friend, who left the cash desk to sit at the piano and play, very prettily, a fragment from *Les Biches*. After midnight, she accompanied the songs of the star who owned the place.

The narrow room differed little from other narrow rooms devoted to songs and alcohol. A layer of smoke clung to the low ceiling, and the size of the room and of the stage left no scope for attempts at eccentric decoration. Lucie waited for a sign from Julie before coming over to sit sideways near her friend and accepting a gin-fizz.

"Oh, Julie, you are beautiful, you know!"

"Have to be," said Julie pensively.

She forced herself to keep up a semblance of conversation. But she was conscious of no reality beyond the thin, dry taste of the gin. All the rest was merely a background to her last actions of the afternoon: removing the stamped paper from the mother-of-pearl box, folding it in a new shape, adding the few words "Do what you like," signing it "Youlka," and sending the whole thing to Herbert d'Espivant. The brevity and the ease of it all left her slightly astonished. She was not regretting her decision; nor did she regret it later during a night of calm insomnia. She only doubted, on the brink of sleep, whether she had really done it, and this doubt woke her up again. She was surprised, in the fine weather of the following morning, to find herself singing, and the morning slipped quickly by. 'How easy waiting is, when one's really waiting for something or someone!' She touched the wood under the table-top three times with her middle finger. After that she had to answer Coco's telephone call. Serene and out of all danger, she dismissed him in affectionate tones.

"No, my dear child, I can't. I really can't. Oh, but it's not a mystery at all, don't be absurd. My brother . . . Yes, him again, as you say. My brother has sold his—what's it called?—his establishment, thanks. Apart from the ducks and the pigs, there's the furniture, which will go for at least a hundred and fifty louis, but poor old Léon hasn't any idea of how to set about it, so I have to. No, really not, not to-morrow. To-morrow I'll be at Ville d'Avray all day. Telephone me there? My dear, just imagine, it's been cut off for the last three months. He hadn't paid the bill. Ah, my brother's an odd card! Fortunately, I've only got one. What? Come here straight away? Oh no, my dear. No, no . . . I really wouldn't."

An urgent voice at the other end kept saying, "Why?

But why?" Julie pondered for a moment and answered in a friendly voice: "Because I'd chuck you downstairs. Yes; that's the gospel truth. Yes. True as I'm standing here."

She put the receiver gently back on its stand and smiled at the world of uncertainty that was opening in front of her. She put on the little felt hat with the wood-pigeon's feather and went down to the street to buy eggs and shell-fish and fruit. The day drifted by with such a soft and imperturbable flow, and Julie's waiting mood populated every moment so densely that the silence surrounding her was like a continual murmuring. 'My letter reached him by the morning post, about nine o'clock. He must have recognised my writing.' In imagination she moved across to the Rue Saint-Sabas and installed herself there. 'At nine o'clock, the mail was put on the little table outside his room as usual. He may be unfaithful, but in everything else he's a slave to habit. Bath. Hairdresser and manicure at the same time. Marianne? It's true, Marianne's there. Smothered in her purple hair, shaped into fringes and coils and shells, Marianne at that time would be. . . . Anyway, who cares? Marianne can do what she likes.' Julie waved Marianne away with her hand and came back to Espivant. 'At ten o'clock he must have looked at his nails before dressing and said, "It's an odd thing, but no manicurist has ever understood the first thing about nails." Then he opened my letter. Then he called Marianne . . . unless he screwed his eyes up and said, "Let's see. . . . Better wait a bit!" '

She lowered her head and clasped her hands between her knees because, saying "Better wait," she realised what a stern gymnastic exploit it can be just to wait. At eight she gave up and went and had buckwheat pancakes washed down with cider at a little Breton establishment, and finished her evening at the local cinema.

She was scrubbing herself in the bath next morning when the telephone rang.

"Run, Madame Sabrier, run for heaven's sake!"

She heard the charwoman answering "Yes, sir," "No, sir," and leapt out of the water. When she saw her naked and dripping, and flowering with crimped yellow seaweed, Mme. Sabrier let out a shocked squawk and fled.

"Hello," said Julie in a high slow voice. "Hello? Who's speaking? Ah! Monsieur Cousteix, of course. How is Monsieur d'Espivant? To-day between four and seven? No; I wasn't thinking of going out. Actually I had planned to stay at home. I won't be going out. Goodbye, Monsieur Cousteix."

Drops of water, while she talked, ran down off her hair in parallel lines, hung for a moment on the tip of her breasts, and fell to the floor. Julie trembled with imaginary cold. She caught sight of her hair and her lashes all stuck together. 'I'm going to look awful to-day.'

She dressed and put on white canvas shoes and walked up and down in the Bois for an hour and a half. Then she came home and cooked herself a well-chosen beef-steak on the ring. 'As thick,' she thought, 'as a dictionary.'

But she left the washing up, and painted her nails red. The hours of the afternoon were faithfully, tritely similar to the swift, exciting hours that precede the arrival of a man one is waiting for. She got ready a tray with two cups and wrapped a bunch of green mint up in a damp cloth to scent the tea made in the Moroccan way. 'Moroccan tea doesn't tire the heart.' Then she lay down in the ox-hide armchair. Now and then she turned towards her reflection and congratulated it with a vague smile on having its hair done neatly, on being dressed in a grey tailor-made and rejuvenated by the lowered shutters. Made for meeting a man and being desired by him, for loving him often and too much, she played with the thought of the man who would soon come in. 'I wish he'd come. I can't go on looking ahead like this. Afterwards . . . afterwards is a long way off.'

She gave no free rein, in her mind, to the thought of physical pleasure. The best part of her vigil was a deep passivity and entire ignorance, for never once in her life had she picked up the threads of a broken liaison, regained the taste for a savour she had forgotten. A faint red flush rose to her cheeks and neck at the thought that perhaps at this moment Espivant might be fearing or desiring the amorous conflict of their two bodies. 'No, no. Of course there is no question of it. To-day's the day when I do my best to get him out of the hole he's in. To-day he'll find out that I'm his real ally in spite of all we've said and done and hurled at each other's heads.'

The sum of money he coveted, the impudent misuse of a few written lines, no longer tormented her. A 'practical joke' either comes off or falls flat. If it's a flop, so much the worse. Nothing had accustomed Julie to thinking of Marianne as a moral creature capable of judging the acts of others. She remained a Marianne whom she had never seen at close quarters, Marianne the millionaire, a precious object calculated to discourage all rivals, a sort of Eastern conquest thrown open to competition once more by widowhood. A slightly sordid mystery did in point of fact surround Marianne. Julie was almost astonished that she knew how to read and write, spoke French, was not a deaf-mute! A woman loaded with so much beauty, with so heavy a fortune. Irritated, Julie gave way to a false little laugh. 'It's almost as if she were a cripple or a woman with six toes,' she thought.

The school clock chimed four and she leapt from her seat to open the shutter and gaze questioningly at the street and the weather, to make sure that the magnificent day and the light warmth had not changed; to chew a leaf of mint and powder her face. At the timid and uncertain ring of the bell, she laughed. 'What punctuality!'—and she gave a finishing touch, before answering the door, to a bunch of cornflowers, and shook loose a sheaf of red poppies that spread round them, along with their dark blue pollen, a smell of dust and opium.

Upright, with her feet together and her mouth slightly open to reveal her white front teeth, she opened the door, 'No, it's not him yet . . .'

"Madame? Yes; it's here."

Automatically her features maintained the half-smile over the white front teeth, the look of impertinent false myopia. 'But—but it's Marianne . . . Marianne,' she said to herself. 'No; it can't be Marianne? It mustn't be Marianne!'

"I am Madame d'Espivant," said the stranger.

Julie dropped her free arm, accepted the reality at last, and stepped backwards.

"Come in, Madame."

She slipped into her duties as a properly trained woman of the world, and Madame d'Espivant gave all the necessary answers. "Do sit down!" "Thank you." "This chair's rather low." "No. I'm perfectly all right, really. . . ." And then they both lapsed into silence. Carneilhan frivolity was already at grips with anxiety. 'It's Marianne. What a story! Lucie will be knocked sideways. And what about Léon? Here, right in front of my eyes, is the famous Marianne.'

"Madame, my presence here must seem . . . strange to you."

"But of course not, Madame."

'We're going to waste a lot of time,' thought Julie. 'She's got a charming tone of voice. Lovely pitch. And downstairs in his driver's seat, Beaupied must be wondering what's going on!'

"But I only came because my husband asked me to."

"Oh? It was he who . . ."

"Yes. He's ill to-day. Really ill," she repeated as though Julie were about to protest. "I waited till it was time for his injection before leaving his side."

"I do hope it's not serious," Julie said.

'A very pretty pitch her voice has, soft, with a something acid in the higher registers. But if we go on like this,' she thought, 'I'll have to ask her to dinner. Fancy going out at four o'clock in a black afternoon dress! And that hat, with its little floating veil! I must say, I don't find the lovely Marianne so staggering after all!'

Then Julie shook off her feminine reactions and began to isolate Marianne from her general renown and from her own private criticism. She searched avidly for "the statue of rose-colored wax" described by Espivant, did not at once discover it, and thought her complexion of untransparent carnation, a complexion with the grain and opacity of marble, had about it a touch of slightly Jewish pallor. 'Yes. In broad daylight it must be pink.'

"Unfortunately, it is rather serious. I believe my husband himself—so he told me—has informed you that the doctors diagnosed his illness as heart trouble."

"Yes, indeed, Madame, indeed. But the future of an organic ailment depends so much on general conditions, and Espivant is supposed—was supposed—to have plenty of natural resistance."

'And so on and so forth, and what lovely weather we are having,' Julie went on to herself. She was regaining her self-control. 'Oh! I hadn't seen the plaits! Oh, what hair!'

Mme. d'Espivant had just thrown back her veil, laying bare part of the red-brown mass of her hair, the brilliant swellings and bosses of a diadem of plaits that crossed and re-crossed and invaded her ears and tightly clasped her temples and her brow. 'It's amazing!' Julie said to herself. 'She's a woman, like certain statuettes, made up entirely of precious materials—jade, green-spangled quartz, ivory, amethyst. Can she really be alive? Yes; she is. And here she is in my flat. Here she is, and not trembling at all, and

193

less impressed at having me in front of her than I am to see her here. Let us get to the point, Madame d'Espivant, to the point!'

"I wish I could share your optimism, Madame," said Marianne, "but I feel I must tell you that your recent demand has greatly alarmed my husband."

She turned slightly in her chair and raised her very dark eyes to Julie. They were wide open, like ancient Greek eyes, and armed with lashes on either lid, and the whites were tinted with blue. 'Lovely, lovely eyes,' thought Julie in admiration. 'And how little she uses them! And she's simple. She must be simple to come and see me, even if he's sent her. What was she just saying? My recent demand? I should think it was recent, my letter only having been posted the day before yesterday.'

"Were you able to judge in such a short time whether my . . . demand had an adverse effect on Espivant?"

The dark eyes fixed themselves on Julie.

"My husband, Madame, even before his illness, suffered greatly from his nerves." 'Thanks for the inside information!' Julie said to herself. The passivity of Marianne, and her gravity, put her out of reach of all irony. ". . . and worry can cause definite ravages on a nervous patient in the space of a fortnight. . . ."

Julie flinched at the word "fortnight." 'Look out! Things are beginning to slip and slide, and I don't quite see. A fortnight? Oh, the dirty dog, what's he been telling her?'

She repeated pensively: "A fortnight?"

"Perhaps a little more," said Madame d'Espivant. "It was

a fortnight ago, I remember, when I came in and found my husband so terribly upset."

'She's got a rim round her mouth like some pretty Indian woman and a little hollow at the corner of her lips. She's a magnificent creature, without the faintest idea of what she ought to wear.'

"Upset, Madame? I don't see my share of blame in this . . . this upset?"

Julie opened her jacket as she was feeling hot, and also, especially, so that Marianne might see her slender throat and the long noble lines of her figure under the grey-and-pink shirt. 'There! She must have seen at once that I'm not a complete hunchback myself!' As she was longing to smoke, she offered her case to Marianne, who refused.

"I hope my smoking doesn't bother you. I was forgetting, Herbert smokes, of course. You said that you held me responsible for his getting worse. It's Monsieur d'Espivant's heart that is causing the trouble? His heart. Of course, his habit of hiding his feelings must have overtaxed his heart. . . ."

'I can wear myself out being ironical; she doesn't even appear to understand. Perhaps that's the most touching thing about her, that vague sadness, that widowed look, that warm-blooded womanish apathy. One thing seems obvious—she's sad, so Herbert must be really ill, as she says.'

"Madame, please believe me when I say that I came here without pleasure and that I speak with deep regret," Mme. d'Espivant said. "You cannot have forgotten that your demand—the legitimacy of which my husband does not question—was accompanied by certain terms."

'She looks a bit matronly when she bridles,' thought Julie. 'It's not a question of flesh, because she's still slim. It's lack of breeding. A miraculously beautiful woman, with something unspeakably common about her. She blushed when I called Espivant by his first name. But, my good lady, you must get used to the idea that there used to be "something," as they say, between Herbert and me. Second Madame d'Espivant, don't lose your head!'

". . . was accompanied by certain terms that could be interpreted in a disturbing way, that made one foresee a . . . a disagreeable publicity round my husband's name, his personality, his honor, even. Am I mistaken?"

'How! What? Publicity! His honor? I can't ask her to repeat it, she'd think I was either deaf or an idiot. If I were at all reasonable, I'd get up and lead her politely to the door, and the farce of the two Comtesses d'Espivant would be at an end.'

"You know, I should quite understand," Marianne insisted, "if necessity or some feeling drove you to use arguments, such as one employs only as a last resort. It's essential that I should not misrepresent what my husband told me, isn't it?"

Julie gazed in stupefaction at this beautiful woman in black who, even in accusing her, displayed such nervousness. 'He did that! He's done this to me. He's put the whole thing on me. Everything, he's put everything on my shoulders. He's made her believe that his idea of a kind of blackmail was really mine. Oh! It's not to be borne. I can't have Marianne thinking I'm capable of . . .' But she was already in the grips of a still more prevailing blindness. She shook her head and cleared her throat.

"Espivant told you the truth, Madame."

She turned away, crushed out her cigarette, saw her hand shaking as she heard her voice shake, and felt an extraordinary joy because of it. 'It's done now. I've said it! I've said what he wanted me to. I'm drowned, lost, done for, everything has happened as he wanted it to. But she must go now. I must tell her to go.'

"So don't think about it any more. Don't let's think about it, Madame," cried Marianne. "A woman cannot always be equal to circumstances," she added with a touch of plebeian *naïveté*. "You mustn't think about it any more."

Julie grew gloomy again as a result of all this encouragement. 'Don't think about it, indeed! Everybody under the sun seems to take it into their heads to give me advice —Coco Vatard, the beautiful Marianne! Don't think about it! As if I'd be able not to think that Herbert's put the whole dirty business on to me, has rolled me in filth. There's still time for me to say the word and put Marianne wise. She's not sure of him yet. She feels that Herbert's cunning white hand is somehow mixed up in all this, and I can change everything with a word if I want to. That, at least, he can't steal.'

A line, written in a jagged, stabbing handwriting, floated in front of her eyes, and she read it through again: "*Youlka, please come.*" She could not help herself, the saliva of sudden tears filled her mouth and she burst out into sobs.

"Madame . . . Madame . . ." Marianne's voice was

murmuring close beside her. Julie struggled in vain, mopping her eyes with the help of a little handkerchief. She heard her own hiccoughs, but was unable to master them. 'Nothing, absolutely nothing worse could have happened to me. In front of her! Crying in front of her! If only she'd go. No, there she is, rooted to the floor. She's watching the damage.' All in a muddle, she thought of her swollen eyes, of the tear-spots all over her blouse, and Espivant's treachery. 'Doing that to me! How sure of me he must be! Surer of me than of his own wife.'

She got herself in hand at last, blew her nose and felt no embarrassment in powdering her nose and smoothing out her eyelashes with a damp forefinger.

"I'm making an exhibition of myself," said Julie, "and a very unpleasant exhibition, too. I'm so sorry."

Mme. d'Espivant made a movement with her hand that simultaneously excused itself, put to rights a tulle collar that nothing had disturbed and felt at her throat for a non-existent string of pearls. 'She took it off to come and see me,' thought Julie, always prompt to change her mood.

"Madame," Marianne said. "I was deeply moved by your tears. Yes, yes, deeply moved. You seem so spontaneous, so . . . so impulsive. Seeing you, I can hardly believe my ears and what my husband was forced to tell me."

They were both standing up, with the folding table between them. Marianne's heavy scent assailed her. She recognised the scented air that had its source in the vestibule in the Rue Saint-Sabas, sailed up to the 'children's room' where Herbert lay in his pearl-grey pyjamas, and then dispersed under the icy fan of the ether. She wrinkled her brows which, dabbed now with her handkerchief, had become completely fair. 'I can clear myself in a few words,' she thought. 'It would be over in a moment. She's waiting for it. She practically invited me to. I'll speak, I'll speak!'

She spoke, without asking Marianne to sit down again. "Madame, the action I took needed no publicity; but I thought, for several reasons, that you couldn't be ignorant of it. I resigned myself to doing it under conditions that were . . . painful and offensive to me."

"Why offensive? The decision was entirely yours, if I understood properly."

'Careful,' thought Julie. 'This middle-class creature knows better than I do myself what I'm talking about, and wants to get me in a muddle. I'd give absolutely anything for a glass of really cold water. Ah, now she's really listening! She'd like to know what sort of man she's married to! Her little ears and her huge eyes are wide open for the truth. But she won't hear it from me. She'll only get a rotten, made-up story out of me, and she'll have to swallow it.'

"Monsieur d'Espivant's extreme frankness doesn't put me on a bed of roses, Madame. The demand that your husband thinks is legitimate . . . ."

Marianne interrupted her. "He only said that he did not contest its legitimacy."

"I'm delighted for his sake," Julie said. "As Espivant has told you everything, you also know how long this *démarche* was delayed. Putting it off was not always easy for me."

"Oh! I quite understand," said Marianne.

Julie leant towards Marianne, smaller than herself, and managed to smile.

"But there's nothing sure about it, or I do not make myself properly understood. Living from hand to mouth, and on very little, is a sort of game for certain kinds of character, a bet that one simply has to win once every twenty-four hours. It's very exciting. I'm a bit of a gambler. . . . And so it went on, until the day when I'd lost everything. And what I did then, you know."

As Marianne did not move, and seemed to be waiting for her to go on speaking, Julie said in a low voice: "I think you know as much about it now as I do."

The intonation obliged Mme. d'Espivant to pick up her bag and her gloves and pull her veil down again, while Julie hastened to guide her to the door. On the landing, they both took refuge once more in automatic good manners and the exchange of commonplaces.

"But really, please don't bother . . ."

"The landing's so tiny that one's in danger of falling when one comes out of my door. I'll get the lift."

"No, no, really. I'd rather walk."

'No, I couldn't have managed five minutes more of it! Oh! And "I hope you don't mind the smoke, Madame," and "I quite understand, Madame," and "the demands I made, Madame." Like schoolgirls playing at visiting.' Julie slaked her thirst with long gulps. Then, driven by some odd impulse, she went and sprawled in the only chair in the dark and claustrophobic little hall. Her mood grew calmer, and she felt grateful to Marianne for having left, for being so far away and already on the other bank of the Seine. 'That woman's superb—or beautiful, actually, rather than superb. She hasn't got that nasty side to her that spoils so many of the Mme. Thingummies one meets. In evening dress, or at home—I'll bet anything she wears tea-gowns!—smothered with her hair and her eyes and with silks and satins and harem-jewels, she must be tremendous . . . tremendous."

She leaned her head against the rough pink plaster. 'Oh dear, I'm no good at that sort of diplomacy. Marianne soon saw that. Nor at any other sort, for the matter of that. I just about got him out of the business by the skin of my teeth, my poor traitor. I'm not quite sure yet whether I did get him out of it.'

She suddenly leapt to her feet. 'And what about the money, the money he wanted? We're no better off if she doesn't give him the money he wants, if she hasn't given it him yet. Poor Herbert! It hurts him here if he stretches his arms out. Poor Herbert needs the wretched little sum, the chance to be a bachelor, his gamekeeper's pension.'

She went and washed her reddened eyes at the tap, telling herself to keep calm. 'He'll ring me up. Or I'll call up Cousteix. What was the good woman saying, all honeyed up with plaits and veils and crèpe-de-chine? That Herbert was *really* ill to-day? After all, perhaps it's true. I'd better wait. If only he'd tell me, or let me know. If it hasn't come off, I'll begin all over again. I'll fix it, whatever happens. Oh Herbert, my greatest love of all, happiest part of my life, and my greatest sorrow!'

She pressed a pad soaked in salt and water on her eyes. Under her eyelids, mixed up with luminous globules and zigzags, little mirages flickered past—a memory, a hope as simple as herself: the small, luxurious table, the fruit, the aromatic fumes of the coffee, a bright sunbeam falling on the burnished silver, and in front of her, pale from his heart attack, the man she was fanning with a napkin soaked in cold ether coming back to life in the hollow of her arm. A rough thirst for rescue work, and unquestioning feminine longing to prove her devotion, assailed her. She made her shoulders and her finger-joints crack to test her strength, promising Espivant all her help meanwhile in threatening tones. 'You'll have your beastly little million. I'll shove it at you on the table beside the cherries, slap in the middle of the bowl of figs, or in your great foot-bath of a coffee-cup. If that Marianne of yours doesn't cough up, I'll have a thing or two to tell her! And if we pull it off, I won't think twice about whatever share of the swag you toss me! I'll snap it up in mid-air like a dog! And, who cares, I'll go and tele-phone.'

She ran into the studio where, from the doorway, her eyes fell on an envelope that looked blindingly white and frighteningly thick. 'Marianne must have put that there! When did she do it? Oh, of course, when I went in front of her to open the door. Nobody could say Madame d'Espivant is the sort of woman to lose her head.'

She felt the packet, weighing it in her hand. 'How light it is! Much lighter, I should have said, than that odd mil-lion of ours. The address is in Herbert's handwriting.'

The top envelope enclosed another in which, wrapped

in several thicknesses of tissue paper, was a bundle of blue and pinkish notes that finally emerged, pinned together in trusses of ten, brand new, and smelling faintly of tallow. 'Is that all? Why, there are only a hundred thousand francs, and not a word. Not even an impertinent little "Thank you,"—not even the sort of joke a cheerful swindler might scribble, to make me laugh?' She looked questioningly at the door through which Marianne had just left, as though she could call her back. 'He split the bundle up into our two stakes with his own hands—those swollen and masterful hands . . . and that's all there is to it. It's the last straw of cruelty. It's . . ."

"It's ten per cent; what a middle-man or a house agent would get," she said out loud, on what she hoped was a cynical and bantering note. But the sound jarred on her.

She rolled up the notes and slipped an elastic band round them, and then, at a loss what to do with them, she went and put them into the mother-of-pearl box. She came back and leant idly over the balcony, vaguely marvelling at the fact that the approach of evening had already assembled the sparrows in the ivy of a dusty neighboring courtyard.

'Not even a line,' she sighed. 'Not a single word to break this silence. The last words I heard him say were "Go away." An hour before, less than an hour, he'd said "Didn't you like it there, Youlka?" '

She was inflicting bruises on herself purposely, trying out the two tones of voice, the harsh and the tender, and she proudly decided that the harsh, the insulting tone, was the one she preferred. It had at least a faint smack of the truth about it, of active jealousy, of flattering iniquity. 'I'd have liked just one word, a word that would have turned us into accomplices, soft on the ear, and comforting to look at on the white paper. He really might have taken the trouble.'

She leant there, motionless under the approach of the violet hour, until her arms grew numb. Then she pulled down the blind and switched on the top light. Making up her mind to go out, she opened her make-up box. 'Oh! No, I daren't show myself this evening.' She felt sorry for her poor face. She made do with another of her scratch meals, with soup and meat replaced by sardines and cheese. She sprinkled sugar on yesterday's fruit which was beginning to shrivel, but she felt defeated by the thought of making coffee. She kept turning, as she ate, towards the telephone, as though demanding an explanation for its silence.

She washed up with deft gestures, and carefully avoided plunging her hands into the dish-water. Everything she did seemed easy and even pleasant, but not entirely satisfying. 'Haven't I forgotten something?' she wondered. When the plates were in the rack and the bed turned down, she gave herself a clean answer to all this uncertainty: 'No; there's nothing I've forgotten. There's no hurry. There's nothing left I can do for him. Or for anybody else.'

As the hours passed, she thought out plan after plan— to telephone to Espivant to thank him, to insult him, but most of all, to summon him to her, to beseech him. 'But beseech him for what? What I really want from Herbert can't be put into words.'

She opened a book. But she had never, in her whole life, succeeded in giving the greatest of books precedence over the most insignificant of worries about love. 'Well,' she sighed, 'I suppose I'd better go to bed. The only thing is, I'm not tired.' She lay motionless in bed and listened to the hours striking. As the clock of the neighboring school tolled the succeeding hours she wondered, 'How could I have stood that clock chiming the hours and the halves and quarters all this time? I'll never be able to get used to it again. I'll have to move.' She fell asleep nevertheless, but woke up with a feeling that something or someone was living in the flat besides herself. At about four o'clock, she got out of bed, slipped into the bath-robe that never quite had time to get dry, and opened the step ladder so that she could climb to the top shelves of the hanging cupboard. There she began reaching and rummaging for things that seldom saw the light of day. After hanging on the back of a chair a beige gabardine coat and a pair of brown whipcord riding-breeches, Julie de Carneilhan sat down under the naked bulb of the kitchen lamp and fell to polishing her riding-boots.

The alarm-clock and the bell in the hall both rang at the same moment. A clear whinnying sound, shrill as a cavalry-trumpet, echoed from the street. Julie, booted, dressed in riding-breeches and a flannel shirt, was tying a white scarf round her neck.

"Is that you already, Léon?" she shouted through the door. "It may interest you to know I'm all ready to be off."

"No, Madame la Comtesse, it's Gayant. I've come for the bags and things."

She opened the door, and shook the dry and horny hand that was held out to her by a little man on the threshold.

"Do you think it is going to rain to-day? I'm taking a mackintosh, just in case."

"No rain, Madame la Comtesse. Mist and dew, and then we'll have the wind and the sun between the stroke of a quarter to seven and seven."

"Is that Hirondelle kicking up such a fuss down there?"

"That's it, Madame. She always knows when the least preparations are in the wind. There's been no holding her since yesterday. She's seen the nosebags and straps and everything."

"Give me my jacket, Gayant. Thanks. Gayant, do you think I'm still up to this sort of trip?"

"I think so," said Gayant. "Madame la Comtesse is a horse-woman. How much does your ladyship weigh?"

"Fifty-five kilos."

"That's all right. Last year your ladyship weighed fifty-six and a half. Fifty-five's all to the good."

The little man with the over-long arms sized Julie up, from her boots to her soft felt hat.

"Do you think so?"

"Yes. Better for Tullia."

"Oh, you only bother about the mares, of course. It doesn't matter if I do myself in! Here, take this and this, and this. Take care, that's our breakfast! Go downstairs and tell my brother to come up. His coffee's ready."

She buttoned up her jacket and saw to it that the fork of her riding breeches fitted properly, with that shocking and masculine gesture with which classical dancers adjust their tights. She felt at ease in these clothes. Her boots and gloves fitted her on the large side, and she was securely hatted against the wind. She slapped herself over the thighs and cursed. 'All this cash is making my pockets bulge. I'll hand half of it over to Léon.'

She gazed at her reflection in the looking-glass, festooned with crops and switches: a tall pale figure, with long, clean-cut legs. Her short and sleepless night, devoted by turns to agreeable preparations and sad thoughts, had just come to an end. She was all ready to go, but she still felt uncertain of her departure. Gayant's discreet "Whoa back there!" rose from the silent street, and the sound of Carneilhan lovingly scolding his mare. Julie could hear the horses moving across the road in the direction of departure. She sat down and wrote a few lines to the *concierge* and the charwoman, leaving a tip for each of them. The sight of the envelopes placed so prominently on the card-table reminded her of the faked-up parcel padded with white paper. She felt weak and agitated. 'I'm not going. No; I won't go! To begin with, I'm no longer up-and-coming enough for this sort of jaunt. And then, nothing decisive has been said yet. Herbert has often played a mouse longer than this, and perhaps to-day's the day he'll send for me, or even come here. I don't want to leave. I'm not going to leave!'

She leant over the balcony, and could just descry the sombre group formed by the two saddled mares, the little harnessed luggage-trap and the two men busy with the three horses. She breathed in the dampness that prevails before daybreak, the smell of ivy, and the impalpable watery powder that hung in the air. She was moved. 'How cool,' she thought, 'this spindrift of fresh water.' Her wounded and versatile spirits veered round to the impending journey and sang in double time the songs that are improvised to and maintained by the gait of a horse; drew rein by a stream under the high timbers of a forest. Quenching their thirst, the mares would tread their hoofs and play their muzzles in the running water. 'La Grosse and Tullia can be re-shod anywhere by the roadside, while Léon will have taken at least four pairs of dancing shoes for Hirondelle. I didn't ask Gayant whether he'd taken the curry-comb and the hoof-picker. But Gayant never forgets anything!'

Julie sat down on her unmade bed. It would never be open again for Coco Vatard. 'What did that sententious young man say? Ah, yes! That he feared I was the woman of his life. Well, it wasn't so wide of the mark, that shop-girl cliché of his. He didn't say I was his Great Love; he'd get it quite clear; he said I was the Woman of his Life. Coco Vatard will have plenty of mistresses and at least one wife. Each of them will open up a wound, an anxiety of which none of them will be the real cause. I'll recover from Herbert once again, I think. And perhaps another man, not Herbert, will hurt me once again. But it will always be from him, that damned "Man of my Life" that I shall draw all my consolation and my desolation.'

She thought she had been dreaming a long while, but, when her brother climbed the stairs, the brow of dawn had not yet risen above the neighboring school buildings, nor painted green the ivy leaves in the walled garden.

Instead of ringing, Léon de Carneilhan knocked three times, fairly hard, on the door: a sound which shook away Julie's dreams and set her once more a-jangle. 'I don't want to go! I won't go! I'll explain to Léon that I've got serious reasons for staying behind. After all, I'm a free agent!'

When Léon came in, she wrinkled her brows, and apostrophised him in the vigorous terms that had become a sort of ritual between them.

"What on earth were you up to down there, taking such a time, I'd like to know?"

"And who do you think's going to tighten the girths? And stow everything that rattles in the bottom of the trap? Including your bags and suitcases? And one of the bins of oats that was leaking through the bottom? Gayant never forgets anything, but he has no idea of how to stow things. If I didn't keep my eyes open, the trap would make as much row as a motor-car, once we got going."

Like Julie, Carneilhan had lowered his reddish eyebrows. He relaxed as he contemplated his sister.

"You know, that kit still suits you, though Lord knows I've never been keen on women riding astride."

Julie could have returned a similar compliment to her brother, who was dressed in some indestructible material.

Russet-colored like their owner, his riding clothes had faded over the shoulders, his coarse and thickly planted hair was going white on the crown, and his forehead, owing to the strange cut of his features, was more deeply tanned than his narrow temples. A meagre Adam's apple shifted up and down his throat as he swallowed his bowl of hot coffee.

"Shall we go down?"

Julie's blue eyes wavered.

"Listen, Léon, I'd rather . . . I'd rather not go. I'm not feeling well to-day . . ."

He interrupted her, moving a step towards her.

"Is that true or not true?"

She pulled herself together, and admitted courageously: "It's not true. I wanted to . . . to stay on a few days, to . . . to please somebody."

Carneilhan's glance slid across to the open bed and came back to Julie.

"Do you mean Espivant?"

She quivered, flinging herself against the suspicion.

"No, no! What on earth are you dreaming of?"

Then she laughed and cried tauntingly, "Really, my dear! You've no imagination. Or else too much."

She lowered her eyes in a comic imitation of bashfulness.

"Poor little Coco. He's very nice, you know."

She seemed to change her mind all of a sudden, and started rummaging in her pockets.

"Here, take this off my hands. Put it in your breast-pocket."

She tossed him half of the roll of new bank-notes.

"What's this?"

"Fifty thousand. Look after them for me while we're on the road. Good old Becker, believe it or not! He sent me that to celebrate his sixtieth birthday."

Carneilhan slowly arranged the notes, fumbling them incredulously.

"Good old Becker. Poor little Coco. It sounds as if you only knock around with saints and martyrs. Espivant will be an archangel soon."

Julie gave a little sigh of exasperation.

"Oh, you can keep that one. He's tougher than a seven-year-old hen. Are we going, Léon, or are we not? We're wasting so much time."

Swift and rose-colored light was already mounting in the sky. Julie's face materialised in the looking-glass, her pallor, the rings under her eyes, her faded air.

"Oh!" she said with a start.

"What's wrong now?"

She pointed to her washed-out reflection.

"I don't think I'm up to it, Léon. I'd be under my horse within a mile from here. I didn't sleep last night, I'm not in training, I . . ."

She turned away, dabbing at her eyelashes. Her brother caught hold of her elbow, and made her swing round towards him. "What a great goose you are! You know what an old armchair Tullia is. Your nice, awful old Tullia, dappled like a circus horse; the beautiful remains of my Hirondelle, La Grosse pulling the old trap with half the paint off, Gayant dressed like nothing on earth. Do you want not to come because you're ashamed of joining such a wretched band of gipsies?"

She put her arms on his shoulders, laughing and crying.

"No, no, no! Of course not, I'm not ashamed! Look at my breeches, they've got two moth-holes in them! Have you still got *the* trap?"

"You don't suppose I went and bought a new one for Gayant? Of course it's *the* trap. There's not an inch of paint left on it. It's peeling all over like a plane tree losing its bark. But it's still got a smart little umbrella-basket, and luckily the rubber on the wheels is still intact. When you're tired, you can get into the trap, and let Gayant ride Tullia."

Julie gazed at the russet-colored muzzle and the piercing blue eyes that were losing their stern and threatening look.

"So I *shall* get tired?" she said sadly. "You see, even you say, already, that I'll get tired!"

"I wouldn't swear to it," said Léon, shaking his head. "But I advise you to. *Be* tired. Come on; let's be off. We're not trying to impress anyone any more. I've got everything I possess on me. I see you're taking your whole fortune. Don't leave anything behind. The road to Carneilhan will be a one-way journey for me. Do you think you can say the same?"

He tightened his leather belt in order to avoid seeming to wait for a reply. But Julie said nothing.

"Off we go, Julie."

"Yes. Where shall we stop?"

"Wherever you like."

She smiled at such an unexpected statement.

"How long do you think it'll take us to get to Carneilhan?"

For the first time Julie saw her brother make a gesture of uncertainty. He raised his arms and let them drop.

"Three weeks . . . three months . . . all our lives."

He listened in the direction of the mares, who were growing restive. They heard the clink of the horse-shoes on the cobblestones below.

"Isn't it an astounding feeling, Julie, having some money and no home, instead of having a home and no money?"

These few words, the lofty voice, the large, quivering nose, the movement of the jaw muscles under the reddened and clean-shaven cheek were accepted by Julie as precious symbols of brotherly affection.

"I want to breathe, Julie. It gets me in the ribs, having no money for oats, no money for straw, for the harness-maker's bill and the blacksmith's."

Julie put her hand on her brother's arm to interrupt a litany that she knew by heart. The arm responded. She felt the muscles move, and rejoiced in so much strength. It seemed a token of hope and support.

"The sun's up," said Carneilhan. "We're going the long way round, Julie. The long way will tire the mares least, and also the horsewoman. We'll be far better off in the by-ways, with grass on either side. Gayant knows some tracks and pathways that are almost Red Indian, they're so remote."

Julie opened her nostrils and her whole body leaned forward in a movement of consent.

"You didn't warn old Père Carneilhan that I was coming too?"

"He'll know soon enough," Léon said, wryly. "If we'd told him, he might have taken to writing again just to stop you starting. Your presence will bother him a lot, at first. He'll have to clear all his stuff out of your blue room, his salt-stores and millet-cobs, his provisions of dried bread, everything that the damp and the rats can get at."

As he spoke, Julie's recollections passed through a porch, sniffed the cold hall and fumblingly hung a straw hat on a stag's antler. 'Shall I still like my home,' she wondered. 'Shall I still love my two Carneilhans enough, with their silence, their pride and their frugality?' She reached a blue room discolored by sunlight under a beamed ceiling. 'I'll re-paint it pink.' The white underside of the aspen leaves cast their light over her memory like the reflections of a river, and she leaned out of the window of the blue room. 'Unless I re-paint it pale yellow!' From her oval room at the top of the tower, Julie de Carneilhan, aged fifteen, with the frontiers of her stubborn forehead marked out by her blonde plaits, peered down at the rounded tops of two lime trees casting their shade upon the terrace, at the brood-mares resting their heads on the railings of the meadow, at Père Carneilhan in his flat cap with his little hazel switch thrust into his coat pocket. So the network of roads, the staircase 'turning like a corkscrew' promised by the candlewoman simply led, as though predestined, to the room she had lived in as a girl?

Careless of the sleep which still enfolded the house, they

went downstairs with an indiscreet clatter of boots and talk.

"Do you think I should take the spirit-stove?"

"I kept out the first-aid set; it's rolled up in a blanket."

When they appeared, the horses pawed the ground affectionately, and Julie greeted each of them with a lump of sugar to make amends and revive their friendship. The saddles and bridles and the stirrup-leathers stretched by long use were shining with age and endless polishing. In order to make much of her dappled mare, such an ugly and meritorious beast, Julie threw her useless quirt into the trap.

Julie, who had been deprived so long of outdoor life and travel, found herself slightly astray among the seasons and the regions; she expected, almost, to gather plums and lilies-of-the-valley on the way, wild strawberries and dog-roses. She longed for the towing-paths and the resilient turf of the heathland. But, above all, she summoned up remembrance of certain sandy pathways, soft under the horses' feet and hemmed in with prickly burdocks and bitter blackberries, with gorse bushes that plucked at manes and tails, and hollowed out pathways that used to force Julie and another horseman, both happy to ride side by side, close up against each other. 'Herbert! And my long hair that used to come down over my shoulders when he tilted back my head.' She pressed her forehead for an instant against Tullia's neck, hiding a last fleeting weakness. Then she turned resolutely towards her brother, at the very moment when the tall mare Hirondelle, immaculately gaitered in white, was coming to search out and caress the hand of Carneilhan with her wide, fanatic nostrils.

'Ah,' thought Julie, 'he, at least, is taking with him what he loves best in the world.'

Chance Acquaintances

Translated by PATRICK LEIGH FERMOR

Chance Acquaintances

I did not acquire my habitual mistrust of nonentities over a period of years. Instinctively, I have always held them in contempt for clinging like limpets to any chance acquaintance more robust than themselves. It is only since I first encountered human barnacles that molluscs equipped with contractile nerve-cords have filled me with horror. We are far too slow in realising that they, though innocent of all personal ill-will, are, in fact, envoys from the nether world, deputised to act as a liaison between ourselves and beings with no other means of approach.

In my music-hall days, Lucette d'Orgeville used to say that I was her best friend. As she was easily pleased, I let her say it, and our intimacy went no further than talk about the weather and an exchange of "How goes it?" between dressing-rooms. "Till we meet again!" she would say when we were about to lose sight of each other at the end of a fortnight's run at the Olympia, and we would happen upon each other again the following winter at the Wagram Empire. She belonged to the half-tart, half-actress category—never more than a few in number—

inevitably thrown up by the music-hall. The real troupers would have nothing to do with her. One girl I remember would never even speak to Lucette d'Orgeville. This was the sixteen-year-old "Jaw-bone" star of a Strong Woman Act, who lifted, between her short teeth, a kitchen table with her mother sitting on it. The Venus Sisters never so much as made way for her when she passed them in the wings.

But I, being on the stage only by accident, was less strict, and often used to drop into conversation with Mlle. Lucette d'Orgeville. She was a quick-change dancer, but totally lacked the self-mastery, abstinence, and breath-control that real dancers must possess. Her mood would vary with her luck, and now and again she would get irritated with the standoffishness of such colleagues as the musical comedian from Milan, the international conjuror, or the celebrated Schwartz family—serious German acrobats with the aloofness and courtesy of princes, and as united among themselves as a nomadic tribe.

It is quite unnecessary for the purposes of this story to dwell for long on the subject of Mlle. d'Orgeville; but I take pleasure in doing so, rather as I might in describing a prehistoric mammoth, or the undiscoverable pear of Prester John. Lucette looked a pleasant enough young woman. Her hair, once chestnut, was now golden blonde. She stooped slightly, but she was healthy and very prettily made. Everything about her was admirable: the curve from shoulders to breasts, which were like apples cut in half; her small, slightly rounded stomach; her ankles; not to mention her smooth and unprominent knees. And her

back view was equally attractive. You will readily under-
stand the kind of beauty she was when I say that she
could not break down on the stage, run away from a fire
stark naked, or lose her drawers in the street, without
these strange misadventures turning out to her glory as
well as to her advantage.

Her pantomime-and-dance sketch, her "number" as we
used to say, produced and directed in all good faith by
Georges Wague and Mlle. Beauvais, was very soon too
much for her. She "faked," blowing kisses to the public
instead of doing a slow pirouette, and covering up a missed
tap routine by a saucy wink and a castanet snap of her
fingers. From acting at the Olympia for Paul Franck, she
suddenly found herself playing third-rate provincial stands
in the off-season. Then, all of a sudden, one would see her
driving up to the Moulin Rouge in a carriage-and-pair.

"I'm leaving *for* Saint-Petersburg," she once confided to
me. Then, thinking of all the risks and fatigues that lay
ahead, she added, "What must be, must be." Four months
later she was back; dead beat, it seemed. A slight quiver
at one corner of her mouth, an expression of alarm and
incomprehension, told their own tale. Among her other
spoils she had brought back a dark sable coat,—immense
and priceless, and apparently also lined with sables—her
"reversible," she called it. She used to put it on every night
to go to *Palmyre* in the Place Blanche for her onion soup,
and to go shopping in at the market every morning. She
had also brought back a whole load of emeralds. Some of
them were cloudy, almost muddy—the color of a mountain
torrent when the snows melt. Others were clear, enormous

stones of a particular green shot with a sublime, indescribable blue flame, and all mounted higgledy-piggledy in great lumps of gold masonry.

I forgot all about Mlle. d'Orgeville, for the simple reason that our paths did not cross for quite a long time. Then I almost tripped over her one day in the Bois de Boulogne, where I was taking my bitch for a walk. We were heading for the lake, the fresh grass and the pine-cones. Mlle. d'Orgeville was sitting bareheaded on the grass, with her arms round the neck of a medium-sized, well-built young man. His hair was a reddish chestnut and he had superb teeth. He belonged, as it were, to the same "family group" as Lucette. He really might have passed for her brother. In the bright sunlight of the clearing, it was obviously a younger brother he resembled. Lucette was looking fine. She had that soft look that seems to fill a woman's eyes when there are no other women to compete with.

After the usual cries of surprise and greeting, she introduced her companion. "It's Luigi! You must remember Luigi!"

I could faintly remember an unpretentious, robust young assistant in one of the trapeze acts. It had been his job to look after the tackle, to screw the braces into the floor, secure the wires, and polish the nickel-plated bars with a flannel rag.

"Of course I do. How's everything going, Luigi?"

"Everything's going wonderfully," Lucette burst out. "We're off incog.—just the two of us—to the mountains above X-les-Bains, within the next ten days or so at the very most. A month and a half's holiday! A spruce little chalet, fresh air, espadrilles, hot milk . . ."

"And love," I added, finishing the sentence for her.

Lucette's only comment was to gaze at Luigi. Luigi, who had been unpacking a frugal picnic from a little imitation-leather basket, was gripping a bottle of red wine between his knees, in preparation to opening it. He made a noise like the pop of a champagne cork, and drank some of the wine straight from the bottle.

"What a little scallywag you are," Lucette said cajolingly, "a proper mechanic. A real garage fancy-man, isn't he?"

She leaned over confidingly and whispered in my ear,

"And what's more, he's a tip-top cook. Lamb's trotters with white sauce, steaks Bercy"—she went through the motions of licking her fingers—"and just as well these days, when one can't afford to be too extravagant."

I saw that it would have been the wrong moment to ask what had happened to the "reversible" and the emeralds, so I wished the lovers a good appetite. Judging by the supple way Luigi sprang up without touching the ground with his hands, by the perfect equilibrium of his poise, and the slim waist fairly set on narrow hips, I decided Lucette had not done too badly in her choice of a sweetheart.

The idyll, however, was destined to shed its petals from the very start. I met Mlle. d'Orgeville a fortnight later in the street. Taffeta was in fashion, and Lucette was a-rustle with dove-grey silk, from her little ruched cape to her flounced hem. When I asked her news, she answered rather vaguely but, as always, in a friendly way, "Nothing much.

I've just been to my dressmaker. It's crazy how tight over the behind the new winter dresses are going to be."

Light as mist in a breeze, the grey-pink bird-of-paradise feathers in her hat kept tickling her cheek and the corner of her mouth. She clutched hold of the precious plumage, tore it out with a gesture of indifference, and threw it away. Her eyes came to rest on mine at last, and, sighing, she said in a gentle voice, "Oh, the things that happen to me!"

Words failed her and she raised both her arms together as though they were handcuffed. Huge square-cut diamonds and lozenge-shaped brilliants, bracelets—regular paving-stones of jewelry—flashed their grudging facets in the sun.

"You can well imagine, as things stand at the moment, a chalet in the mountains is out of the question."

She said no more. I could tell from her silence that her regret was genuine. One does not console a young woman overpowered by half a hundredweight of diamonds.

"Wouldn't *you* like to take over the chalet?" she asked at length. "Just think, three hundred francs for six weeks! Or rent free, if you like. I mean it, really! I'm fed up with everything."

"I wasn't thinking, this year . . ."

"Oh, that's all right. Forget all about it! Better not to think of anything this year."

She gave a forced laugh. Her gold-flecked eyes and her upper lip, slightly elevated by the curve running up to her nostrils, gave her a look of Mme. Emilienne d'Alençon.

"I'd rather someone I knew took over the chalet. I'd

much rather. I'm sailing in ten days," she added to convince me.

She enlarged no further. But, from her reserve, I was given to understand that diamonds and aigrettes and foreign travel were pale attractions compared to a cottage in the Daupiné with Luigi—at the cost of not more than three hundred francs for six weeks. I believe I can only have given way in order to keep the conversation going.

When she came to see me two days later, to "talk business," she again voiced a mood of resignation. She told me that one can't always do what one likes, that the head can be stronger than the heart, but that the clouds sometimes have a silver lining. And there her confidences came to an end.

The suddenly acquired riches of Lucette—the many facets of that mass of jewelry—shed purple and orange and blue flashes on the tray and the port glasses. They spilt color on the card-table cloth nibbled by cigarette ends. I thought of the village church where, with a number of other little girls, I used to play as a child "doing a masque," moving to and fro in the bright patches of color cast by the stained-glass windows. With no respect whatever for the sacred precincts, we would shout, almost at the top of our voices, "I've got a blue nose!" "My forehead's yellow!" One of us, more brazen than the others, screamed, "I've got a red behind!" and the rest all told her that she would go to hell.

So I became sub-tenant of the chalet, at cost price. It was called *The Knick-Knack*. At the last moment I very nearly called off the deal because of that name.

After Lucette had left I cursed my lack of backbone.
I was honest enough not to confuse it with a spirit of
adventure. Who on earth first put it into my head that
I possess adventurous instincts? The very most of which
I was capable was a hasty "Yes," in the hopes of getting
a little peace: and, since I was once again in search of
peace and quiet, the "Yes" had slipped out. In part, too,
because of my cat, who was badly in need of fresh air
after a long year in a Paris flat. She was a striped cat that
I had picked up in the fields, where animals have a hard
time of it. She had been completely wild to start with,
scrabbling at the walls when I locked her up; but she grew
steadily in courage and confidence until she became—or
so she thought—the Queen of Cats. She used the elevator,
had meals in the *bistro*, rode in taxis and travelled by train
like an ordinary person, showing off a splendid, fastidious
and classically striped face and two green eyes filled with
a supernatural radiance. One day, when I was scolding
her, she took a flying leap at my face, hardly using her
claws,—on principle, just for the fun of the thing. Few
she-cats are ready to compromise on questions of preced-
ence. Toms are the ones that argue and then give way,
provided you pretend to take seriously all their palavers,
war-songs and tail-lashings, which turn out to be mere
intimidation parades.

The striped cat was called Peronnella at first, then Prrou.
You'll find the two names in my earlier novels; but these
names fell to shreds on her like second-rate clothing. She
became an unclassifiable, private-edition cat, and—as is
universally known—cats with strong personalities need no

names. She was called "Come here!" she was called "Where have you got to?" and she was called "Let's be off!" not to mention other fancy names, invented at moments of enthusiasm or tenderness, such as "Light of the Mountainside," "O striped to the utmost of stripeability," "Bird-cat," and so on. No one made much of a fuss of her, not even me. She was never called on by reporters, and she granted no interviews. We lived together. When I had to leave her behind with my mother during a long absence, the striped cat took it into her head to die: and she died. If I mention her in this tale now and again it is not because I want to give her any special prominence in it, but because she was part of my life.

A few days later every conceivably foreseeable disappointment lay in wait for me behind the little door leading into *The Knick-Knack*. As far as construction went—millstone granite and unseasoned wood—the chalet vied with any jerry-built bungalow in the suburbs of Paris. If it had not looked out on a skyline of mountains, I could have believed myself at Vernouillet. As it was only the beginning of July, a little chalky snow still sprinkled the distant peaks. The striped cat jumped out of the old-fashioned four-wheeler that had driven us up from the station, and shook her bells like a horse in full harness. Then, to cure herself of the effects of a night in the train, she at once began eating the tufted grass between the slats of the paling. A woman came out of the next-door chalet, which was a replica of *The Knick-Knack*, and said she was at my disposal for any housework I might need: with the stricture, that is, that she was pledged to the ladies of *The Mistletoe Bough* from nine to ten; that the lodgers of *Rudolph-and-Daisy*—she pointed to a third chalet identical with the others—had been employing her since the first of July from eight to nine; and that the young lady in the family way at *Gathering Peascods* felt too tired, between half-past two and half-past three in the afternoon, to do her own washing-up. She also informed me that, for meals, I had the choice of the *White Rabbit* or the *Inglenook*. Meanwhile, I was admiring Lucette's foresight in choosing a companion who was "a tip-top cook" into the bargain.

I entered *The Knick-Knack* in the wake of the woman-who-had-no-time-to-do-my-housework, and peered into the dining-room. It was embellished by a circular bronze chandelier studded with lumps of colored glass. "You could fix up an extra bed in here," the caretaker observed. I waved passing approval of the first-floor bedroom, with its bed in the middle and the dusty frills of its bedside lamp, and of the bathroom with its enamel basins and warped wood. I smiled at the kitchen with its two saucepans, its milk jar and cord for hanging up the washing. Nor did I forget to glance at the adjoining lavatory and look into the living-room with its wallpaper sprinkled with a highly decorative pattern of cockle-shells and its cushions of ribbed sateen. When I had seen the lot, I said "Perfect!" and, picking up the cat, went down to the cabby who was waiting to be paid and said: "To the Hôtel des Bains!"

The cat sat beside me on the antiquated seat cover the color of greenish lichen. She wore her most flippant and scornful expression, with moist nostrils high in the air as though she found our departure as normal as our arrival. As we drove down the hill, we gazed at the remainder of the housing development, and I counted ten or twelve more chalets, all whelped from the same litter. One of them was called *Beethoven*, another *Sweetie Pie*.

Little need be said about the Hôtel des Bains. It is merely one more in my long list of hotels. I have not travelled much, but I have had to put up at a great many of them in my time. It was striking twelve as we drove up and my arrival caused a flutter of curiosity among the Bath-addicts and drinkers seated round the tables outside the Hôtel des Bains. It was a stone's-throw from the Casino and its terrace, from which it was separated by a huge bed of begonias and a circular road-junction. The colonnade of the Thermal Establishment ran between these two pleasure domes and completed the setting.

"Look, a cat!" the children shouted, clustering round. "A cat!"

The cat, however, looked them up and down in a way that made them fall back, and the expressions on their faces changed as quickly as if they had run forward to greet a total stranger by mistake. It was still cool in the shade, and a light breath of mountain air, taking my Parisian lungs by surprise and filling them with delight, wafted both the scent of orange blossom, from the magnificent trees arranged in tubs round the terrace, as well as the reek of the sulphurous waters—a mixture of marsh gas and rotten eggs.

A quarter of an hour later, I had chosen the spot for my brief sojourn. The very Frenchness of the hotel and the date of its construction almost improved it. A new storey with a balcony had recently been added, but this was carpeted with a dirty old drugget, whereas the gloomy first floor had claimed as a matter of course the right to a brand new pile carpet, of purple edged with yellow. And, on the sovereign principle of "Never throw anything away, it might come in useful," a small, cracked, and quite useless sideboard, dating from the Presidency of Jules Grévy, had been hauled up to the landing of the newly built top floor.

I found this object, all too familiar as it became, equally repellent each time it was confronted by me. Who shall say whether we become more attached to things that disgust us or to those we find attractive? At that unsettled period of my life, I had simply to dust out the drawers and cupboards in some temporary lodging, sprinkle the sheets and mattress with half a pint of Vétiver water, shift the bed, ask for a writing-table and a tray of sand for the cat, and then put flowers in every available vase, to consider myself, till further notice, at home.

While I was soaping myself in the bath-tub, the cat began to wash herself meticulously, lying on the bed in the very middle of my travelling rug. She was no doubt aching for her midday meal; but she was a cat that never demanded food, supplication and complaint both being alien to her nature. She must have retained the memory, from some former life, that neither were able to melt the stony heart of man. By banishing hunger and fear from her mind, I had made her more silent than ever. She was always ready to oblige, but she was also in full possession of her free will. She insisted on freedom of choice in her sleeping quarters, and would wait patiently for whatever food I might choose to offer her. She had an appetite that would tackle anything. I will always remember the way she would drink, like a dog, in the middle of the street if anyone turned on a pavement hydrant, and as she drank she would tremble, no doubt mindful of the terrors of bygone days.

Now that I was saved from *The Knick-Knack* and the housing development, I reviewed my present plight, as I sat on the balcony provided with a table and a wicker chair for my own private use. Similar objects on my neighbor's balcony were a reminder that hotels are as mass-produced as vacation chalets, and I noticed a folded vicuna shawl on the chair next door. The table was strewn with illustrated papers. 'Oh well, for as long as I'm here . . . ,' I said to myself, and I went downstairs, firmly believing that a train would carry me back to Paris the next day, or the day after.

When I went up to my room again, everything appeared to be altered, for the cat was no longer in the middle of the bed, neither was she in the bathroom, nor on the balcony. And when I called, "Where on earth are you?" there was no reply. I hunted high and low. I looked inside the varnished mirror-wardrobe, stretched myself flat on the floor alongside the bed, leaned over the balustrade of the balcony—but there was no gathering of people down below to suggest that a little black-and-fawn-striped body had fallen all the way from the fourth floor. There is a suffocating difference between a room where a feline presence has a moment ago been reigning and the same room, empty.

"Now wherever are you?"

"She's here," came from the neighboring balcony, in a rather coarse and rasping voice.

"Here, and as happy as can be," said a deep, pleasant, and more masculine voice.

"Thank you," I gasped. "Would you please mind telling that wretched cat . . . Or, better still, blow on her nose, she can't bear that, it'll send her back in no time."

"Indeed I won't," said the voice. "She'd take against me at once. I wouldn't mind getting into the bad books of a tom—but a she-cat . . ."

I smiled in the direction of the voice with a stirring of sympathy. "Hand the creature over to me!"

"What if she scratches me?" from the mannish voice.

"Let me do it," from the less masculine.

I went closer and took the truant from the hands of a man still young, whose general aura of blue and grey pleased me at first sight. At his side, a woman of thirty-five greeted me in husky, virile tones, while the man, in a charming veiled tenor, counselled the cat to remain patient and gentle. Then he introduced himself as Gérard Haume.

"And his wife," his companion added briskly.

My hands encountered, under the cat's fur, bony fingers beneath a soft skin.

"It's very kind of you both. I'm idiotically fond of this animal."

"Oh, we know all about it!" cried M. and Mme. Haume, and Mme. Haume added, "We're not so behind the times as we look. And how's Toby Dog?"

"He's as well as he can be, Madame, since he is dead. If he were still alive, he'd be—let me see—sixteen, seventeen, or eighteen. Bulldogs don't live to a great age."

"You can let yourself go with us," the woman warmly assured me in her thick voice. "We don't keep any animals in Paris, but at Aussorgues we have three cocker spaniels and twenty-six parakeets, and we've given up counting the fan-tailed pigeons."

Gérard Haume smiled tolerantly while she was speaking. I saw him take a furtive peep at his wrist-watch.

"Thank you once again, Madame. I musn't keep you from luncheon any longer. Besides, I'm only here for a moment. I'm hoping to leave again for Paris this evening. Give my regards to the three parakeets and the twenty-six cockers!"

Mme. Haume laughed loudly—a laugh impaired by some sort of chronic hoarseness. Her husband only smiled. I shook their hands—each so different—over the grid through which the cat had strayed.

But that was not the last of the Haume couple. Our tables on the terrace of the Casino were almost touching. How could I refuse to turn my chair round and put my coffee-cup on theirs? Ought I to have shaken off the weariness due to a night in the train, and have run to make sure of a sleeper on the eight-thirty? Paris in July holds no terrors for one who realises its dangers and its possibilities. But who or what was there to make me hurry back? Nothing. . . . Nobody.

When my thoughts return to that distant hour—the sun advancing across the terrace and, by the end of the meal, since the awning protected our table and our faces, reaching no further than my feet, where it lay like a warm dog—when I recall it, I can think of no motive for my staying except that I longed to sleep between smooth sheets and let the sun-blind and its wavering shadow cast dreams of boats and mills and waterfalls over my resting body.

"You really ought to stay on for a few days," Mme. Haume said. "There's a good orchestra at the Casino."

"There are plenty of excursions one can make without tiring oneself out," said M. Haume. "Look, you can see it from where you're sitting, that little white cube between the Mont d'Enfer and the Saut-du-Berger."

I could see nothing. I was under the influence of every sort of drowsiness—the drowsiness of afternoon concerts, of lectures, of childhood hours during dictation, of cate-chism classes, of waiting for a train at three in the morning when on tour, of every conceivable state of over-powering exhaustion. Already their words were filtering through to my mind in fits and starts. "This craze for bobbed hair really looks like catching on," Mme. Haume was saying.

Under the strength of the sun at its zenith, the high lights on the mountains were beginning to fade, unless the draining of color was due to my sleepiness. A gilded white cloud, the shape and almost the size of *The Knick-Knack*, distintegrated into powder with the crash of a saucer breaking, and I woke up, without realising that I had fallen asleep in front of two people I hardly knew, to find that piece of china in smithereens at my feet.

"You're half-dead with sleep, I can see that," said Mme. Haume.

Deftly raising a blue linen cuff off his wrist, M. Haume remarked that it was two-thirty.

"My gargle!" cried Mme. Haume, jumping to her feet. "I insist on your dining with us this evening, Madame Colette! Seven-thirty, and don't forget to bring down a woolly—after all, we're six hundred metres above sea-level!"

She readjusted her stays, pulling them down and smoothing out her waistline with both hands—a gesture women rediscovered in 1939. Mme. Haume was wearing a cool dress of a thousand and one blue stripes with a grosgrain riband round her waist. The hem of her skirt just touched the ground. It was what used to be called a short dress. She wore her hair in much the same way as most women at that time if they had not yet had it bobbed; that is, waved and brushed straight up off the neck, leaving the nape bare, and fastened high on the head so that it fell in a natural wave over the forehead. A very becoming coiffure: one that allowed for personal variations, and set off the head to advantage. The brim of her tilted hat rested at the back on a cluster of dark blue forget-me-nots, hiding the comb.

A woman eager to conform to prevailing fashion must always resemble any number of other women. With her bright coloring—probably she was too tightly laced—her wide open eyes, and her strong narrow mouth, Mme. Haume reminded me of Boldini's portrait of Mme. Salvator in the Luxembourg. Helleu, though slimming them down in the process, also drew a number of Mme. Haumes. A thin gold-mesh bag and a platinum chain set with small diamonds as a necklace—I was almost forgetting the pointed light brown shoes—completed, on this particular specimen, the 'turn-out' then considered correct for a spa. It is a species one would be mistaken in thinking could ever become extinct. There will always be women who suffer, on principle, from the heat in summer, from the cold in winter, and from facial congestion after meals. Just as, somewhere in the world, there is always an opera house where *Carmen* is being performed, and always a woman to say, "*I* never lie down after meals. My shoes? Oh no, they never pinch me—I've got the kind of feet that melt. . . ."

I roused myself from sleep only to drop a small brick. Misled by the fact that Monsieur was spare rather than thin and by the belief that his greyish-brown complexion hinted at some bilious disorder, I had assumed that he was the less robust of the two. So it was to him I addressed the remark, "I suppose your treatment is fixed at strictly regular hours?"

Madame Haume began to laugh. "But he's not undergoing any treatment! Not he! Why, the man's a rock! I'm the one who's doing a cure—for gravel and various other miseries. Nasal douches, steam-rooms, flushing the kidneys, gargles—all that's my concern. If you peep from your door at seven in the morning, you'll catch sight of me dressed as a Dominican friar, along with all the rest . . . all the rest, I mean, except Gérard, of course! I weep tears of exhaustion when I get back. . . . Don't you think there's something odious about a man who's never ill?"

I made the ascent of the "rock" with my eyes, and answered, in all sincerity, "No. Indeed I don't."

Fear of strangers. Contrariwise, the fear of displeasing strangers whose reaction has been amiable, whether or not with a hidden purpose. I tiptoe past a closed door, to avoid being obliged to say good morning if the door should be opened. Contrariwise: the need to send Mme. Haume a big bunch of the yellow irises that grow beside the mountain streams. The desire to place the illustrated weeklies alongside Mme. Haume's white suède shoes outside her door. Withdrawals . . . Advances. . . .

So I must have felt the need to write of my bad luck over *The Knick-Knack*, of my meeting with the Haumes, and of what ensued. The rediscovery of this sheet of paper is proof of it. It dates from the time when I had not yet exchanged my habit of passivity for a certain definite unsociableness.

Four days after my arrival, I was still at the Hôtel des Bains. My liveliest gesture of activity and independence consisted of a regular morning walk down to the Park with my cat, between seven and seven-thirty. The geraniums and winter cherries, watered overnight, still glistened with an iridescent dew that the first rays of the sun effaced. Not that I have any special admiration for the winter cherry, but its name fills me with astonishment, and the flower as well—the color of ox-lung fibrillated with blood. As for the damp red geraniums, they breathed from every pore the scent that turns one's thoughts to love and makes one regret that one is not in love. There were also some blue cinerarias, to set off the red geraniums.

I strolled about. I offered the cat freshly drawn milk, which could be bought at a little sky-blue dairy-stall in the Park. She would then go straight to the cropped lawn and lick the milk plebeianly from her whiskers; ferociously, too, as if it were the blood of an enemy. I often told her she had the manners of a hardened campaigner. Then she had to roll in the dew, giving voice, as she did so, to a great tuneless, incongruous chant—some fragment of a recitative dragged from the depths of her former poverty and freedom. After that she became immersed in the business of feline cleanliness. When these rites were accomplished, she would sit and wait beside me while I read the paper, with spasmodic interludes of play and an occasional choke of disgust when she encountered a worm; then she would shoot up a tree with an impetus so swift and paradoxical that it reminded me of the films one used to watch being run through again in reverse, when a factory chimney one had just seen topple and crash suddenly reassembled itself even quicker than it had collapsed.

This place was never referred to otherwise than as "the Park," and there was no apparent limit to its southern extent. Flat and well-tended, it seemed to stretch away as far as the sudden escarpment where the Dauphiné mountains rose sheer in the distance—just as the apparently boundless ocean seems to end abruptly at the barrier of the sky. I have never acquired either the craze or the habit for mountainous scenery. This over-kempt garden, with its neatly hewn boundary-stones here and its blue buttresses there, could never, never be what I call "the country." But the air, the light, and the balmy breezes—one very soon ceased to notice the sulphurous reek of the springs, except when the barometric pressure was low—the evenings heavy with the smell of orange trees like those at Blidah, and the crystalline early mornings, all these brought their healing touch to my long-neglected weariness, to cares and troubles cast aside before they had been remedied. After five days, I looked at myself in the morning and found my cheeks rounder and myself possessed of a more provident aptitude for dealing with improvidence. In a word, I confronted the uncertainties of the seasons ahead without the requisite courage to encounter them. Idleness cures all ills.

The cat and I would turn homewards at last. Near the Thermal Establishment several spectres were to be seen, scurrying along, garbed in thick wool of every shade of white, except the golden-white—rubbed here with rose-colored clay or there with brown, dirty and luminous—that glows like ripe fruit under the sun at Marrakesh and Fez. One of these figures, seated on a sort of stretcher, waved to me, and I saw that it was Mme. Haume. The cat took an instant dislike to these spectres: she fell into step beside me at first glimpse of them. After a few days in this land of Cockaigne her fur had turned glossy and radiant with that immaculate beauty—the prerogative of striped cats, whose secret lies hidden, except for the initiated, somewhere under the alternating black and tawny stripes of their well-fitting coats. She levelled her magnificent green eyes—so sure of themselves, so ultra-green and vari-able—on everything around her. It was the masculine look of a she-cat who has decided to make frequent evasions of her gender and to live a life of comparative sterility.

Within ten days of turning down *The Knick-Knack*, I was abreast of all the details concerning X-les-Bains and the Haumes that interested me least. I knew, for instance, that the Haumes, with a brother of Gérard's, were the owners of a family enterprise: one of those turbulent paper-mills where a mountain torrent keeps the wheels turning, somewhere in the Cantal or Corrèze district. Year after year the Haumes and their factory had seen their prosperity decline. A factory in the country, a car and small flat in Paris—these were the credentials proffered to my indifferent ears. Mme. Haume called me "Colette," with a trace of bravado in her voice, a challenging note which specified: "I'm broad-minded. The company of a music-hall actress, and a writer into the bargain, holds no terrors for me."

"Call me Toni," she said. "It's gayer than Antoinette."

The Haume species in general—haunters of fashionable watering-places—has both its uses and its justification. My swift adoption by this couple and their company protected me from other Bath-goers who had pretensions to being "artists at heart," and who were, in fact, highly dangerous organisers of theatrical matinées and *thés dansants*. Their semi-provincial, bourgeois background fitted somehow into my former background of the village middle-class variety. Antoinette had opened proceedings by angling for "spicy" tales of my music-hall life; but, when she found I disliked talking about anything that encroached on my private life, she gave it up, from natural kindness rather than from simple politeness.

It amazed me to see her, on more than one occasion, in the throes of real suffering. Hers was a malady that demanded treatment of throat, nose and ears, a malady that would silence her ravaged voice. She never complained. I like courage in women. I like to watch the ingenuity it gives rise to in organising a life of suffering. I admired Antoinette's patience and the way she would sit without speaking, wrapped up against the wind in a little shawl of patterned satin, edged with mink, which I thought atrocious, while she cut the pages of a novel. Her wisdom appealed to me in much the same way as her powerful wrists, her strong and by no means ugly mouth, her firm, thick neck—a smooth column instinct with exceptional power. And, however colorless and lacking in personality her conversation, it was, to say the least, not entirely without profit.

As for M. Haume! To be frank, I think I first took a

liking to him because I have always been fond of blue. Let me explain. Gérard Haume underlined the rare shade of his eyes with the color-scheme of his clothes. Against the background of light-colored suits of that rather mealy texture so popular among Englishmen of a certain age, his blue-grey jerseys, his shirts and handkerchiefs, his socks and ties were dazzling, by virtue of the very moderation of their grey and blue shades. Except for this fixation, he might have passed for a "smartly dressed man." But any affectation in a man's clothes threatens the impressiveness of the whole. And, when I saw M. Haume take from his pocket, as the ultimate flower of refinement, a cigarette-case of blue-grey sealskin, I pulled a face I made no attempt to hide. He noticed it.

"Is all this," I asked him, indicating the carefully matched cigarette-case, tie and handkerchief, "because of some vow?"

"Oh no," he answered guilelessly; "it's very fashionable."

He realised he had spoken like a very young man, blushed, and shot me a swift and covert glance. I remember that it was from this look that I first understood that he did not find me attractive. When a man is made fun of by a charming woman—and that I certainly was, in those days—he has at his disposal a dozen ways of keeping his end up; gaily, wittily, or by a sort of amorous masterfulness. I could read no actual hostility into Gérard Haume's look; but then again, no desire to please. There can hardly exist a woman who would not be faintly offended at such swift and silent proof of her own harmlessness.

A lean nose with the skin stretched almost transparently

over the bridge; a moustache curling upwards in two little wings above a rather reticent mouth, which nonetheless had no fear of scrutiny; slate-blue eyes, deeply set in bistred sockets, not unlike Gabriel Fauré's; a left-side parting and hair still dark but flecked with white—thirty or forty years ago this male type was the acknowledged slayer of young women, and of young girls even more so, who in their gullibility believed all such men to be weary and ardent sensualists. Without comparing M. Haume to the Comte de La Palferine, whose eyelids, according to Balzac, held promise of "horrible fatigues and infernal pleasures," I thought I discerned in M. Haume that fixity of expression which is sometimes to be seen in the eyes of men who have been hard-living in their youth. At other times, I concluded that he was merely somebody with very few thoughts in his head.

Women are quick to attribute such signs of indifference to the cause of mental deficiency.

That afternoon a storm was threatening. A purplish rain-cloud as solid as a pile of apples overhung the nearest mountain buttresses.

"How blue it is! Look, the sky's on your side," I said to Gérard Haume, pointing to the blue of the oncoming storm.

"None too soon, either," he answered in a level voice.

He looked at his watch. It was a frequent, rather furtive mannerism, of which he seemed unaware. The smell of the orange-trees pressed down by the weight of the thundery air submerged us, and the flies skirmished over our bare hands. A mob of children burst out from the room in the Casino allotted to them for their recreation.

"That means the dancing-class is over," cried Mme. Haume. "What's the time?"

"I've no idea," said M. Haume.

"But," I observed, "you just looked at your watch!"

"Did I? Why yes, I'm so sorry."

He lifted his left cuff once again with his right forefinger. "Twenty-past three."

Antoinette Haume gave her customary strangled cry and jumped to her feet.

"My nasal douche! Will you wait for me here, Colette? Gérard, what are you going to do?"

"I want to catch the post . . ." Gérard began.

Without waiting to listen, his wife hurried off towards the Thermal Establishment, with quick little steps and a tapping of high heels. As I watched her back bobbing up and down, the huge tray of her mauve straw hat, the wasp waist, the voluminous folds of the shantung skirt gathered up and held in her hand, I wondered what I was doing there and why on earth I was on Christian name terms with this good creature.

But, in turning my chair round a little to face M. Haume, I ceased to wonder why I was sitting there, under the shadow of a storm that labored across the sky, beside a man who had not shown the slightest sign, by prolonging sighs or a brightening of expression, that he derived any pleasure from finding himself alone in my company. There we were, alone in the middle of a thermal agglomeration devised for those of moderate income. Alone, surrounded by exasperating flies and noisy, idle children; alone, spied upon by girls of thirteen to fifteen just out of their dancing-class and still innocent of the fear of men and of physical bashfulness.

Gérard Haume mopped his damp forehead with a handkerchief, as if his wife's departure had suddenly given him permission to breathe.

"Are you sensitive to thunderstorms?" I asked.

"I am rather. And all these flies!"

"Why don't you go indoors? Here comes the rain. Watch its effect on the swarm of 'innocents!' "

This was our nickname for this bevy of formidable young girls. It is my belief that the wave of shameless abandon, which, a few years later, was to strip puberty naked, by the same token deprived of its bitter tang the taste for this "green fruit." And about time too. At X-les-Bains, the older girls had little to do with boys of their own age; but any youngish married man with a family, any elegant middle-aged bachelor or fifty-year-old musical comedy star who happened to be there to cosset his voice, each and all were liable to be pestered, to the point of victimisation, by young girls running in and out among the tables and pretending to be children.

"Hide me, Monsieur, hide me! Hide me or they'll catch me!"

At that moment a tall, knobbly girl with bare knees came bouncing up to our table. She squatted behind M. Haume, flung her golden arms round his waist and thrust between us a mop of frizzy black hair and a frenzied little face that did not appear to see us. Thirteen, or perhaps fourteen. She panted there for a moment or two, then shouted "Coo-ee!" but received no answer. Gérard Haume had not stirred. The girl grew tired of waiting, and said "Oh! I'm so sorry, Monsieur!" in tones of false ingenuousness. Then she made off to rejoin a whispering, giggling group of girls, all of them equipped with dangerous charms —hair like streamers waving, precociously developed breasts, freckles, ruddy complexions and stilt-like legs: nymphs, in short, with an appearance not unlike the ideal pursued by the present-day women of twenty-five.

"A well-directed assault," I remarked to M. Haume.

He shook his head. "Oh, I'm a tough nut to crack. Even the blonde girl over there, the lovely . . ."

"The one we call Miss Morphy?"

"Yes. She even tried the dancing-lesson trick on me. 'Monsieur, do teach me the Boston, Monsieur!' But I'm not Louis XV!"

He smiled serenely and glanced at his watch.

"Is she late?"

"Who?"

"Madame Haume."

He raised his brows in astonishment. "I wasn't thinking of her."

"You looked at the time."

"Automatically." He repeated the word, blinking as if secretly pleased with himself. "Auto-mati-cally."

A great star-shaped raindrop landed on the table like a grasshopper. Others followed within a few moments and M. Haume made no secret of his dread of the rain. Not without a touch of malice, I took my time in crossing what, in X-les-Bains, they call "The Esplanade."

My wide-open windows let in the scent of the orange blossom and the rain-whipped dust; also the cavernous but far-distant rumble of thunder. My well-behaved and independent cat, who was watching the deluge with perfunctory interest, turned to smile at me. When I sat down with a book open on my knee and the cat beside me on the arm of my chair, I had another attack, brought on by the sound of the rain and the cat's warm contact against my arm, of unaccountable uneasiness, of a vague longing to be happy—but that was as far as it went.

The storm glided away to the west and the rain with it. In the room next door—for the Haumes had two communicating rooms—Gérard Haume began to sing. A very ordinary voice, but in tune. He was humming a pleasant, spineless little English waltz that had been popular some years before. I recognised the tune and the words, based on a pun on "you" and the letter "u".

> *You, you, you,*
> *Only you, you, you,*
> *I, J, K, L, M, N, O,*
> *P, Q, R, S, T, you, you, you.*

To the devil with all mind-readers, oracles, fortune-tellers—to the devil with all women, in fact! From the moment I heard M. Haume singing *"Only you,"* I felt convinced that he possessed some hidden secret. I derived an agreeable zest from this conviction, as though

I had suddenly taken a firm resolution to learn to play bridge or the piano or to embroider a set of chair covers in cross-stitch.

Ghosts, even flesh and blood ghosts, do not appear unless they are summoned up. The fact of spying on your neighbor is enough to turn him into an evil-doer.

The day after hearing M. Haume break into song and then as suddenly break off, I went for a walk. My cat guided me between lawns revived by the downpour and borders of cherry-pie and geranium. As a result of our tardiness in rising, we found the dairy crowded with children and governesses, and we passed the bedouin figures already on their way back after treatment. We altered course owing to the lateness of the hour, steering in the direction of a fruiterer where they sold delicious wild raspberries—so full of taste and of such a deep red hue under their faint bluish haze. I was handed them in a curly cabbage leaf, as many as it would hold, and I sat on the wall of the little formal garden to eat them. There were only a few shopping streets at the back of the large buildings in the centre of the town, all of them well shaded in summer, and here were to be found the wool-shop, the souvenir-shop, the chemist, and the Post Office. The old out-of-the-way Post Office frowned from the depths of a courtyard and the pediment of its archway was adorned with two horses' heads. It must all be sadly changed to-day!

While I was eating my raspberries, a grey-blue man

emerged from the Post Office yard and walked away quickly in the opposite direction with a light step. I was in no hurry to return to the Hôtel, especially since my cat, who had been honoured by the inhabitants of this health-resort with the name of Puss-on-the-Lead, had to receive certain offerings on the way back, such as small pieces of gruyère cheese, a red rosette to set off the twin black zebra stripes on her neck, and a little celluloid ball with a lead pellet inside.

When I got back I found pushed under my door a note from Mme. Haume. "Look in and see your neighbour. She's feeling a bit off color. Toni." Before calling on her, however, I changed out of a terra-cotta-colored pullover into a white blouse. M. Haume came to the door.

"Is Mme. Haume not feeling well?"

He made a vague gesture, halfway between sorrow and impatience. "No. She's caught a chill. Tell her she's looking well." He then added with similar brevity. "Anyway, she *is* looking well."

I had never seen Mme. Haume in bed. Her ideas of sick-room elegance scouted any idea of illness, but not of accident, for my first impression was that she had been laid out on her bed in haste and fully dressed. She was wearing a sort of bed-jacket in two shades of mauve, em-broidered and ruched with lace. Her knees were covered with an openwork tea cloth and a bunch of pansies was resplendent on her bedside table. Through the door I could see M. Haume's room and his unmade bed. Mme. Haume was, in fact, looking well; but a faint olive-colored, feverish tinge, especially noticeable round her eyes, had crept over her powdered cheeks. The lovely, strong neck I envied so much was smooth and bare, supporting a beautifully waved head of hair. She closed the pages of a new novel to greet me.

"Well, Toni, what is wrong with you?"

"Absolutely nothing, my dear. I've caught a chill, that's all. Sit down on the end of my bed."

Her strong, hot hand drew me down. Her voice was worse than I had ever heard it. I gazed, as though for the first time, at her great brown eyes, at the curls that half covered her forehead, at the false gold of her hair, which that morning made her look older. I liked her face. No single feature was delicately molded, but there was nothing ugly about it. Her husband stood anxiously not very far from the bed, his hands deep in his pockets. It occurred to me that his anxiety was a little too obvious.

The cat heard my voice from the room next door. She floated across the barrier between our balconies as lightly as a silk scarf and came in to join us.

"The family's complete," said Mme. Haume. "What can I offer you?"

"Nothing. I've just treated myself to a heap of wild raspberries. I'd have brought you some if only I'd known you were not going to the Baths this morning."

"If I'd thought you wanted any," M. Haume broke in, "I'd have gone round to Besnus. . . ."

This deliberate lie filled me with conceited satisfaction. I threw up my head like a charger at the sound of a trumpet-call.

"So you'll stay in bed all day, Toni?"

"Yes, I think so. . . . Dr. Ruhl is such a martinet. He's coming to see me at eleven."

Mme. Haume was stroking my cat and she kept her eyes lowered. Her cold, or the beastly mauve of her bed-jacket, took the color from her complexion to a disconcerting degree.

"Don't let her do anything rash," I said to Gérard Haume.

He had not moved, and it was the fixity of his attention, no doubt, that lent him his air of distraction. But he heard me.

"Of course I won't," he answered. "Do you mind if I take the cat back to your room? I'm afraid she may tire Antoinette."

In spite of the fact that the cat made it quite plain, by stiffening in his arms, that she knew how to walk by herself, he carried her as far as my door.

"It's nothing serious, is it?"

Gérard Haume passed a hand across his face. "Serious! No, not if by serious you mean dangerous. But her treatment is interrupted after fifteen days. We were supposed to be leaving in nine days' time."

"Well?"

"Well, we won't be able to go. Dr. Ruhl won't hear of it. A journey, a change of air at this stage. . . ."

He dug his hands deep into his pockets, pulling his grey flannel jacket out of shape. "Her temperature's well over a hundred."

"Well over a hundred!" I repeated. "At this time of day! Where did she catch cold?"

"She likes going into the church, which is icy. You see, Antoinette is delicate. She's . . . she's in danger."

"I didn't realise. To look at her, I'd never have thought . . . So she'll have herself looked after here for a few days?"

"A few days! We'll be lucky if we get away from here inside three weeks."

He made a soft, sneering sound, let his hands fall to his sides and with an expression of despair rested his head against the glazed panel of the door. I was touched, and at once all my suspicions were allayed.

"At least I hope you're not going to wear that expression in front of her!"

"Oh, don't you worry. But this accident throws me into an abyss of complications!"

The last word took me aback. M. Haume looked at the time on his wrist-watch, clasped his hands and made his knuckle-joints crack. The fumes of morning coffee came up to us from the stair-well.

"It's not yet ten. Can't the doctor come before eleven?"

"What doctor? Oh, yes. I'm sorry. No, he's busy with his morning consultations, as official doctor to the Establishment. Anyway, there's no hurry. Antoinette knows her own case only too well, and so do I. It's not the first time."

He looked me in the face, and then said, rather strangely, "Oh! if only I could be three weeks older at this moment —or a fortnight—even a few hours. What a mess! What a tangle of complications!"

He certainly seemed attached to that word, which to

me sounded oddly irrelevant. I stared at him with that disagreeable brand of pity one reserves for a man whom one would have preferred to find strong and sure of himself. He looked at me from the remote blue depths of his eyes like a blind man, and with an air of bewilderment that I found particularly distasteful. He consulted his watch and left me hurriedly.

To watch a woman struggling in the throes of affliction may certainly be called an edifying spectacle. I have not seen sufficient sick men to make a comparison between the male and the female reactions to the arduous duties of recuperation and of living with exemplary diligence. If Antoinette Haume's congestion of the lungs proved less serious than her husband seemed to fear, it was because she was determined, from the very first day, from the depths of her fever and at grips with the agonies of pleurisy and the anguish of her shortening breath, to try to get well. She reduced everything—movement, complaints, impatience—to an heroic minimum. Each time I went into her room, where a female attendant from the Baths, promoted to the duties of nursing from those of administering showers, was at her bedside, she insisted on being given one or other of the mauve or biscuit-colored bed-wraps, which made her look as if she had gone to bed in a tea-gown. Dr. Ruhl had recommended her to speak as little as possible, and she remained silent— if I may so express myself—with an air of urgency. At the end of the second week she insisted on wearing a tulle veil to hide her forehead, since it distressed her that I might see the brown roots of her golden hair. For after a fortnight I was always there, of no great practical use, and confining my services to a one-sided conversation with this silent woman; to taking her mind off things, to pressing a lemon into a tumbler with a dissolving aspirin, or arranging a few Alpine cyclamen and gentians in a small vase. When she was not absolutely prostrate, I told her stories. I told her, for instance, why one of the eyes of a sole is set askew, and why it is safer to have a wolf in the house than the offspring of a domestic dog crossed with a wolf. I discovered some really mossy rose-galls one day up on the slopes behind the Park, and I put these briar tumors on her counterpane so that they might spread, as they dried, their delicate smell of pine and rose. M. Haume moved softly from room to room with an almost winged step. During the second week I noticed that the little creases in his checks had lengthened and that he had developed a mania for walking. He spent little time at his wife's bedside. When I went out, I came across him everywhere. Finally, I suggested a game of cards in his room after dinner, when Antoinette, arranged and settled for the night, was slow in going to sleep. There was a hint of "That's as good as anything else" behind his gesture of acceptance.

We made no noise as we played, for we spread a blanket over the wooden table. After the worst nights were over, the "Bath-woman" used to leave at ten. From the door of Antoinette's room I was unable to tell at a glance whether she was really asleep, for there were deep shadows over her huge eye-sockets even when she lay awake. She used to strike the side of the bed with the flat of her hand to let me know she was still awake, and I would go back to the game—piquet or écarté—and sit down again opposite her husband, whose distracted and altogether discouraged appearance seemed proof against the doctor's optimism. On some evenings the open windows would let in a grey flurry of insects and very small silkworm moths that fell like snow all over the room; and there was always the smell of the orange blossom and the sulphur fumes of the springs.

"I'm afraid I don't play very well," I ventured to murmur.

M. Haume acquiesced in silence.

"As we're not playing for money, you might give me a little advice."

He refused with a shake of his head. "You'll never make a good player."

"Why?"

"You seem to expect a miracle, as if a fifth ace or an unexpected king would suddenly come to your rescue. Besides, I play too well."

"Are you a gambler?"

"I've gambled in the past."

He dabbed his forehead, glanced at his watch, and shuffled the pack. Under the lamplight, the blue of his eyes acquired a transparency that abolished, or nearly so, all that we incorrectly term 'the expression' of the eyes. The first evening of Antoinette's convalescence was celebrated with champagne. She raised her glass from the little bedside table and said, "To your health, both of you! You've been wonderful. Now go and finish the bottle in Gérard's room."

I was moved by the sound of that deep voice, so long silent and now so enfeebled. I made some sort of joke as we settled down facing each other. My opponent said nothing. After about a quarter of an hour's play, Gérard Haume laid down his cards on the table saying, "Please forgive me, I simply can't go on," and covered his face with his hands.

"Please don't apologise; it's only natural. It's the reaction."

He made a violent gesture of denial and picked up his cards again. I looked at him, from time to time, with unjust severity. I have never had any leanings towards flirtations over a sick-bed—fingers coming into contact over a cup of herb-tea, and whisperings behind doors of "my poor friend!" But I failed to grasp why this man—"a rock" as Antoinette had called him—was not looking more cheerful, now Antoinette was on the mend.

The cat, reconciled now that the rooms were free of fever, came in from the balcony in accordance with Cat Law—that is to say, as if by magic—suddenly materialising in a place where, a moment before, she had not been. M. Haume shuddered and dropped the card he had just picked up.

"I'm sorry," he said. "I'm . . . I'm all on edge."

I too must certainly have been less calm than usual, because I made the mistake of giving him a curt answer, and without raising my voice.

"Well, I can't spend my life forgiving you. And when, oh when, will you get tired of glancing at your watch the whole time?"

The fleeting enmity that flickered for a moment over his features gratified me rather than the reverse. He pointed in the direction of his wife's room to enjoin prudence.

"Antoinette is expecting the hairdresser to-morrow, and a manicurist, and the pedicure from the Baths. It was no good my pointing out that it's still rather early days. As you go out early every morning, may I offer you, and the cat, a glass of fresh milk to-morrow, or a black coffee at the dairy in the Park?"

"All right."

"At eight?"

"At eight. . . . I've got a point of five."

"And it's no good."

"Of course!"

"Of course."

Gérard Haume contemplated his excellent hand with a sad eye. But, till the end of the game, he fought against his gloomy mood like a man who has come to a decision. When I went back to my room, Mme. Haume was fast asleep, her head resting on a folded arm, her hair carefully enveloped in a white snood. There was just enough light from the lamp, over which a mauve scarf had been thrown, for me to see that she was looking younger again. But she also looked worn out, for her strongly defined mouth stood out from between her hollow cheeks; and she looked happy, on the other side of sleep, in the knowledge that the end of her suffering was in sight. Ugly or beautiful, I felt quite certain that no harm would ever come to her through me.

Does the church at X-les-Bains, tightly squeezed as it was against an outcrop of rock a few feet higher than the building, still occupy the same humble position? I remember that water from an oozing fissure dripped over its roof, turning it green and contributing to the cellar-like temperature of the interior. I did not go to church, but I remember its discolored belfry chiming out the quarters from afar. At eight the next morning, I sat down at one of the round tables of the dairy. The cat was served first. She was a beautiful and devoted wild animal not more than five years old: full of that rather rough gaiety which was her special characteristic; sleek, glossy, shimmering with her thousand stripes, her coat still sombre despite the summer season; calmly vigilant and applying to everything—except to me—her impenetrable judgment. Far-sighted, like many cats, she saw a familiar figure approaching in the distance and drew her ears closer together. I re-tied my banana-colored scarf, the prettiest I possessed, and readjusted the fit of my yellowish jacket with black edging. The only child there, a fat, fair-haired little boy, was drinking his milk under the eye of his nanny. When he paused for breath he forgot to wipe his mouth, so that, at each of these pauses, his face was barred with huge white moustachios like an elderly general.

Gérard Haume, dressed in grey flannel and white shoes,

sat down at my table; and I felt grateful that he spared me any preamble for the benefit of the dairymaid, the nurse, and the child with the moustache.

"Did Toni have a good night?"

"Oh, a very good night. She never stirred. She's almost down to normal and entirely concerned with making herself look beautiful. She has amazing powers of recuperation."

"How lucky for her!"

"Yes. . . . Do tell me, had you noticed that I look at the time . . . rather often?"

"Rather often, if not more."

"That's very odd. My wife has never noticed it."

He put his soft hat on a chair. I would have liked to have asked him to put it on his head again. Something, I did not know what, had wrought a great change in him óver the last three weeks, something that was particularly noticeable about the cheek-bones right up to his temples, and, without exactly knowing how a forehead can become thin, I thought, 'How thin his forehead is!' Along the crude lines characteristic of a woman's thoughts about a man who makes no effort to charm her, I also said to myself, 'Another three months of such havoc, and he'll be fit for the dustbin.'

We hurried through our breakfast, and then turned our chairs to face the restful mountainside, which the sun had already abandoned. As he shifted his basket-chair round, Gérard Haume looked at the time on his wrist, thinking that I hadn't seen him. . . .

"Madame," he began, "I think I can trust you."

"That all depends."

He smiled with a shake of his thin forehead, and I had to admit that this man 'fit for the dustbin' still possessed a certain charm.

"I'm resolved to pay no attention to what it all depends on, and confide in you. I've gone seventeen days—no, eighteen—without any news."

"News of whom?"

"Of the woman I love, Madame."

"Oh . . . well," I said gloomily. "So that's what it is."

"That's what what is?"

"Why you look so tired. And why you go to the post before nine every morning."

"Yes; that's it."

He pressed his closed fist against the metal table top, time and time again.

"That's it, that's absolutely and horribly it. And for seventeen days, not eighteen, as I said, instead of a letter every day at the *poste restante*, there's been nothing at all. So . . . I just can't go on. I don't know what's happened and I don't know what's going to become of me."

"Have you sent a telegram?"

"Yes. After waiting much too long."

"None of your letters have been sent back—from the Dead Letter Office?"

"None."

"Is this . . . is this person in Paris? Why don't you ask a friend?"

He interrupted me in a tone of intolerant asperity.

"Really, Madame! I'm not a child! I've been acting a part

for two years now. But remember that we live at Aussor-
gues just as much as we do in Paris, and my brother———"

It was my turn to lose patience. "Good. Now for the
brother! Do you realise that you're telling me all this as
if I were acquainted with all the people involved."

My companion begged my forgiveness with a look of
abject misery.

"Madame, I beg you to be patient with me. I won't take
long. My elder brother is called Georges Haume; he's the
owner of the factory; an excellent man. I'm only Gérard
Haume, the one who used to be known, not so very long
ago, as the black sheep of the family. Oh," he continued,
vigorously shrugging his shoulders, "I might have done
worse things than gamble and borrow and hang about
night clubs and waste money. Nevertheless, without my
wife, heaven knows what would have become of me! My
wife is someone who exceeds excellence, someone—and I
beg you to believe me—I'm fonder of than anything in the
world. Out of respect, out of affection for her, my brother
fixed up everything and kept me in the business; but . . .
but I'm not much good at it. Anyway, that's not what I
wanted to talk about."

"May I ask you a question? Does Antoinette suspect
anything?"

He swore that she did not, with his hand across his
heart, a familiar gesture with weak characters and liars.

"She knows nothing about it. But there's a double dan-
ger. Who is sending the letters astray—the ones I don't
receive? I only hope no person is making use of them!"

"And the second danger?"

Gérard Haume threw away his cigarette, looked at the time on his wrist-watch, and then questioned me with a glance of inane intensity.

"The second danger? Oh yes! The second danger's me. I'm . . . I'm literally going to pieces—literally, I can't help it. Supposing I had a . . . I don't know . . . a nervous breakdown, and began to talk and ask for . . . ."

'A rock,' I thought. 'She says her husband's a rock. A rock composed of bread-crumbs, and a fool as well!' While I was accusing him, mentally, of stupidity, he observed, not unskilfully, "I'm not bringing on this crisis by talking to you about it like this. I'm delaying it. To whom could I talk when I felt like shrieking out loud?"

Even to-day I still do not know whether one should talk about "profound male ingenuousness" or "profound male diplomacy." The man beside me seemed, on the surface, a fairly commonplace type. Nevertheless, his instinct taught him that a confession might put him out of harm's way; that, by revealing himself in all his weakness, he might perhaps find help; that I might point out to him some escape-route leading to the relief he was so slow in finding for himself.

"The break in correspondence doesn't coincide with any quarrel, any . . . ?"

"Impossible."

He repeated the word "impossible," and he half closed his eyes in an expression of security and self-satisfaction.

"Supposing . . . supposing she'd just stopped writing to you?"

"How do you mean?"

"I mean, supposing she'd suddenly decided, for some reason best known to herself, that all was over between you?"

It took him a moment to grasp my meaning. Then he began laughing, in the way actors laugh on the stage. "Ha ha ha, ha ha, ha ha, . . . I don't, I really can't see that happening. No, no!"

"Why shouldn't it happen to you?" I asked acidly. "It's certainly happened to me."

He calmed down, but still wore his expression of superiority.

"Obviously you don't understand! The attachment between us, between her and me, is of such an extraordinary kind."

"Like all attachments."

"Oh, please! It's not at all ordinary, or usual, that two human beings should be capable—for two whole years—of hiding nothing from each other, that every hour of a woman's life should be devoted to the same sentiment, to the same man—to such an extent that this man can look at his watch"—he looked at his watch—"at any moment of the day or night, and say: 'It's nine o'clock, she's home; it's midnight, she's plaiting her lovely hair before going to bed; it's———.'"

"Really, please! We haven't got time now to go into the way each of the twelve hours is filled."

"I'm sorry, but what do you think of such an ingenious love, a love that enables the distant lover to see right across intervening space?"

I only answered with a sigh. I had already learned that

silence is invaluable when dealing with certain kinds of triumphant blindness.

"Has this . . . ? Is this lady in a business profession?"

"No, no!" M. Haume protested, as if I had intended an insult. "She's the simplest, the most unselfish of women, she manages with one maid . . . whom I could wish was more worthy of her, more suitable to the delicate state of her health. Oh God, oh God, when I think that for eighteen days . . . Eighteen days!"

He broke off, pressed both hands to his forehead, and I could hear his breath coming faster.

Total absence of humor renders life impossible. M. Haume's conviction and the catalogue of his woes were already becoming tedious, and it was I, for once, who asked what time it was. I could think of nothing further to say. Then—as though suddenly inspired—I cried "Have you tried to get Paris on the telephone?"

He brushed my suggestion aside with a sweep of the hand.

"No; it's not possible; really it isn't. There's not even a connection at night! The Post Office shuts at seven, the girl at the exchange is away for lunch from twelve to two, and betweenwhiles there's always a two hours' delay. So——"

"Obviously."

Obviously Gérard Haume had resigned himself to pining away: he was prepared to die of a broken heart, but not to wait two hours for a telephone call. In point of fact he was right, for the whole of X-les-Bains wandered about the Post Office between the hours of ten and midday and again between two and five. Telephone conversations were audible through the thin partitions of a booth that was more like a rustic privy. . . . I made one more attempt.

"But why haven't you gone to Paris by train?"

"Because I had no motive or excuse, especially while Antoinette was ill." Gérard Haume's answer was honest enough. "Antoinette comes first. But it doesn't stop me being miserable. I don't know which way to turn. I could never have imagined——" He cast a morbid glance at his watch. "Five past nine!" he cried. "The time she's handed my letter every day of the week."

It was a real cry of anguish, and no mistake. All sorts of questions that I longed to ask him came into my mind. "What did this lady, your mistress, do before you knew her? What does she do all day? Whom does she see? Has she got friends and relations? What are her tastes? What does she read?" But, instead of asking some sensible question, I opened my mouth merely to suggest another commonplace.

"Couldn't you get in touch with her *concierge?*"

"Her *concierge!* There's a specimen for you, a thoroughly evil old bird if ever there was one! I've done my best to get round her, but she always glares at me. The *concierge* indeed!"

He hunched his shoulders and put his hands in his pockets, muttering indistinctly. It was not difficult, from my knowledge of the average Frenchman, to interpret these mumblings. M. Haume was afraid of the *concierge.*

No doubt he anticipated, and very logically, my next question. He allowed himself a romantic smile.

"As for friends, it's now the twenty-sixth of July, and

Paris is deserted. And you've no idea how few real men friends one has if one's life has been obsessed by women. Otherwise, of course . . ."

He made up his mind to look me in the face: a contrite expression full of meaning. I tossed my head. "I see. It would suit your book admirably if I were to go to Paris?"

He had not the courage to deny it, but turned his moist blue eyes away from me. To quell any wish to retract, I took a letter out of my bag—they were called "reticules" then—a letter I had received the day before, and handed it to him. Looking very worried, he shivered and fumbled, hesitating to take it from me. Then he became acquainted, as he read, that my friend and colleague Georges Wague was in the habit of addressing me as "The Rat," that there was a proposal for our going on tour in October, and that if I turned up in Paris, at Buysens', the agent, on the twenty-seventh of July at four o'clock . . .

"The twenty-seventh! That's to-morrow!" he murmured. "You never said a word about it."

"I meant to send a telegram, followed by a letter, leaving everything in Wague's hands. I didn't mean to go myself, because . . ."

I felt myself blushing, and fell silent, idiotically.

"But why? Why?" M. Haume asked in an urgent voice.

"Well, because . . . How odd you are! Because, if the deal had failed to materialise, Buysens would never have paid my travelling expenses."

"That's ridiculous," M. Haume said, in a low voice. "And when you're finished with your agent, where would you go?"

"Nowhere. . . . I thought of staying in Paris."

With salvation in sight, his face lighted up and his eyes became slate-blue and inquisitorial. He declared that the coincidence was an act of providence.

"Don't worry about it. I'll see to everything," he said, rising to his feet. "Yes, yes; you must come back. I know you're fond of Antoinette. Please come back! Oh yes, and don't forget your letter. Here it is—you must show it to her when you go in. She'll call me and show it to me, and I'll advise you not to let the deal slip. Before luncheon, I shall have the honor of presenting you with a return ticket. Oh, really, I implore you, we mustn't have any fuss about it! When one does anybody a favor such as you're doing me . . . Send Wague a telegram and see What's-his-name, the agent. But keep an hour to go and see Suzanne!"

He walked back to the Hôtel with such quick steps that the cat thought it was a game and went galloping across the lawn.

"We'll look after the cat for you," he said, as if clinching the argument. "Yes, yes, I know she has to be locked up at night. I'd better not try and take her for her morning walks, had I, during the next two days? All right, I'll get fresh milk for her straight from the dairy. Do you need a small suitcase? My wife's got one she'll lend you if you want it. I hope Antoinette will be looking better when you get back."

He thought of everything. He had recovered the presence of mind and skill of someone who is used to moving female pawns about on a chess-board full of hazards. He spoke of Antoinette without a trace of embarrassment, and pronounced her name with his blessing, perhaps—as if it had been a magic formula. Nothing seems shady, or even cynical, in the eyes of a man who, certain of one faithful love, is at liberty to suffer for another.

Everything worked out as M. Haume had planned. I did not forget to toss Wague's letter on Antoinette's bed. Her hair was glittering with fresh gold, and she was wearing a new "bed-jacket"—of blue velvet with a few sequins—that looked like an evening wrap. She voiced a few hoarse complaints when she learned of my departure, and hugged the cat to her breast as a hostage. Her husband gazed tenderly down at her and glanced at his wrist-watch. She wanted to lend me a suitcase, her travelling-clock, a blanket; to load and attach me with presents that would bring me back more quickly. When her husband said he would take me to the station she cried out, with a flourish of the little spoon she was using to eat a large sweet-scented peach, "And don't forget, if you clinch the deal early enough, there's a train with sleeping-cars to-morrow night at 9:57 that gets you here at 5:30 in the morning! Think how pleased your cat would be—she's only expecting you back the day after to-morrow night!"

In the station buffet, M. Haume handed me a sealed envelope. "You see the address—Madame Leyrisse, Rue du Mont-Thabor. May I suggest you call on her either at ten in the morning or at three in the afternoon? The masseuse, who looks after Suzanne's circulation, is usually finished by ten. You could talk to her during the hour's rest she takes after massage. Or if three suits you better . . ."

"But wouldn't it be best to arrange the time before-hand by telephone?"

M. Haume, with his gaze lowered reflectively, was stirring a lump of ice round in his glass. It refracted the rays of the setting sun. All round the jumble of station buildings a cool mist was beginning to spread over the little gardens and across the meadows. High up above was perched the real-estate development, with *Beethoven* and all the other *Knick-Knacks*. Breathing in the smells of the evening and of crushed grass, and thinking of the heat of Paris, I told myself that I was more than half an idiot.

"No," M. Haume said at last; "don't telephone. She might be suspicious."

"What of?"

"I don't know. She's suspicious by nature. You'll soon find out. But you'll manage. There's no reason why she should refuse to see you. At least, I don't foresee any."

"All right. Would you like me to send you a telegram, *poste restante*, after I've seen her?"

He had it all weighed up in advance. He shook his head.

"No. If, by any chance you should catch the train to-morrow night, the telegram might arrive later than you. I'd much rather learn whatever is to be learnt direct from you yourself. Here's your train. Not a very good one, unfortunately."

He jumped with agility into the compartment, gave me a hand up, let down one of the windows, and arranged my suitcase and my coat and the magazines with efficiency. I let him do it, having lost the habit of a man's attention many long years before.

"Come back safely!" he shouted egotistically.

A flat left empty for a few weeks takes advantage of your absence to alter its appearance. Mine, a modest one, which needed my constant attention to be tolerable, was not expecting me. A book lying open on the divan-bed, a crumpled letter beside the waste-paper basket, the window curtain caught up—nothing more was needed to create the impression that my arrival had put to flight heaven knows what phantom. But I had no time to waste on ghosts.

It was striking eleven when I dropped in on Georges Wague. At ten to twelve we were discussing matters with Buysens the agent, who turned out to be pink, peevish, and tough. An hour later, I was sitting with my back to the scorched leaves that sifted the Parisian sunlight—at a table in the small garden of a *bistro* up on the Butte—where we were doing justice to a shoulder of lamb and a bottle of white wine. Below the garden wall other Montmartre gardens were dozing, each dotted with saucers of food for the cats, tumble-down summer-houses, and little, starved-looking currant bushes. Further down the slope chestnut trees in bloom barred the ascent from Paris. I noticed, last year, that they were still flourishing.

About half-past two I found that my spirits were beginning to flag: a state induced by the company of my friend, by the white wine and by the "nice little" contract

I had just signed: *Bordeaux* (Rue Judaïque, with an orchestra conductor called M. Juif); *Biarritz* (end of season); *Montpelier* (four days that always pay for general expenses); *Nice* (yes, but only at a small place); *Monte Carlo* (Oh! but not at the Grand Casino!); and *Beausoleil* ('What's wrong with Beausoleil? They've got a wonderful set-up there'). My understandable gaiety began to wane, for in thirty minutes I should be meeting, in her own home, the punctual, the modest, the delicate stay-at-home, Mme. Leyrisse.

Sad verso of the sunny Rue de Rivoli, the Rue du Mont-Thabor can boast several ancient houses whose whole architectural charm lies in their interior: sweeping staircases and banisters, doors and fanlights made cheerful by Directoire cross-sashes. Looking up to check the street number, I saw that the "To Let" sign would provide me with a beginning worthy of *Fantomas*.

In the peaceful shade of the courtyard, a *concierge* was washing some leeks.

"Madame," I began, "I've come to ask about the flat to let."

"The flat! Well, you've not been long in finding out about it!" She shook the water from the pallid tufts of her leeks and came closer to get a better sight of me. "Who told you about it?"

I launched into fiction at once. "Through Madame Leyrisse. Is she——"

M. Haume's enemy interrupted me. "Oh, so that's how it is! I understand. She wanted you to occupy it after her."

"After her?"

"Yes, seeing she put you on to it. Up till this very morning the owner had hopes of a possible lodger, that's why there was no notice up, but he fell through. But seeing as Madame Leyrisse sent you . . . Do you know the flat? It looks much bigger without the furniture. Would you like to see over it again? I'll open up for you, then you can have a look round and give me the keys back on your way out."

As one might imagine, I remained prudently silent as I followed the *concierge*. She left me on the threshold of a square, dingy living-room, whose fine oak parquet, laid chevronwise, groaned under my feet. Another room led out of this, but the walls showed the marks where the bed had been, and the paper bore shadowed traces of a high rectangular wardrobe and a large oval looking-glass. A young and commonplace scent lingered in the bathroom, from which I was chivvied, not unwillingly, by my own reflection in the mirror over the basin. A few words had been scrawled on the pale blue panelling of the bedroom: *Dédé will be back in half an hour with the taxi.*

M. Haume had foreseen every single thing, except the most probable. I hastened out again into the welcoming summer heat.

"How did you like it?" the *concierge* asked me briskly.
"Not at all bad."
"It'll be snapped up in no time, I can tell you, if you don't make up your mind."
"I'm sure it will. There'd been some talk of a sub-let between Madame Leyrisse and myself. But I see she's taken everything away at the last minute. If she comes back, would you mind giving her this."

I handed her M. Haume's letter, accompanied by a folded banknote.

"Thank you very much, Madame. But I can only say that I'll be very much surprised if Madame Leyrisse does call back. She squared up everything when she left and let me see now, that would be Sunday fortnight. I think Madame ought to take the letter back."

I took back the letter. There was a smile on the lips of the *concierge* behind her little flame-colored moustache, which had obviously been bleached with peroxide. I had no inclination to persist or to get myself still further involved. To be addressed as Madame, in the third person, was all that my heavy tip had achieved. One ought to know exactly how much people are worth before one starts trying to bribe them. The note had been too big.

I was delighted to think—as I travelled back by the night train that Antoinette had advised me to take—that the flight of Mme. Leyrisse had precluded all chance of my meeting her. And, without having yet decided how best to deliver my report, I cursed Gérard Haume and, on the rebound, myself. 'I'm bored with that fellow and all those blue color-schemes of his! And it wasn't very decent to Antionette, my taking on the unsavory business. So the good lady has done a bolt, has she! Well, she's bolted, and he'll have to get used to the fact.'

As the train left Paris further and further behind, the stifling night air became lighter and warmer, then cool, and thereafter steadily colder as we passed through meadowlands and a large forest with invisible streams. The forgotten pleasure of being cold overcame me a little before dawn, at the same time as sleep, and I woke to step down on to the small, deserted platform, where I found the horses of the Grand Hôtel omnibus half asleep between the shafts.

I opened the door of my room silently, yet I did not take the cat by surprise. She greeted me with a kind of dispassionate pleasure. Perhaps, forewarned by some seventh sense for which man has not yet discovered a name, she had seen me coming. She simply pushed her forehead roughly into my hand, purring, and watched me attentively while I brushed and combed my hair. Mingled smells of orange blossom and hydrosulphuric vapor from the mineral springs floated in strong drifts through the slats of the venetian blinds: precursors of another hot day. I managed not to bump into the furniture, or let the locks of the suitcase snap, and I was careful to turn the taps on with as little noise as possible.

'And now,' I thought, 'all I've got to do is to wait for the awkward moment.' But my apprehension was not unaccompanied by that evil, deep-rooted cheerfulness, that faint shock in the region of the stomach, that are proof of a human being's hostility to the rest of his kind. Nobody laughs when a horse falls or a dog is run over, but it is often hard to behave properly if the worthy lady in front of one slips up on a frozen puddle, or if the gentleman with the parcel labelled "with care" misses the edge of the pavement.

Gérard Haume, as the betrayed lover, was steadily losing place in my esteem. In our latitudes, women are without pity for men who have been deceived. It's true that Gérard Haume had become involved with a mistress of fifth rate quality, the kind that makes off with the furniture, covers her tracks, and then gloats—"Just think how he'll carry on!" All the same, the less commendable side of me was also entranced by the idea of how M. Haume would carry on. Men who are too exclusively taken up with women receive their punishment, in due course, from the women themselves.

Time was by now running short. Should I tell him the truth? Should I pretend I had never been to the Rue du Mont-Thabor? A faint scratching sounded outside my room. I tied the belt of my kimono round my waist, and half-opened the door.

"I heard the omnibus," whispered Gérard Haume. "You can imagine I was quite unable to sleep. May I come in a moment?"

"You certainly may not!"

"Why not?"

"Because someone might see you going out. I mean, because of Antoinette. Is she all right?"

"She's much better. But tell me something reassuring, in Heaven's name!"

He spoke with his face thrust through the gap of the door, and I did my best to avoid his breath; the breath of a man before breakfast, who has smoked a lot and then brushed his teeth. He was wearing a blue scarf round his neck, and he had certainly not slept for two nights. Yesterday's beard was sticking out through the long creases on

his cheeks like the bristles on a brush, and I told him that
he might at least have had the decency to shave after hear-
ing the carriage! For the first time, I saw his thin bare feet
in his slippers. For some reason, they filled me with horror.

"Did you see her? Is she alive?"

The last question, uttered in a deep and slightly insane
voice, gave me a chance of making a positive answer.
"Very much alive. Do go away. We'll talk later."

"No. Now."

"What do you mean?"

"I mean, at once."

"That is, if I want to! Really!"

I was irritated beyond all reason, and entirely because
he had given me yet another proof of his total indifference.
He closed his eyes as though about to faint and continued
his insistence in a humbler tone. I let him come in because
I thought I heard a step on the staircase. I pointed to the
only armchair and went to sit on the edge of my bed, as
far as possible from this man who, it was all too clear,
could barely contain himself. And here was I about to
hurt him!

"Well? Did everything go off all right? When did you go
there?"

"At three."

"Bravo!"

"Why 'Bravo!'?"

"Because I feel like cheering everything you tell me
about her."

He smiled. The overwrought angularity of his face became softer, and his eyes shone with a different shade of blue. He was once more exerting his charm.

"She hadn't had to leave Paris? She's very pretty, isn't she? You did see her, didn't you? You called on her? Is it really true?"

He got up and walked between me and the window, forcing me to turn my head towards the daylight.

"She must have been surprised! Wasn't she? What dress was she wearing? The green one, with the heavy frilled collar? No? The silver grey, with the embroidered red leather belt? Oh, have I guessed right?"

I made a gesture that might have meant yes, and M. Haume came a step closer to me.

"I was positive. You're lying. You never went to the Rue du Mont-Thabor at all!"

"Oh, but I did!"

"No. Because Suzanne has never worn green: she's much too superstitious. And the silver-grey one only exists in my imagination. You weren't expecting that, eh? One can't be ready for everything!"

He grinned triumphantly, dabbing at his forehead and glancing at his watch.

"Now," he said, "we must begin all over again. Anyway, I don't care a damn. I'm through. I'm leaving for Paris to-night."

He strode up and down, losing one of his slippers and collecting it again by curling up his big toe. It was whitish and well cared for, and I could not bear the sight of it. He suddenly swung round on reaching the door.

"Why have you done this to me? You should have told

me you wouldn't go! What did it matter to you? You should have told me!" He was shouting in a low voice, as one shouts in a dream. "Unless she didn't want to see you? Unless . . ."

He fell silent, waiting for what was to come.

"Don't go to Paris," I said. "I did what I promised you. There's nobody at the Rue Mont-Thabor now. The flat's to let."

His silence seemed intolerably long.

"To let?" he asked at last, in a plaintive voice. "Why to let?"

"It's empty. I went there. The *concierge* told me the occupant left a fortnight ago without leaving an address."

The man whom I had just dealt such a heavy blow appeared to be lost in a profound reverie. I listened anxiously for the sounds of steps in the hotel, thinking that Antoinette might by now be awake.

"You were saying . . . ? You were saying that you visited the flat? And that it was empty?"

"Quite empty."

"Quite empty. . . ." M. Haume repeated it like a singsong, "Quite empty. . . ."

"Do you realise it's a quarter to seven? Do go, please!"

"Yes. . . . Quite . . . emp . . . ty. . . . Not even a scrap of paper or a chair? Not a book? Nothing?"

He scratched his unshaven chin absent-mindedly. He was paying no attention to me.

"Yes," I said; "there was something written in pencil on the wall."

"Something for me?"

"I don't think so. It ran, '*Dédé will be back in half an hour with a taxi.*'"

He did not seem to have heard what I said, and I did not dare repeat it.

"Why do you tell me all this?" he said at last.

"What? The writing on the wall? But you'd just asked me if there was anything."

"Tut, tut," he said, raising his hand to interrupt me. "Don't play with words. There was absolutely no need to tell me what you've just told me. It's not a useful piece of information. Nor is it friendly information. It looks like . . . like personal spite on your part."

"I'm quite overcome. It's charming of you to think so."

He waved his hand as though he wished to say there was no need for thanks, or that he was indifferent to my opinion. Pulling his dressing-gown tight round his thin body, he walked towards the door.

"Wait! There's somebody on the stairs."

He waited a few seconds while the sound of footsteps died away and then went out with a slight valedictory gesture. Fully occupied as he was with the present disaster, would he attempt to retrace events to the sudden whim, to the little turn of chance that had brought me to X-les-Bains? He had other things to worry about. But I, alone once more, stood there linking up the chain of coincidences, reassessing the chance I had been offered of living, or not living, at *The Knick-Knack*. This was where Mlle. d'Orgeville came in, dragged down by the weight of her heavy jewels.

What a shame that Mlle. d'Orgeville, smitten with a

passion for mediocrity and love without complications, should have bumped into a man from the distant Americas! I went back no further along this sequence of omens, and mishaps and *mektoubs*. As George Wague was in the habit of saying—"If Adam and Eve hadn't 'got up to tricks,' I wouldn't have my house in the Ile de Bréhat!"

I did not allow myself to malinger and, by half-past eleven, I was in Antoinette's bedroom. She was up, and her skin was pinker, more transparent and more radiant, than any really strong woman's could have been after an illness.

"I'm having luncheon downstairs!" she cried. "To-day I'm allowed to! But not on the open terrace, only on the veranda. Well, what about your tour? Did you fix it up?"

"Yes. It's all fixed."

"I *am* glad! And you're not too tired? And how much was it?"

"How much was what?"

"How much money for you, of course."

She opened her eyes wide, puffed out her lips, and made herself look greedy on my behalf.

"But that's not how it works, Toni! I have a fixed sum guaranteed me, and when the takings are more than a certain figure, I get so much per cent on top."

"Oh, that doesn't sound half so nice. How's Paris?"

"All currant bushes, with chestnuts in the background, and overhead a bower of vines and lime trees "

"What is she talking about? Did you hear, Gérard?"

Gérard, in the recesses of his room, vouchsafed no answer.

"I can only tell you what I saw in Paris. I had luncheon in an open-air *bistro* in Montmartre! The cat hasn't been out this morning, so I'll take her down, and see you again in the dining-room at twelve sharp."

At noon, Antoinette was waiting for me, slightly out of breath, with a light coat over her shoulders, very excited about her first venture downstairs and exchanging jokes with the *maître d'hôtel.* I laid a bunch of red poppies in front of her. They were full-blown, with the blue-black stain at the base of the petals showing plainly.

"Look, what lovely creatures they are! In full bloom, like you! Is your husband coming down?"

"No. Just think, he's not feeling well. He doesn't want any luncheon."

"Really! The Rock's feeling indisposed?"

"Yes," said Mme. Haume in a hesitant voice. "He's gone back to bed again. I called to him when I was ready, and he answered something I didn't catch. And I believe—forgive me for mentioning it—I believe I actually heard him throwing up!"

"What did you say?"

I laid my crumpled napkin on the table. Mme. Haume became agitated.

"Do you think I ought to have gone in?"

"But why didn't you?"

"I couldn't. He'd bolted the door. If you only knew how fussy he is! He hates being seen doing anything unbecoming."

"And he was feeling unwell?"

She looked at me, and her face at once reflected the anxiety she must have read in mine. There was no question of going on with the meal.

"Don't run, Toni; please don't run," I said, running myself. "I'm sure your husband's got nothing worse than indigestion."

"He had a syncope once," panted Mme. Haume.

"When was that?"

"Oh, a few . . . I've forgotten . . . but he's forbidden me to mention it."

The rest is not hard to imagine. Antoinette begged me not to, so I did not go through the door into his room. Gérard Haume, who was a weak man, only capable of sudden passionate decisions, had already vomited the major part of the poison he had swallowed in a massive and violently emetic dose. Dr. Ruhl, even if he did have his own mental reservations, hid them under an abundant flow of words which succeeded in convincing Antoinette. She repeated them the following day for her husband's edification, as he lay flat and exhausted in his bed.

"When you want to throw up," she expounded, "you should stick a finger down your throat, instead of meddling with things you know nothing about. Throwing up is quite simple. I'm a past-master at it. I leave the room for a couple of minutes and then come back and nobody has the faintest idea I've just thrown up."

She insisted on the phrase so much that I began to feel faintly sick myself.

"You were in serious danger of dying, Gérard. Do you realise that now?"

"I've a vague notion of it," replied a weak voice from under the mosquito-net; for the warm, windless rain had carried with it from the west clouds of harmless moths, flies, and poisonously armed mosquitoes.

I rarely entered Gérard Haume's room during the week he was bedridden. If I did go in, he turned over and faced the wall. Through the mesh of the muslin, I was just able to follow the automatic gesture with which he consulted the watch strapped to his wrist. And, in my heart, I was sorry for the man who felt so unhappy and rancorous towards me.

The fine cool weather returned, carrying off the mosquitoes and bringing a breath of spring. The foothills turned green with short-stemmed wheat and with the still paler green of the rye. The hours lay heavy on my hands. I decided to leave for Paris; but I stayed on because Gérard Haume wished me ill. I fixed the date of my departure and then I stayed on again merely because Gérard Haume wished me ill.

When the mosquito-net was rolled up to the ceiling again, his blue eyes still gave me no hint of the thought behind them. They seemed to have grown paler in the gloom. He accepted his wife's care with a tender condescension that made her brim over with happiness.

One morning, when she had an appointment with her hairdresser, she asked me by a sign to watch over her convalescent. As there was nothing he needed, I thought I would be able to perform this duty from a distance, so

I settled down with my cat and a book in Mme. Haume's room. I was suddenly overcome with impatience, and went in to M. Haume's room.

"Gérard Haume," I began, "I plan to leave in four days' time."

He never took his eyes off the blue-and-yellow horizon. "I'm very sorry to hear it."

"I'm not," I went on. "We've finished the season badly. But I shan't regret a word or a gesture, no, nothing at all, if I can feel when I go that nothing bad is in store for the person I privately think of as the admirable Antoinette."

M. Haume fingered the folds of his pyjamas: they were light blue drawn with darker blue thread. He brought the face of his wrist-watch under his eyes with the usual faddish gesture. He looked as if he were about to speak, but he said nothing. He suddenly unfastened the leather strap of his watch and threw it out of the window.

If he had not—from shame or sorrow?—laid his forearm over his eyes, I should have liked, out of some sort of gratitude, to have pressed the bare wrist stamped with a whitish circle. But, bold as they are to do hurt, women are often clumsy when the moment comes to show emotion, or simplicity. So I refrained from touching the exorcised wrist and went back into the other room, where I did not even wait for Antoinette's return. I set off on a formal visit to *The Knick-Knack*.

I drove there in a green and mildewy cab drawn at the trot by a horse that was lost in its last earthly dreams. The tufts of grass between the palings had turned yellow, and the little privet hedge that no one had watered was languishing with thirst. I did not cross the threshold of the chalet which had given me no cause for either pleasure or reproach.

Where, and under what auspices, was the real lessee now dancing and suffering and loving? A half-rotted envelope, stuck to the bottom of the ramshackle letter-box after the recent rains, divulged nothing and almost turned to pulp in my fingers. Nothing remained of the letter Mlle. d'Orgeville had written me except long tears of violet ink and the faint letter-head of a yacht's burgee. But I did not regret that it was illegible apart from a few words of generic importance, majestically commonplace—"never . . . storm . . . hundred thousand . . . ill . . ." What more did I need to know?

The half-dissolved letter, falling from my hands in sodden tatters, dispersed the first true revelations Mlle. d'Orgeville had ever entrusted me with. The day when, weakly raising her fetters of diamonds, she had interrupted her confidences as soon as begun, was the day that her unfinished gesture had dispatched me in her stead towards an uncertain goal: to Gérard Haume, the guardian of a secret, which this time had to be shared with somebody else. The rôle of proxy—mine in this case—is a risky one! At the cost of a small and almost negligible bruise, I found that out once more. Then, bidding farewell to *The Knick-Knack*, I went to collect the few personal belongings which, at that time, I held to be invaluable: my cat, my resolve to travel, and my solitude.

"But why do you want to see *The Knick-Knack*? It's so ugly."

Antoinette half-closed her eyes, and tilted her head to gaze in artistic fashion at the yellow and blue mountains.

"Because it's thanks to *The Knick-Knack* that I got to know you. I haven't many hopes of seeing you again. No, no; please don't protest!"

"I didn't say anything."

"One doesn't start up a chance acquaintance all over again, one doesn't meet a second time in a little watering-place like this. You yourself confessed to me that you'd never rented a horrid little chalet in your life before, nor taken the advice of anybody like Mademoiselle d'Orge-ville."

Good, safe Antoinette! I let her prattle on. It was better for her not to know that an outcrop of coincidences is equivalent to a sort of responsibility, that there is system and routine in the unexpected. A circumstance only seems unique to us because we are not subtle enough to discern that it is the fellow of some past and identical chance occurrence in a new disguise.

"Antoinette, chance events go in couples, sometimes even in dozens, and then they are enough, by their monotony, to fill an entire existence with despair."

"For whose benefit are you saying all this? For mine or for your own?"

"For neither yours nor mine. I hope we are sufficiently adult to be happy or unhappy with spirit, variety, and freshness we haven't let go stale."

"Yes. . . ."

It was a rather vague yes, but it contained, all the same, more thought behind it than was usual in Antoinette's conversation. Half lying down, as Dr. Ruhl had ordered, she neglected her needlework on her lap—something in openwork cambric on a background of green oil-cloth. The smell of the oil-cloth and its crude, pathetic color, reminded me of the fruitless activity of my eldest half-sister Juliette and of her hard and nimble little seamstress's fingers. When the recumbent Antoinette fell silent, and her needle-point went astray on the green cloth with the waxy smell, I raised my head, astonished to find that the woman sewing was this stranger, Mme. Haume, and not my half-sister, so pretty yet so plain beneath her turret of plaited hair.

"What is that stuff called—that needlework you're doing —Antoinette?"

"I don't a bit mind answering; but, do you know, you've already asked me that three times! It's the kind of embroidery known as Colbert."

"Thanks. I'm sure to ask you again. Go on, Antoinette; explain your ideas about luck."

"Oh, really, I'm not much good at——"

She stopped short, as though from modesty. We talked no more about what she called her "indisposition." Now that it was so much warmer, she had on a light dressing-gown. All the color had returned to her cheeks, turning her into a beautiful woman—really beautiful—and, thanks to an almost normal daily temperature between five and eleven at night, as blooming as a Montreuil peach. Did she think, without confiding her thoughts to anyone, that her future, and the part that luck would play in it, depended on no more than a single and complacent "Yes"?

"I *do* want to see *The Knick-Knack*, Colette!"

"Well then, let's go and see *The Knick-Knack!* Whichever day suits you best."

For I had delayed my departure for another week, a decision in which my chilly reconciliation with M. Haume played no part. It was dusty, golden weather, damp enough in the early mornings to make the cat's nose moist, as well as the leaves and the tables of the dairy kiosk. It gave Antoinette a persistent little cough, scarcely audible compared to the deep rasping of her voice. But, on days when the foothills were shrouded in level banks of white mist, she would declare that "it wasn't damp weather, properly speaking, only misty."

The July Bath-addicts were succeeded by the Bath-addicts of August. There were fewer children in X-les-Bains and more pretty women. A good-looking young man with pale hands and hollow eyes was noticeably attracted by the charms of Mme. Haume, her rounded bosom and well-corseted waist. Antoinette told me in confidence that her husband had soon "put things straight," that there had been an "exchange of words" in the vestibule of the Casino. She was radiant with pride, not so much on account of the young man's attentions as of Gérard's intolerance.

"The poor young man was obviously an invalid. There was no need for such a dressing-down. But Gérard's like that."

Whether he was really like that or not, Gérard, wrapped

up in his grief like a grub in its chrysalis, had abandoned all idea of a desperate solution. I had proof positive of this when some weighing-machine tickets slipped from his pocket as he was taking out his blue-grey handkerchief. They were from the machine in the chemists' where he used to buy porridge.

But his thoughts were still far removed from us. I like suffering to be discreet and I force myself to be so when the occasion arises. Often, during a fly-infested meal or a game of cards, I felt like interrupting his distant suffering with a shout or a wave. "Cheer up! Don't give in! Another fifty strokes and you'll be in your depth!" But one can't do these things.

One day Antoinette said: "Aren't you wearing your watch any more?"

"No," Gérard answered. "I've lost it."

"Really! How like you! When did you lose it?"

He took some little time to answer, as if he were trying to remember.

"Oh . . . yesterday. Or the day before yesterday."

No covert glance roped me into his distortion of the truth. He followed the road to recovery alone. I noticed that, courageous after his fashion, he had cured himself of the gesture of looking at his wrist.

A hired landaulet, making as much noise as a threshing-machine, took the three of us off for our drive. We had planned to have a look at *The Knick-Knack* and then drive up to the Saut-du-Berger. Gérard Haume sat facing us, on the flap-seat, and I felt I should not be able to bear for very long his efforts to seem cheerful and gay.

"Why don't you sit beside the driver? It's much the best place."

"It's nicer here," he answered politely. "If my long legs aren't a nuisance for the moment, I'll change places after we've seen *The Knick-Knack*. I imagine you know the legend of the Shepherd's Leap?"

"Oh, yes indeed!" I cried. "Nobody has let me languish in ignorance of it: neither you, nor the Bath-woman, nor the waiter, nor the little Italian hairdresser, nor the young woman at the dairy. I'd like to know the peak in France from which a shepherd or shepherdess has *not* leapt into the abyss—only to be saved in mid-air by the Virgin, an angel, a winged sheep or a haloed goat."

"No," Antoinette gravely observed, "not by a goat. Never by a goat. There are some kinds of animal one is never saved by!"

"And some kinds of persons," added Gérard Haume.

I took it into my head that I was included in that kind of person, and blushed. M. Haume looked down at X-les-Bains, vanishing deeper into its hollow as the road climbed. There was no more than a tourist's interest in his passionate and variable blue eyes. 'In a fortnight or three weeks,' I thought, 'those long creases in his cheeks will have filled out for certain, if he takes regular meals. His eyesockets won't seem so deep then. I shan't be there to see the younger version of Gérard Haume. Only the pupils of his eyes will remain the same. They are more blue-green than blue, because there are pale gold streaks in them, radiating like the spokes of a wheel, while the rim itself is dark slate-colored. . . .' Ah! there we are

at last! There's *The Knick-Knack,* and be damned to it!
A quick look, and away!

"Driver! That's the one!"

"No, no, not that one," Antoinette said. "There are people living in that one."

We were both right. I might have been mistaken about the yellowing grass between the palings, the dried-up privet and the bulb over the door, looking like a swan's beak on the end of its tube—the neighborhood bristled with them. But when I saw the woman sitting on the top doorstep, there was no longer room for mistake.

Sitting on the doorstep with her knees wide apart, her elbows resting on her knees and her chin in her cupped hands, Mlle. d'Orgeville seemed to be waiting for us, although—five hours after getting-up time—she was dressed only in a printed kimono and imitation silk mules, and her curly, medium-length hair was loose over her shoulders. She recognised me as I sat there hesitantly, rose, and said without a trace of astonishment, "Well, what a surprise!"

Then she smiled, recovering her natural grace in a moment. "I'm hardly dressed for the occasion, but please come in."

Gérard Haume got out to help me down, and I effected the introductions.

"How do you do, Monsieur? How do you do, Madame?" said Lucette.

She tried to gather up her hair and the sleeve of her kimono slipped along her arm, revealing an undepilated armpit and a black birthmark that suddenly made Lucette's presence real to me. On the stage, Mlle. d'Orgeville used to accentuate the size of this birthmark with grease paint.

"No, no!" cried Antoinette. "Don't put your hair up, it's much prettier as it is! What lovely hair!"

"*Hennedor 22*," Lucette said with engaging sincerity.

"*Hennedor 22*," Antoinette repeated. "A precious piece of information like that won't be easily forgotten, I can promise you."

"I've only just arrived," Lucette went on, "and the house is too topsy-turvy still for me to offer you anything."

"Don't dream of it! We've just had luncheon! Anyway, we ought to be off at once if we're to get to the Saut-du-Berger before five."

"Oh," Lucette looked downcast. "If it's a hard and fast date . . . But perhaps Monsieur would like a drink or something?"

Monsieur was waiting a little to one side, with his hat in his hand. I realised, from the slight jut of his hip and the care he was taking to keep the level of his glance raised so that the blue of his eyes should not be lost, that he was "backing into the limelight," as I call it, for the benefit of Lucette.

A few minutes later I was alone with Lucette. I peered at her for any signs of a sea voyage, shipwreck, or exotic adventure, and at last permitted myself a question.

"You don't suppose," she answered ironically, "that one makes much headway on a yacht in six weeks, do you?"

We were sitting side by side on the doorstep, and once more she had sunk her face between her hands. Scattered hairs strayed across her tired young face.

"But surely it gave you plenty of time for a nice trip?"

She shrugged her shoulders with an air of indifference.

"Oh, what you find doesn't always come up to what you leave behind! I fell out with that chap on the yacht. Things weren't going too well, even when I wrote to you."

"The chap with the diamonds?"

"Yes. The chap's gone, which is a good riddance, really. But the diamonds have gone too."

She put up her hand to screen a yawn.

"Oh? How did that happen?"

"It just happened. It's the same old story all over again, you know, more or less. A chap who is as kind as anything to start with suddenly becomes the very opposite. He had me tied up and locked in my cabin. So it was easy for him to get his jewels back."

"Tied up. What a terrible story! It's horrible! How did you get out of it in the end?"

"I managed somehow," she said laconically. "But I did get out of it; that's the chief thing. And then, I came here to save money, mainly. The lease lasts till the fifteenth of September. Then I'll go back."

For a moment I suspected that she was "piling it on." But her complete state of calm and the gloomy tone of her voice were evidence enough for me that she was speaking the truth. Adventures happen to people who, by their composure, their unshakableness, and their scorn of the unusual may be said to deserve them. They leave little or no trace. Lucette yawned again and apologised.

"It's just tiredness. And the food in the train was awful.

So I'm doing myself proud this evening with a tomato salad, a veal cutlet as thick as both my hands, a huge bowl of raspberries and some goat's milk cheese."

She smiled greedily. "So you stayed down at the Hôtel with your friends," she went on, "instead of taking my 'cottage?' Who are these people?"

"Nice people."

"So I see."

"I'm sure they thought you were ravishing. In fact, that wavy hair. . ."

"Yes," she went on seriously. "It's a hair-do I'm still working on, it's not quite ready yet. For I can't go on pinning up my hair."

She raised both arms, gathering up her hair, and her well-placed breasts rose under the kimono.

"Why?"

"Because of a scar. It looks horrid. It was that tiresome wretch on the yacht again. And on top of everything else, he went and put me ashore in the middle of the night on a little promontory in the Balearic Islands, all covered with rocks and cactuses and prickly things. I caught it all right. And this thing on my neck hasn't healed up yet. So there it is!"

"Didn't you think of bringing an action against him?"

"There were more important things to think of"—she was still smiling—"I'm expecting Luigi."

"No?"

"Yes. By the eight-twelve."

She blushed scarlet, lowering her voice. "So I said to myself, 'After all, why bother to get dressed?' "

She crossed her arms energetically over her rebellious breasts, and took a deep breath of the mountain air which was heavy with particles of golden dust and the first mists of evening.

When the Haumes returned to pick me up, she paid them only scant attention, but shouted "Bye-bye!" to them most cordially as we drove away.

Then it was that Gérard Haume, relaxed at last and bringing into play a new and delicate charm, set out to win my favor. But, when intrigue is called into play, a woman never forgets that feminine instinct is the older in guile. When Gérard began by presenting me with the latest novel, with cakes called "wells of love," and finally produced a huge bunch of wild flowers, picked on the slopes by village children and tied tight with osiers so that they were stiffer than a bunch of salsify, I gazed at the gifts in my lap without a trace of pleasure. Antoinette benefited by a pretty pair of scissors molded to lock and open like a stork's beak, as well as by an old-fashioned chatelaine in filigree steel with all its accoutrements. Seeing him gay and rather excited, her face lit up. He kept coming and going, and throwing himself into armchairs on the terrace as petulantly as a young man. Five or six quiet days slipped by, and Antoinette extracted a promise from me to "sacrifice" a further week to her.

One day M. Haume joined us over our daily orange-juice.

"I bumped into that charming Mademoiselle d'Orgeville," he said. "Just imagine, she's asked us to tea tomorrow."

"Where?" Antoinette asked.

"Why, up at *The Knick-Knack.*"

"Where did you meet her?"

"Over there . . . near the chemist's, if I remember rightly."

"And what did you say?"

M. Haume rather overdid his discretion. "Oh, nothing definite. I answered that I was the humble slave of all your projects . . . and of Madame Colette's, of course."

Antoinette, from under her enormous white straw hat, gave me a bright look that seemed to leave the answer in my hands.

"Was she alone?" I asked.

M. Haume raised his shoulders in a slightly offended shrug. "Alone? Yes."

"Ah!" I said. "Perhaps Luigi hasn't turned up yet."

"Luigi?" asked M. Haume curtly. "What Luigi?"

"Her Luigi," I said, with well-feigned simplicity.

"Oh! I'm sorry," M. Haume said. "I didn't know."

"Perhaps you thought," Antoinette interposed brightly, "that Mademoiselle d'Orgeville had sworn a vow of chastity? Listen, Gérard, be a dear. I'll give you a note of apology to Mademoiselle d'Orgeville, because I won't be going up to tea with her. Would you take it to her this afternoon, when you go for your walk? You will? You're an angel."

In the course of the evening I mentioned a name which evoked no response. Antoinette, flushed and bright-eyed, stitched away at her embroidery—was it Louvois? or Colbert?—as if at a set task, while her husband read Fabre's *Entomological Memories.* My cat and I alone enjoyed our undisguised idleness without shame. But, at about half-past ten, I was overcome by an urgent necessity, that of taking leave of X-les-Bains without losing an hour. It occurred to me that boredom, the well-known boredom that haunts all watering-places in the long run, was weighing me down. I went off to bed, followed by my cat. She danced for joy at the approach of one of our silent nights, of her impending communion with the stars and her descent among the dreams that smoothed her striped coat, made her eyebrows and whiskers twitch, and sometimes parted her lips to show dry and transparent gums like those of a dead cat.

About noon the following day I went up to *The Knick-Knack*, where I found Lucette alone. She looked, in a cotton dressing-gown and with her hair in curling-pins, both younger and smaller, with something of the air of an attractive housewife. She threw the turkish towel she was holding round her neck, but not quickly enough to hide a terrible scar low on the nape of her neck. It was still soft and pinkish, and it made me think of an attempted decapitation.

"It's not that I'm trying to hide it from you," she said, "but that business on my neck is not nice to look at. They say the sun's good for it."

"What about Luigi, Lucette?"

"He's gone down to the market," she answered serenely. "He's got plans for cooking a rabbit in white wine. Come and sit in the garden, if you've a moment to spare."

She dragged an iron chair into the space between the fence and the steps leading up to the chalet, took a quick look around over the palings, and came back to where I was sitting.

"What a scene you let me in for."

"A scene! Who with?"

"That chap, your friend, Gérard."

"Gérard . . . ?" I repeated.

She began to laugh and gave me a tap on the knee. "You're not your usual bright self. Perhaps it's the waters. Going and telling Gérard about Luigi! Well, I mean to say! But how were you to know that Gérard would fall for me like that? So I bear you no ill-will."

"Fall for you?"

"Yes, for poor little me."

"But," I began stupidly, "he's married."

"Lucky him."

She sat down on the highest step, and let her slippers fall to the bottom of the flight. I watched her misshapen toes, which had danced on so many a stage, as she wriggled them under the mesh of her stockings. She lifted her short face up to the white-flecked sky. In spite of some superficial marks, her face was as fresh as an apricot that an insect has faintly nibbled. She had a tiny black spot here, a blemish under the skin there, a faint wrinkle further on, and one of her eyelids was traversed by a scar. The sun sank deep into her light-brown, orange-speckled eyes.

"But," I ventured, "Madame Haume, his wife . . . You know, she's awfully nice."

"I'm delighted for his sake," Lucette answered, condescending to bow her head.

"If she heard about it . . ."

"Do you think he'll go and tell her?" She turned a hard smile on me from the top of the wooden steps.

The novelty of this expression, beneath hair held up in curlers that revealed the round architecture of her head, turned her into a stranger for me.

"Lucette, listen, you must see that it wouldn't be very decent of you, if . . ."

I was counting on an interruption that was not forthcoming; so I fell silent. In the presence of this combative creature, who had escaped all those improbable but really dangerous adventures, I felt myself to be the very personification of female irresolution.

It chimed twelve down in the village and I rose to go.

"You make me laugh," Lucette said in a voice that was neither high nor low.

I slammed the gate I had just opened.

"You're the one who makes me laugh. Do you imagine that Haume's a rich man? He's up to his eyes in debt, his wife told me."

Lucette nodded her head sagaciously.

"A man who's in debt is compelled to have ideas about finding money all day long. Don't worry. When a chap has to lay off, he lays off."

She clenched her hands on her hips and, by a twist of her mouth, her whole expression became altered.

"And how are we to eat? Soon Luigi and I will have nothing left. I've battened on his savings ever since I got back."

She lowered her eyes and then stared at me again with

an expression of stupidity and horror. "He'd scarcely a bean, and I've spent the lot. True as I stand here!"

"Hasn't he got a job?"

"He's just gone down this morning to try the Bathing Establishment. It seems their electrician's had an accident, and they're in a bad fix."

"Is Luigi an electrician?"

"I'll say he is!" Lucette proudly exclaimed. "I'd like to know what he isn't! He knows absolutely everything! He said to me, 'Don't wait too late for me. Cook up anything you like for lunch. Whatever happens, I'll bring back a rabbit for supper to-night.' "

As she repeated these words culled from the lips of her beloved, she assumed an expression of genuine piety that made her look young and kind again. Her face hardened as she added, "It's not my fault. Your friend, that man Haume, just happened to be the chap at the end of the wire."

"What wire?"

"The wire of the electric bell. Haven't you ever been tempted by the button of a door-bell, when you're in a strange place? I am, often. I say to myself, 'I'd like to know what's at the other end of that wire. Suppose I press that button? Perhaps it'll bring the police, or cause an explosion, or a peal of God's thunder. . . .' So, in the end, I press the button, and a head waiter turns up with tea and toast, mistaking me for someone else; so I keep the tea and toast. That's how," she went on with a laugh, "I rang Haume, and he turned up with the tray. Not a very heavy one, but if you're feeling peckish . . ."

If it hadn't been for Antoinette, I might have been amused by the tale of Gérard Haume. But there was Antoinette.

"Lucette, have you any music-hall plans?"

She kicked at a pebble peevishly. "What, at the end of July? You must be joking. There're not many contracts about where I've just come from. And this beastly thing's got to get better. It hurts . . . and I'm not what you'd call a milk-sop, either. Do you know anything about wounds?"

"My brother's a doctor," I said, keeping strictly to the truth.

She took off the towel and uncovered her wound. I did not like the color or the consistency of the two lips of the scar. They were thick, flabby and still moist.

"Lucette, show it to Doctor Ruhl. Or to one of the other doctors here."

"All right," she said cheerfully. "I'll get Pa Haume to stand me that."

I laughed, rather treacherously, as if her impertinent conduct—the manner of a young woman leading an old fogey by the nose—avenged me for some insult.

"That's the way I like you," said Lucette. "How you glared at me! Twelve-twenty—I'll go and cut up the tomatoes for the salad. Suppose I put on a compress of salt water? This thing aches."

I put a handkerchief soaked in salted water on the nape of her neck. I noticed that she was shivering slightly.

"Yes, it makes me all trembly, really it does. Specially at night. I'll go and see the doctor."

As there was no writing-paper in the house, I wrote down Dr. Ruhl's name on the edge of a newspaper, and hurried down to the village. The cat sniffed at my hands with her mouth half-open, as was her habit with certain impure smells. I scolded her, deeply humiliated. But I washed my hands carefully.

"Antoinette, you haven't by any chance grown a shade thinner this week, have you?"

"I have," said Antoinette. "Five hundred and fifty grammes."

A mauve shadow on her lower eyelid—the shape of a spear-head—added to her good looks. But she seemed absent-minded: friendly during conversations, but remote as soon as she withdrew into herself over her embroidery or a new novel.

"Antoinette, it's silly. Are you eating enough?"

She raised her head and smiled at me. "I don't care for porridge."

We had arranged that my departure should coincide with that of the Haumes. I had not seen Lucette again, and I had as little as possible to do with Gérard Haume, who, lean and as though winged, set out—and returned—with great strides, with an inappropriate smile on his lips. And I was sorry to be leaving Antoinette so soon, in much the same way that I have frequently regretted such chance acquaintances. This particular companion was endowed with great and good qualities in which I am lacking: patience, a gift of observation that put mine in the shade, and courage, beside which my bold gestures were hardly more than temporary whims.

She finished embroidering the scallops round a trefoil, stuck in her needle, and laid her work aside.

"Tell me . . . how do you find my husband?"

"A handsome cavalier, i' faith, as Madame Valtesse de la Bigne said about Edouard Detaille."

She laughed, from mere politeness.

"That wasn't quite what I meant. Don't you think there's something a bit odd about him lately?"

I pretended to get angry.

"Listen, Antoinette. Don't force me to declare myself! We all know your husband is charming and that he's got the most beautiful eyes in the world; but you've spoilt him terribly, and you go right off your head the moment he has so much as an eyelash out of place!"

"No, no. I don't mean as far back as the time when 'I flicked off every speck of dust,' as you call it. I simply wanted to ask you if you'd noticed that there's been rather a queer smell about him these last few days."

"A queer smell? What smell? Scent?"

"Not only scent. A smell. . . . He smells," she went on, her eyes still holding mine, "he smells of phenosalyl and geraniums."

"Phenosalyl? Really? What's that?"

"Your brother's a doctor, and you don't know what phenosalyl is?"

"Well, I imagine it's some kind of phenol. . . . But what's Gérard got to do with the stink of carbolic?"

I thought to myself, 'She's getting warm. She'll be on to

it soon. Now that she's following the trail by scent and scent alone, nothing can stop her catching up with the quarry. If only that idiot with the bad neck had stuck to salt and water!'

"Stink? Stink?" said Antoinette, quite scandalised. "There's no question of stink. I said 'phenosalyl *and* geraniums.'"

"All right. But what are you getting at?"

Antoinette placed her kind, patient, heavy hand on my arm. "Madame Colette . . . I'm so sorry, my dear Colette, but do answer me frankly. Can you assure me, quite sincerely, that nobody is ill at Mademoiselle d'Orgeville's?"

This direct question and the honest friendly face robbed me of any wish to prevaricate. "No, I can't assure you of that, since I've had no contact with *The Knick-Knack* for five days. I repeat, none. I've had no message, I haven't met Lucette, and there's no telephone at the chalet. But" —at the last word, the prominent chestnut eyes and the firm mouth became riveted with attention—"but the last time I saw Mademoiselle d'Orgeville she had a sort of dressing on the nape of her neck."

I cursed my half-lie and my half-need to speak the truth, my semi-honesty that made me first want to hush up Mlle. d'Orgeville's goings on and then try to protect Antoinette. But my heart was on Antoinette's side.

"A dressing on the nape of her neck," Mme. Haume repeated avidly. "And what's the matter with the nape of her neck?"

"Antoinette, I'm not her doctor."

To my great astonishment, Mme. Haume seemed satisfied with my ambiguous reply.

But it did not satisfy her for long. Three days later, while Antoinette was busying herself over a trunk-drawer balanced on her knees, carefully packing handkerchiefs and blouses, gloves and nightgowns, a bell-boy knocked at the door and handed me a note without an envelope. I saw at once that it was a page torn out of a notebook, neatly folded into a triangle, like an old-fashioned *billet-doux*. It was a sort of curt obituary notice in telegraphese and read: *Lucette deceased Hospital Sainte-Marie-Glorieuse two hours after noon septicæmia. Luigi.*

"What's the time?" I asked automatically.

"Half-past four. But I'm a few minutes slow according to the Casino clock. Do you want tea already?"

"No thanks. . . . Just as you like . . . Antoinette, look, here's a message that tells you what you wanted to know!"

She read the note and, with the aid of her small lorgnette with square lenses, read it through again. She did not exclaim out loud, but the violent pulsation of her blood brought on a fit of coughing.

"Poor young woman," she said at last.

"Yes, poor young woman."

She handed me back the note; but I did not take it, so she put it on the table between us.

"Are you going there?"

"Where do you mean?"

"To the hospital?"

"Oh, no! Certainly not!"

"What sort of a hospital is the Sainte-Marie-Glorieuse?"

"I've no idea."

Antoinette went back to her packing, but I noticed how nervous she was with her hands, mixing up the handkerchiefs with the scarves.

"What do you think she died of?" she asked.

"Septicæmia. That's blood-poisoning."

There was a shade of irony in the tone of her answer. "Good heavens, I know that! But what caused the poisoning? You mentioned a dressing. . . ."

I shrugged my shoulders in token of ignorance; but I would have liked to have shouted: "She died because she was chained up in a ship, more or less tortured, and then cast upon the rocks; she died because she lived surrounded by pirates in a world of rape, stolen diamonds, doubloons, loaded dice, shipwrecks, royal sables and rough tavern wine. She died of a savage wound that looked like a gash from a pair of shears or a terrible hack with a bill-hook. It all seemed natural enough to her. She died in the arms of her kind-hearted tough, who was waiting for her each time she came back from the ends of the earth, in a galleon, a car, or a cart, or barefoot and gashed to the bone. A kind, humble tough, a real lover, capable of facing the death of his vagrant mistress and announcing it without any fuss, and of never getting over it. Dear Antoinette and sensitive Gérard, I'll try not to think too much of this couple when you are close at hand in case I should find the pair of you a bit colorless by comparison. . . ."

A bit colorless! Was that what I was accusing them of so unjustly? Unjustly, for both of them—Gérard by wishing first to die and then going on living because he was in love, and Antoinette, by forcing herself to the duties of life—touched the limits of human energy. No doubt all that was wrong with them was that it had been their lot to be caught up by and steeped in their desire to become my friends. It must also be said that the places where the Gérards and Antoinettes congregate are no training for the violent propensities to which one may loyally and willingly surrender. . . .

Something faint and feebly pencilled smudges the outlines of a couple like the Haumes. They can be rubbed out with a finger, they are worn thin by time. But chance, because they had delayed my departure, had spread all round them one of those queer-shaped, expanding stains that at one and the same time resemble—according to the observer's eye—a monkey, a death's head, a female backside, or the island of Borneo. I still regret not having deciphered more clearly the cartographical meanderings, or seized the meaning hidden in those hungry gulfs and beaklike promontories.

All I saw of M. Haume, when I passed him on the landing on the way back to my room, was a pair of shoes. They were white with dust and they had obviously covered a lot of ground. I kept out of the way of my neighbors till we met in the restaurant.

The days were drawing in, and the electric globes were already casting a mauve lustre over the tables on the veranda. Antoinette was dressed in pearl-grey. It suddenly occurred to me that this half-mourning was designed to spare M. Haume's feeling, and I nearly gave way to one of those mad temptations to laugh which all of a sudden assail one in the middle of a funeral service, or during the performance of a truly gloomy tragedy, or halfway through a serious oration. But I kept a hold on myself and watched Haume, who, I had to admit, was behaving himself well. Perhaps the novelty, the lack of depth of his new misfortune, left him in better command of his features. And perhaps the death of a mistress whom one adores is easier to bear than her unfaithfulness, or her flight. At any rate, all I could read into his face was a faintly hypnotic rigidity and a change of complexion that might have been due to the mauve lights overhead. Antoinette also behaved admirably, save for a very slight tremor, springing from the anxious alacrity which affects all of us when there is a mishap which, in crushing our neighbor, either prostrates us too, or sets us free. When we had finished eating some clammy cod disguised as brill, she spoke with a certain diffidence. "Suppose," she said, "we were to drink a little champagne?"

It was an innocent suggestion, of the kind to which, as a rule, her husband hastened to agree. This time, however, he rather smugly refused, as though his wife were sinning against the most rudimentary formula of such secret obsequies. It was all that was needed to stir up in me the evil spirit of laughter and scorn. I applied myself to being "brilliant," and went a little too far. I alluded to people who pass from one love to another in less time than it takes to mention it: I even compared them to brood-mares that, the moment they have foaled, are once again—if I may so describe it—put face to face with the stallion.

"What's the matter with her this evening?" cried Antoinette. "What's come over her?"

I also propounded that to exaggerate the sorrows of love is tantamount to an indiscretion: that it reveals the lack of that precious faculty, a sense of the ridiculous. I stopped only when I saw pale blue signs of anger—an admirable antidote—driving the sorrowful tints of slate and violet from the eyes of M. Haume. Then I begged to be excused on account of a splitting headache, and went upstairs to pack my own two suitcases.

My cat took a shrewd and practised share in these preparations, kneading my favorite woolen things with her paws as if they were dough, and thoughtfully measuring the depth of a shoe with an outstretched paw. She switched from one suitcase to the other with leaps that resembled, according to her mood, the flight of a fairy or the clumsy floundering of a filly. When it was all over she joined me in bed, nestling beside me instead of settling down somewhere cool and smooth. I think she had understood it all, and that she was appealing to me yet once more to extricate both of us from chance acquaintances and from bitter disappointments—the full horror of which I had been hiding from myself—from fortuitous towns and strange rooms and all the rest of it. She was imploring me to blaze a trail just wide enough for my feet and for hers, a trail that would be obliterated behind us as we went.

JUDITH THURMAN's 1999 biography of Colette, *Secrets of the Flesh: A Life of Colette*, was a finalist for the National Book Award and winner of the Los Angeles Times Book Award for Biography. It has been translated into eleven languages. Her 1982 biography of Isak Dinesen, *Isak Dinesen: The Life of a Storyteller*, won the National Book Award and was the basis for Sydney Pollack's Academy Award–winning film *Out of Africa*. Ms. Thurman, a staff writer for *The New Yorker* and a contributing writer to *Architectural Digest*, lives in New York City.